A LOVE STORY VEILED IN MYSTERIOUS ALLURE

VELVET SHADOWS

BOOK ONE

A KEYSTONE SERIES

LORAIN RIZK

Praise for Lorain Rizk

"Velvet Shadows" is a mesmerizing tale of love, betrayal, and self-discovery. The author weaves a captivating narrative, introducing intriguing characters like Jake and Dylan Dalton. The delicate dance of love unfolds with unexpected choices and thrilling revelations. A must-read for romance and mystery enthusiasts.

— Martha Reynolds, Book Reviewer

"Velvet Shadows" offers a unique perspective on love and self-discovery. Madelyn's journey, torn between past betrayals and newfound connections, is compelling. The mysterious characters add depth, and the intertwining of passion and mystery keeps the story engaging.

— Ron Perth, Book Author

In "Velvet Shadows," Madelyn's role as a wedding planner adds a distinctive touch to the story, offering insights into both personal and professional endeavors. The author skillfully combines the haunting echoes of past betrayals with the allure of newfound connections. Dylan Dalton, the enigmatic millionaire, introduces layers of complexity. The book's strength lies in its ability to blend romance, mystery, and the intricacies of Madelyn's profession.

— Laura Weber, Editor

Disclaimer: This is a work of fiction. Character names and descriptions are the product of the author's imagination. Any resemblance to actual person, living or dead, is entirely coincidental.

Copyright © 2024 by Lorain Rizk

All rights reserved.

No part of this book may be reproduced in any form or by any electronic or mechanical means, including information storage and retrieval systems, without written permission from the author, except for the use of brief quotations in a book review.

To request permission, contact lorainrizk@gmail.com.

Cover by The Paper House

Edited by The Paper House

ISBN: 979-886-916-3387

Published by The Paper House

www.thepaperhousebooks.com

Contents

Foreword	ix
1. The Preparations	1
2. A Breath Of Fresh Air	11
3. The Struggle	21
4. Digging Deep	37
5. The Spark	51
6. The Birthday	71
7. Conflicted Hearts	91
8. More Secrets	105
9. The Decision	115
10. Pure Passion	139
11. Consequences	161
12. Reality Check	171
13. New Beginnings	185
14. The Wedding	199
15. The Secret	213
16. Doubts	233
17. Again	251
18. Enough	261
19. Moving On	273
20. Letting Go	287
21. Real Life	297
Afterword	311
About the Author	313

Velvet Shadows is dedicated to all of you hopeless romantics. That no matter what happened to you and the heartbreaks you had to endure, you still believe and seek real love.

And of course, to my husband Mo.

Foreword

When I first met Lorain Rizk, her passion for storytelling was immediately evident. Through our conversations, it became clear that Velvet Shadows and the Keystone Series was not just a project, but a journey—a culmination of experiences, dreams, and the relentless pursuit of understanding the complexities of love and relationships.

In Velvet Shadows, Lorain Rizk weaves a narrative that is both captivating and thought-provoking, inviting us into the world of Madelyn, a wedding planner that finds herself at a crossroads torn between the haunting echoes of her husband Steve's past betrayals and the irresistible allure of Jake, the man she accidentally met at her favorite bookstore. This book arrives at a time when social media is overtaking the world making relationships hard to last, offering a fresh perspective that is both necessary and welcome.

Having had the privilege to witness the evolution of this story, I can attest to the depth of research and the personal

FOREWORD

dedication that has gone into its creation. Lorain invites us not just to read, but to question, to feel, and to explore alongside Madelyn.

I encourage you to embark on this journey, to find within these pages not just a story, but a mirror, a challenge, and a companion. Welcome to Velvet Shadows.

— Martha Reynolds, Book Reviewer

CHAPTER 1

The Preparations

A GENTLE BREEZE wafted through the open window, carrying with it the faintest scent of jasmine from the garden below. I sat cross-legged on my living room floor, surrounded by a sea of fabric swatches and floral brochures, the detritus of my once-fervent passion. Sofia perched on the armrest beside me, her gaze piercing as she sifted through the chaos of my thoughts.

"Lauren's birthday is coming up, and Dylan Dalton's wedding—those are opportunities, Maddie," Sofia said, her voice slicing through the haze of my indecision. "You need something to ground you, and what better than focusing on what you love most?"

I plucked at a corner of ivory satin, its smoothness a stark contrast to the rough storm inside me. "Planning parties isn't going to fix my marriage. It feels like... like putting a band-aid on a broken bone."

"Maybe not," she conceded, reaching down to still my fidgeting hands with her own. "But it might give you the space you need to think. To breathe." Her hazel eyes locked onto mine, willing me to find the courage I had misplaced.

"Space to breathe..." The words resonated within me, but doubt clawed at their edges. Planning Lauren's tenth birthday should be a joy, not a strategy for distraction. And Dylan Dalton's wedding? That was work, a professional obligation that now felt tangled in personal conflict.

"Think of it this way," Sofia pressed on, her tone softening, "this isn't just about distraction. It's about remembering who you are when the world isn't pressing in on you. You shine when you're bringing joy to others, Maddie. Let that light guide you through the rest. I have known you for fifteen years, and I am your best friend. I know you more than anyone else."

I hesitated, my mind a carousel of images—Steve's distant eyes, Lauren's expectant smile... Could I really compartmentalize my life so neatly?

"Lauren would love a vintage tea party, wouldn't she?" I found myself saying, almost despite myself. A vision of pastel tablecloths and fine china began to form, a tiny flame of excitement flickering to life.

"And Dylan's wedding," Sofia nudged gently, "it's a chance to create something magical, something that speaks of elegance and true love—even if it's not your own."

"True love," I said, the words bittersweet on my tongue. I let out a shaky breath, allowing the possibility of escape to settle around me like a shawl. Maybe Sofia was right; perhaps immersing myself in the beauty of celebration could help untangle the knots in my heart.

"Okay," I whispered, my voice tinged with a hope I wasn't sure I felt. "I'll do it. For Lauren. For... clarity."

Sofia's smile bloomed, warm and reassuring, illuminating her striking hazel eyes that sparkled with the vivacity of a woman truly alive. Her flowing black hair framed her face in gentle waves, a touch to her natural elegance and strength. As my best friend for the last fifteen years, she stood beside me, her mid-30s bringing with them a fierce loyalty and an honesty that was as refreshing as it was rare.

"That's the spirit," she cheered, her voice not just a sound but a presence, embodying the comfort and encouragement that only someone who had been a constant in my life could offer. Her hand, warm and reassuring, squeezed my shoulder, reminding me of her unwavering support.

Despite her busy life as a stay-at-home wife, Sofia always found the time to stand by me, especially when it came to organizing events that mattered to both of us. Her commitment to our friendship and her ability to balance her responsibilities at home with her eagerness to help was nothing short of remarkable. She grabbed her bag from the floor, her movements exuding a purposeful grace that was all her own.

"But for now, I have to go. I'll be back as soon as I can. Promise." The words left her lips with a playful blow of a kiss, a gesture that was quintessentially Sofia—vivacious, loyal, and unafraid to speak her mind. She ran out the door, leaving behind a trail of warmth and the promise of her quick return. In that moment, I was reminded of the fortune in having Sofia in my life, not just as a friend but as a beacon of strength, honesty, and unwavering support.

She always knows how to lift me up, I thought.

And so, with a mixture of trepidation and determination, I pulled myself to my feet, the blueprint of a plan slowly etching itself into my mind. Lauren's laughter, the look of awe on guests' faces, the touch of grace amidst the chaos—it was all there, waiting for me to reach out and grasp it.

For now, that would have to be enough.

The moment my fingertips grazed the smooth expanse of my event planning binder, a familiar warmth blossomed in my chest. It was an old friend, this binder, its leather cover worn at the edges from years of use showcasing thousand decisions made, a hundred themes explored. I opened it reverently, pages bristling with tabs and notes, a different hue representing a different piece of the intricate puzzle that is a perfect event.

"Okay," I murmured to the quiet room, "let's create something unforgettable."

I began with Lauren's birthday, sketching out preliminary ideas on a blank sheet of paper. The pencil danced in my hand as if it were an extension of my thoughts—swirls for the centerpieces, lines for the layout of the tables, dots marking where balloons would bob against the ceiling like captured clouds.

"Whimsical," I said aloud, picturing Lauren's bright eyes sparkling amidst a sea of fairy lights and soft, flowing fabrics. "She loves the garden fairies... maybe a midsummer night's theme?"

The thought took hold, tendrils of excitement unfurling within me as I envisioned tiny lanterns nestled among greenery, with a smell of jasmine and rose. It would be a tableau drawn straight from a child's dream, ethereal and touched with starlight.

Turning my attention to the Daltons' wedding, my heart clenched with a pang of envy before professionalism smoothed the wrinkle of personal emotion away. This was about them, their love story. I tried to narrow the focus until nothing existed but the vision taking shape beneath my pen.

"Classic elegance," I decided, speaking to the empty room as if to assert the idea into existence. "Timeless... like their love should be." I began listing vendors, venues, and musicians with a meticulousness that bordered on obsession. Every detail mattered—the curve of the calligraphy on the invitations, the subtle fragrance of the floral arrangements, the balance of flavors in the menu.

"Tables draped in ivory linen," I whispered, sketching fervently, "crystal glassware catching the light, a gentle clink of toasts to happiness and futures bright."

Here, in the realm of satin ribbons and softly spoken vows, I found a measure of peace. My world narrowed to textures and hues, tastes and sounds. It was as though by orchestrating the joy of others, I could silence the cacophony of my own doubts.

"Madelyn, you can do this," I encouraged myself, my voice a soft but determined whisper among the chord of rustling papers. "You were born to bring dreams to life."

And as I poured over vendors and quotes, lost in the rhythm of creation, the tangled threads of my emotions began to weave themselves into a tapestry of renewed purpose. Each choice, each flourish and embellishment, became a stepping stone away from confusion and towards clarity.

"Lauren will feel like she's dancing with the fairies," I promised into the hush, "and Dylan... Dylan will look back on his day as the beginning of forever."

Satisfaction unfurled within me, a quiet bloom of contentment in the midst of the storm raging in my heart. Here, among plans and possibilities, I found solace—a sanctuary built of hope and the promise of celebrations yet to come.

The evening had surrendered to the velvet cloak of night, and a hush settled over my workshop like a promise. I stood before my vision boards, their surfaces a mosaic of

THE PREPARATIONS

colors and textures that mapped out Lauren's birthday extravaganza and Dylan Dalton's nuptial celebration.

"Looks like you've found your groove," I mused aloud, my voice steady in the solitude. The reflection in the window pane revealed a woman with purpose in her expressive green eyes, a stark contrast to the Madelyn who once waded in insecurity. Her wavy chestnut hair framed her face. Madelyn, in her mid-30s, had always been introspective, her mind a constant whirlwind of thoughts and emotions. Compassion was her gift, extending to everyone around her, save for herself. Creativity flowed through her veins, manifesting in every event she planned, every detail meticulously chosen to create harmony and beauty.

Yet, beneath this façade of control and precision, my insecurities whispered incessantly, casting shadows of doubt over her achievements. I struggled with an internal dialogue that questioned my decisions, my relationships, and my worth. This battle with self-doubt was my constant companion, a specter that loomed large over my moments of solitude.

But today, something had shifted. The reflection did not just show a woman changed by time, but by experience. The insecurity that once clouded my green eyes was dissipating, replaced by a glimmer of confidence. It was as if the very act of acknowledging my growth aloud had fortified me. My journey through the mire of self-doubt had not been easy, but it had taught me the value of trust—

trust in my intuition, my abilities, and the love that surrounded me.

Though the insecurities might never vanish completely, I was learning to navigate them with grace. I understood now that my doubts did not define me; rather, it was my response to them that shaped my character.

The solitude that once echoed my fears now resounded with the promise of growth. Madelyn stood, a beacon of my own making, my green eyes reflecting not just the woman I was, but the woman I was becoming—more confident, more certain, yet ever compassionate and creative. The reflection in the glass bore witness to my evolution, a reminder that even amidst uncertainty, one could find their groove, their purpose, their light.

I ran my fingers over the fabric swatches, a tactile proof of the progress I'd made. With a decisive movement, I pinned the final choices onto Lauren's board. "She'll adore this. It's joyful, vibrant—just like her."

My phone buzzed—a gentle intruder in my sacred space—and Sofia's name lit up the screen. "Hey, you're still working? So sorry, I got caught up," she said, her tone tinged with concern.

"Still? No, it's..." I glanced at the clock, startled by the hour. "It's passion that keeps me here, not obligation." My laugh was light, a sound I hadn't heard from myself in too long.

"Passion is good. It guides you, doesn't it? Just don't forget, you need rest too."

THE PREPARATIONS

"Rest can wait. There's something exhilarating about solving puzzles, piecing together fragments of ideas until they bloom into something tangible." I cradled the phone between my shoulder and ear, hands busy sifting through sketches of floral arrangements.

"I'm glad you listened. I love when this passion comes out."

"Every choice I make for these events mirrors a step I'm ready to take in my own life." I paused, picturing Lauren blowing out her candles, Dylan slipping a ring onto his beloved's finger. "These aren't just parties. They're milestones—reminders that every moment is precious."

"That's beautiful. But remember, you're allowed to be happy too, not just the architect of others' joy."

"Creating joy for others is my path to finding it for myself," I confessed, a smile spreading as I envisioned the guests' reactions, the smiles and warmth. "I think I'm finally starting to understand that."

"Good. Hold on to that feeling, okay?" Sofia's voice was soft but firm. "You deserve all the happiness you're putting out into the world."

"Thank you, Sofia. That means more than you know." I placed the phone down, letting her words sink into my bones. They became a silent mantra.

"We will continue working on these events on Thursday at the office. Leave some things for me to do, please."

"Alright, alright, I'll go to bed. Good night," I said.

With every detail confirmed, every doubt acknowledged and set aside, indecision was fading. My heart hummed a rhythm of newfound hope, synchronized with the tick of the clock—the heartbeat of my aspirations.

As I switched off the lights, the outlines of my dreams lingered, etched against the darkness. In the silence, I held onto the day's revelations—the clarity that had emerged from chaos, the determination born from rediscovered passion.

CHAPTER 2

A Breath Of Fresh Air

I STEPPED over the threshold of my sanctuary—Quill Haven—the little bookshop nestled between a bakery and an antique store. The visits were like returning to a cherished friend's embrace, and today, it felt more vital than ever. The familiar smell of old books—a mix of musk and vanilla with a hint of aged paper—filled my senses, grounding me in the moment.

"Back again, Madelyn?" Mr. Partridge, the owner, called out from behind the counter, his eyes crinkling as he smiled.

I returned the smile, the kind that reaches your eyes. "You know I can't stay away for too long."

"Find something to get lost in," he said, gesturing toward the shelves.

"Always do," I replied, my voice almost a whisper.

As I wandered through the aisles, trailing my fingers across the spines, my heart felt heavy. There were days when I felt like a character out of one of these novels, caught in a life I had not entirely chosen, my own plot twisted by doubt and what-ifs.

Then, like a soft light in the dim room of my thoughts, a book caught my attention. It was wedged between two larger, imposing volumes, its spine worn, the title etched in faded gold letters. I leaned in, my curiosity piqued by the promise of escape it offered.

"Come here," I murmured, as if coaxing a timid creature.

My fingertips brushed the spine, gently coaxing the book out, but my usually steady hands betrayed me. In a clumsy dance, the book slipped from my grasp, tumbling down in a cascade of sound that seemed far louder than it should have been.

"Shoot!" I kneeled to retrieve the fallen treasure, my cheeks burning with embarrassment. "Clumsy much, Madelyn?"

I picked up the book, dusting off the cover with a tenderness reserved for things we cherish, and sighed. "It's just one of those days."

Perhaps it was symbolic, the way I kept knocking things over—not just books, but the carefully arranged aspects of my life. Steve's distant gaze at breakfast this morning came flooding back, and the uncertainty I saw mirrored there unsettled me more than I cared to admit.

A BREATH OF FRESH AIR

"Plans getting to you again?" I asked myself, tracing the embossed patterns on the cover. Lauren's birthday was around the corner, and I wanted nothing more than to make it perfect, to weave a bit of magic into her world despite the chaos in mine.

"Let's hope you're worth the trouble," I whispered to the book, a faint smile touching my lips. Maybe within its pages, I'd find the inspiration I needed, a guide to navigate the labyrinth of my own emotions—or at the very least, a temporary reprieve from the nagging doubts that filled my days and nights.

"Here, let me help you with that." The voice, warm and unexpectedly close, caught me off guard as I was crouched on the floor. I looked up to find a pair of kind brown eyes looking back at me, framed by tousled dark hair that had a mind of its own. "You dropped your keys on the floor."

"Thank you," I breathed out, a little startled by the sudden company but grateful nonetheless. My fingers brushed against his as we both reached for the keys, a current of something undefined sparking between us.

"Are you okay?" His concern was evident, and it resonated within me, vibrating softly like the string of a violin long after the bow has been lifted.

"Yeah, just a bit embarrassed." I offered a faint smile as we stood in unison, the keys now safely cradled in my arms.

"Embarrassment is the mind's way of keeping us humble," he said with a chuckle, sliding his hands into his pockets nonchalantly. "I'm Jake, by the way. Jake Evans."

"Madelyn," I replied, tucking a strand of chestnut hair behind my ear. "Madelyn Montgomery." His gaze felt like sunlight—warm, bright, impossible to ignore.

"Madelyn," he repeated, rolling the name around as if tasting it. "A beautiful name for someone clearly passionate about literature."

"Passionate might be too strong a word," I countered, feeling my cheeks flush. "I just... love getting lost in stories, you know? They're like compasses when reality gets too overwhelming."

"Ah, so you're an escapist reader." A teasing glint danced in Jake's eyes. "Tell me, Madelyn, what genre guides you today?"

"Actually, I was reaching for this one." I held up the book, its title embossed in gold against the deep blue cover: 'Whispers of the Past.' "Historical fiction. It's like time travel without the risk of altering history."

"An excellent choice." He nodded approvingly. "History has so much to teach us, doesn't it? The lives entwined with ours through the centuries, their whispers echoing in the pages we turn."

"Exactly!" The excitement bubbled inside me, finding resonance in Jake's words. "It's incredible how strangers from another era can feel like old friends, isn't it?"

"Indeed." His smile widened. "And sometimes, strangers from our own era can surprise us in similar ways."

For a moment, I allowed myself to indulge in the fantasy that destiny might have had a hand in this chance meeting.

"Have you read it?" I asked, gesturing toward the book.

"Many times. The readings offer a new perspective. But I'm eager to hear your thoughts once you've journeyed through its pages."

"Perhaps I'll take you up on that," I said, the notion of discussing the book with Jake suddenly very appealing.

"Consider it an open invitation," he affirmed with a nod.

"An invitation to discuss books or to discover new perspectives?" I teased lightly, surprised by my own forwardness.

"Both," he replied, his eyes locked onto mine, "if you're inclined to accept."

Each word we exchanged weaving a tighter web of connection. Madelyn Montgomery, the woman who planned every detail of her life down to the last petal on a birthday cake, was teetering on the edge of something new, something terrifyingly wonderful.

"Let's just keep this conversation going, okay?" I proposed, surprised by my own eagerness to dive into the unknown depths of whatever this was—or could be.

"Nothing would make me happier," Jake replied, his smile genuine, lighting up his entire face and sending a flutter through my chest.

We continued to talk, the world outside the walls of the bookshop growing dimmer as the bond between us brightened, casting a glow on the path ahead—one filled with the thrill of uncharted territory and the promise of discovery.

"Would you like to grab coffee sometime?" Jake's voice was tentative but hopeful, a gentle invitation hanging between us.

I hesitated, the question stirring a whirlwind of emotions inside me. I wanted to say yes—I wanted it more than I'd admitted to myself during our entire conversation. "I think I'd like that," I replied, my words cautious but sincere.

"Great." He pulled out his phone, his fingers dancing over the screen before he looked up at me expectantly. His sharp, angular features and warm brown eyes gave him a confident look. A neatly trimmed beard adorned his chiseled jawline, adding a touch of rugged charm. A faint hint of his masculine cologne spread in the air as he extended the phone toward me, making me blush. "Your number?"

"Right, yes." Fumbling in my purse, I retrieved my own phone, our digits exchanged in a digital handshake. The screen lit up with his contact now saved—a beacon in the fog that had been my thoughts for too long.

"Jake," I typed under his name, and as I handed his phone back to him, our fingers brushed—a brief, electric connection that made my heart skip. It was such an inconsequential touch, yet it resonated with promise.

"Madelyn," he mimicked, showing me his phone screen with my name neatly entered. There was a smile in his eyes, one that spoke of secrets and the beginning of something new.

I tucked a stray lock of hair behind my ear, a nervous habit revealing the fluttering in my chest. "I should get going," I said, reluctant to break the moment yet aware of the life awaiting me outside the safety of these book-lined walls.

"Of course," he nodded, stepping aside to give me room to pass. "I'll call you about that coffee."

"Please do." The words came out softer than intended, a whisper of longing.

As I moved towards the door, I could feel Jake's gaze on me, warm and unwavering. I pushed it open, the sound marking the end of one chapter and the tentative step into another.

I felt like a teenager again. *What the hell is wrong with me? Did I really just get butterflies?*

Outside, the late afternoon sun was painting the pavement in hues of amber and gold. I allowed myself a moment to just breathe, my pulse still racing.

What am I doing? My mind reeled with the possibilities, one more thrilling and terrifying than the last. Steve would be waiting, dinner would need to be cooked, Lauren's birthday plans required attention—yet here I was, entertaining the thought of coffee with a man who was practically a stranger.

But hadn't I yearned for this? For change, for connection?

Yes, there was guilt, a gnawing sense that I was teetering on the brink of betrayal. But there was also excitement, the kind that bubbles up from within, unbidden and irrepressible.

With every step away from the bookshop, the mix of emotions churned and blended, creating a cocktail of anticipation and fear. The possibilities lay sprawled before me, a landscape both daunting and inviting.

"Change," I sighed, the word a key turning in the lock of my heart. "You're overdue."

My phone vibrated, a sudden jolt that sent my pulse racing again. I fished it out, the screen lighting up with a message:

"Great meeting you, Madelyn. Jake."

The words, simple and direct, cut through the fog of my indecision. With a shaky breath, I typed a response, my fingers bold where my voice feared to tread.

"Looking forward to coffee. And conversation. M."

Sent. Done. No going back now.

Life's too short, I thought, the statement taking root. The city unfolded around me, indifferent to the seismic shift within one woman's world. But to me, it was everything— the flutter of anticipation, the weight of choice, the silent acknowledgement that the course of my life might have just altered with the gentle push of fate.

A BREATH OF FRESH AIR

"Maybe it's time for the next chapter," I said to myself, the words a vow to the woman who stared back from shop windows, her green eyes brighter now, reflecting the streetlights, the stars, and the spark of something new.

CHAPTER 3

The Struggle

THE MORNING LIGHT filtered through the gauzy curtains, casting a warm glow on the wavy chestnut hair spread across my pillow.

"Steve?" The name hung in the air, a tentative whisper against the silence of our home.

From the bathroom, the sound of running water ceased, and Steve emerged, his presence as commanding as his arguments in the courtroom. His tall, athletic frame was silhouetted against the stark white tile, an embodiment of the discipline and rigor that defined both his personal and professional life. His short-cropped dark hair, usually so meticulously styled, now lay damp and unruly, a rare glimpse into the less guarded version of the man who wore the suit. Deep-set blue eyes, the kind that could intimidate a witness or charm a jury, scanned the room with an intensity that was both captivating and slightly unnerving.

"Yeah?" The word delivered with the curt precision of a lawyer who was trained to weigh each word, yet it was tinged with a distance that was uncharacteristic of the charismatic man known to his colleagues. The easy banter that once echoed through these walls seemed like echoes from a distant past, replaced now by a silence as dense as the legal tomes that lined his office.

Steve, a man whose life was a series of battles fought and won, was not without his personal struggles. His profession demanded a façade of invulnerability, a trait that served him well in the legal arena but created barriers in his private life. The strong exterior sometimes served to mask a vulnerability he was reluctant to acknowledge, even to himself. As a lawyer, he was trained to communicate with precision, yet at home, words failed him, and emotions remained pent up, leading to tensions that he couldn't quite cross-examine his way out of.

Jealousy was a familiar adversary, one that he often, maybe too often, found himself grappling with. It was a reflection of the possessiveness that sometimes comes with deep passion—a passion that made him an excellent lawyer but also left him feeling exposed in more intimate settings. Steve was indeed a 'manly man,' but this archetype, this role he felt compelled to play, often left little room for the expression of softer emotions, which were there, albeit buried deep like case evidence waiting to be discovered.

In the stillness of the post-argument atmosphere, Steve stood, not just as a lawyer, an embodiment of justice and argumentative prowess, but as a man—a man wrestling

THE STRUGGLE

with the complexities of love, communication, and vulnerability, seeking a verdict that would grant him peace both at home and within.

I pushed myself up, tucking my hair behind my ear as I watched him avoid my gaze. "We need to talk about Lauren's parent-teacher conference."

"Already on my calendar," he said, brushing past me with a brusque energy, the scent of his cologne a fleeting reminder of better days.

"Is it? Because last time..." My words trailed off.

"Last time was a mistake. I'm not going to forget our daughter." There was a defensive edge to his voice, a shield raised preemptively against criticism.

I bit my lip, feeling the familiar stir of doubts that haunted every corner of our relationship. Was this tension ever going to ease? Could we find our way back, or were we fumbling in the dark, grasping for a connection that had long since frayed?

"Fine," I replied, though the knot in my stomach tightened. "Just make sure you're there."

"We've gone over this," Steve snapped, the impatience clear in his tone. "I will be."

"Of course." My response was automatic, but inside, my thoughts churned. We were like two actors rehearsing our lines, perfecting the performance of a happily married couple. But the cracks in our façade were too deep, too raw to ignore.

I got out of bed, the floor cold under my bare feet. There was a distance between us that spanned more than the few feet of carpet—it was filled with unsaid words and unresolved issues. I moved towards my dresser, my movements deliberate, my reflection in the mirror a stranger with haunted eyes.

"Madelyn..." Steve's voice softened slightly, a hint of the old warmth seeping through. "I know things have been rough, but..."

"But what?" I turned to face him, my heart aching with a mix of hope and resentment. "Do you know how hard it is for me to look at you some days?"

He flinched, the vulnerability in his deep-set blue eyes flickering before he masked it with frustration. "I'm trying here, okay? What more do you want from me?"

"I don't know," I confessed, feeling the sting of tears. "Sometimes I don't even know what I want from myself."

"Great," he muttered, walking away, the finality of his footsteps echoing in the hollow space between us.

I collapsed onto the edge of the bed, my hands trembling as I fought to quell the emotions threatening to spill over. This wasn't the life I had envisioned—the love that was supposed to sustain us now felt like a puzzle with missing pieces. How did we get here? Where did we go wrong? Then, Jake invaded my thoughts, and a tiny smile slowly grew on my face.

THE STRUGGLE

But Lauren, for the tiny heartbeat of hope that still lingered, I would try. I would fight for us, even if it meant facing the darkest parts of our marriage. And maybe, just maybe, we could find our way back to each other in the wreckage.

"Steve," I murmured to the empty space beside me in bed, the name feeling like a shard of glass on my tongue. The wound of his infidelity was still fresh, its sting a constant companion. "How could you?" No response came, of course; he'd left for work minutes ago, leaving behind the scent of his aftershave and a bunch of words only in my head.

I sat up, wrapping my arms around myself as if I could hold together the pieces of a life fractured by cheating. My mind replayed the moment I found out—the late nights I had brushed off as business meetings, the lipstick stain on his collar I wished I could dismiss as my own. But the truth, much like the early dawn outside, had a cruel way of illuminating lies.

"Trust is a fragile thing," I whispered to the reflection in the mirror, tracing the lines of stress that seemed etched deeper every day. Expressive green eyes that once held dreams of forever now searched for a semblance of normalcy in their depths.

Shaking off the cobwebs of hurt, I stood and moved with purpose. There were events to plan, lives to celebrate— even if my own felt like it was on pause. I got in the shower to wash off the morning bad feelings, and I made my way to the office.

The familiar hum of WedLux welcomed me, the small office space filled with fabric swatches and floral arrangements; this was the world I had built from the ground up. WedLux was more than a business to me; it was a world I curated with the tenderness of an artist, breathing life into every detail. The boutique office, nestled in the heart of downtown, hummed with creativity and the soft rustle of silk and tulle. It was here that I poured my heart into crafting moments that would live on in memories and photographs; the events showcased love's grandeur— perhaps even more poignant because my own love story had faltered.

"Okay, let's see," I muttered, scanning the list of tasks for the upcoming wedding. "Seating chart for the Henderson reception... check. Confirm delivery for the peony centerpieces... check." I took pride in my work, details meticulously arranged, elements pieces of artistry crafted with care. If only life could be organized with such precision.

"Are you sure about the blue hydrangeas? They might clash with the bridesmaids' dresses," I imagined a client saying, their question pulling me back to reality.

"Trust me," I would answer, the words bitter on my lips. "I know how to make things work together." If only I could apply the same confidence to mending the distance between Steve and me.

A sigh escaped me as I placed a call to the caterer, confirming the menu. "Yes, everything needs to be perfect,"

I insisted into the receiver, my voice steady even as my hands trembled slightly.

"Darling, you always make everything so beautiful," I could hear my clients praise. If I could channel even a fraction of that dedication into piecing together my fractured marriage, perhaps there would be hope for Steve and me.

"Steve..." His name was a prayer, a plea for understanding that maybe one day, I could look at him without seeing what he had done. Every choice I made, every event I planned, was a step toward something resembling forgiveness—if such a thing was ever truly possible.

"Lauren needs us both," I reminded myself, picturing our daughter's bright smile. She was the anchor in the stormy sea of my doubts, the reason I couldn't simply let go. For her, I needed to find a way through this, to navigate the choppy waters of mistrust and pain.

"Mommy will make everything okay," I promised, though the rooms of my heart echoed with skepticism. Would Steve and I ever find our way back to what we used to be? Or would we remain adrift, two souls lost amidst the wreckage of what used to be?

As I continued my daily routine, the precision of my work in stark contrast to the chaos of my emotions, I clung to the hope that the future held answers. For now, all I could do was wait, plan, and endure.

After tucking Lauren into bed with a story and a kiss, I retreated to the sanctuary of my home office. I let my thoughts drift to Steve once again—the man in the room next to mine who once completed the picture of our perfect little family. Now, every memory was tainted.

Lauren, with her curly brown hair sprawled across the pillow and her breath steady in the quiet of the night, remained oblivious to the storm brewing in the hearts of the adults around her. Her innocence was a stark contrast to the mix of emotions that filled our home. Lauren's eagerness to learn, to explore every nook and cranny of our lives together, often brought a much-needed lightness. Her happiness could cut through the thickest tension, reminding us of simpler times.

She was the bridge between Steve and me, her very presence a constant reminder of the love that once bound us together. Even in her absence, her drawings pinned on the fridge, her toys scattered across the living room floor, and her endless questions about the world around her kept the essence of her spirit alive in every corner of our house.

Lauren's curiosity about love and relationships often caught me off guard, her questions piercing in their innocence. "Why do people who love each other get sad?" she once asked, her big eyes searching mine for an answer that I struggled to find. It was in these moments that I realized how much she was absorbing, like a sponge, the emotional currents that flowed around her.

Her relationship with Steve was uncomplicated by deception and disappointment that clouded ours. To

Lauren, her father was a hero, a figure of unconditional love and support. Watching them together, I often felt a pang of longing for the naivety that allowed her to love so freely, without reservation or fear of heartbreak.

It was a balancing act, shielding her from the pain while nurturing her growth into a compassionate, strong individual. Lauren's bright smile and boundless energy were constant reminders of what was at stake, pushing me to fight through the darkness for the sake of our little girl, who was the embodiment of the purest form of love and hope. *Is it still love if trust is shattered?* I thought. My reflection in the mirror was a ghost of contentment, eyes haunted by what-ifs and might-have-beens.

I sank into my chair; the leather cool and unyielding against my back. My mind wandered to the weddings I orchestrated with such precision, where vows were exchanged with a certainty I envied. Could those promises endure the trials that had torn at the seams of my own marriage? I craved the simplicity of my clients' beginnings, with no time and error.

"Madelyn?" Steve's voice filtered through the half-open door. His silhouette lingered on the threshold, a hesitant intruder.

"Lauren's asleep," I said, not turning to face him. "We should try to keep it down."

"Right." He paused, the space between us swollen with unsaid words. "I don't want to fight anymore."

"Neither do I," I admitted, my throat tight. "But wanting isn't enough, is it?"

"I'm trying to be better, Maddy." There was a plea in his voice, one I'd heard before.

"Trying doesn't change the past." I spoke to the reflection of us, distorted in the glossy surface of the desk. "Every time I look at you, I remember, and it hurts. It hurts so much."

"Let me make it right." His voice broke.

"Can you?" My eyes met his in the reflection, searching for the man I married ten years ago. "Because I need more than apologies—I need to know why. Why her? Why us? We were so freaking happy. Or at least I was. So stupid!"

"I don't know," he whispered, the truth in his skepticism. "It was a terrible mistake. She never meant anything to me. You know this. I want us to be happy again. "

"But with your assistant... how can I ever trust you again? I can't even be at peace when you're at work. Then how can we move forward?" The question unanswered.

"How about we start by not talking about this anymore?" Steve suggested, his voice a mixture of frustration and desperation.

"Mommy, Daddy, stop it!" Lauren's cry from the doorway jolted us both out of our heated exchange. She stood there, small and frightened, clutching her stuffed bear tightly to her chest as if it could shield her from the harsh realities of the world.

"Lauren, baby, go back to bed," I urged, my heart breaking at the sight of her distress. I rushed to her side, kneeling to be at eye level. "Everything's okay," I whispered, trying to infuse my voice with a calm I didn't feel.

"Please don't be sad," she begged, her voice quivering as tears brimmed in her wide, fearful eyes. Her innocence in that moment was a piercing reminder of the impact our actions had on her, an embodiment of the love and security she deserved but was threatened by our discord.

Steve and I exchanged a look, a silent agreement passing between us that this was not the time nor the place for our grievances. He approached slowly, his expression softening at the sight of our daughter's distress.

"We're not sad, sweetheart," Steve said, his voice gentle, attempting to reassure her with a tenderness that seemed foreign in the tension-filled room. "Mommy and Daddy were just having a grown-up conversation. We promise, everything is going to be okay."

But the assurance felt hollow, even to me. How could we promise everything would be okay when we were so far from okay ourselves? Yet, for Lauren, we tried to bridge that gap, to protect her from adult emotions and conflicts.

"Can I sleep with you tonight?" Lauren's small voice broke through the dead silence, her eyes moving between Steve and me, seeking solace in the storm.

"Of course, baby," I answered immediately, lifting her into my arms, her stuffed bear now sandwiched between us.

Steve nodded, his earlier defensiveness replaced by a concern for our daughter's wellbeing.

As we made our way back to our bedroom, Lauren's trust and need for reassurance grounded us. In that moment, our roles as parents—to provide love and protection—overshadowed our personal turmoil. Lauren's presence, her need for peace and assurance, became a silent vow to try harder, to navigate with more care, for her sake if not for our own."Sweetheart," I knelt, brushing away her tears with a thumb. "Mommy and Daddy are just... working on things. We both love you very much, and that will never change."

"Love fixes everything, right?" She looked between Steve and me, hope mingling with sleep in her gaze.

"Love is powerful, darling," I said, sharing a look with Steve. "But sometimes, it needs help."

"Like glue?" she asked, her innocence piercing me.

"Exactly like glue," Steve answered, joining us on the floor.

"Will we be okay?" Her voice was small, a reflection of the vulnerability in my own heart.

"We're going to try our best," I promised, holding her close. "That's all we can do."

As Lauren nestled against me, her breathing soon deepening into the rhythms of sleep, I wondered about the strength of that glue—whether it could mend the fractures or merely hold the pieces together long enough for us to pretend they weren't breaking apart.

THE STRUGGLE

"I'm done fighting," I whispered. "I can't do it anymore." I slowly lifted Lauren, carried her to her room and tucked her in.

"Can we talk? Really talk?" Steve's shadow fell across my sketches, the dark shape merging with the outlines of floral arrangements and seating charts.

"About what? The weather? Lauren's soccer practice?" I asked, my tone edged with a frost that belied the warmth he once ignited in me. My heart pulsed with a painful rhythm, a metronome out of sync with his intentions.

"About us. About this distance that's now between us." He moved to sit beside me, his proximity a reminder of a time when such closeness offered comfort instead of confusion.

"Steve, there's an ocean of silence filled with words you never said and actions you can't take back," I replied, my voice barely above a whisper, betraying the tempest within. "I don't know how to bridge that."

"Maybe we start with a single step. I've been going to counseling, trying to understand why I... why I hurt you," he admitted, his blue eyes seeking mine, searching for a foothold on remorse's slippery slope.

"Understanding doesn't erase disloyalty," I said, closing my sketchbook with a soft thud, a definitive end to one conversation, an uncertain beginning to another. "It doesn't rebuild trust overnight."

"I'm not asking for overnight. I'm asking for a chance," he implored, reaching out to tentatively touch the back of my hand. "For us, for Lauren, for the life we dreamt of."

"Life isn't a fairytale. Not all dreams come true," I pulled away, my heart aching at the gesture, at the hope I dared not entertain. "Some stories are meant to be cautionary tales."

"Is that what we are? A cautionary tale?" His question thick with fears and unshed tears.

"Maybe. Or maybe we're just at a crossroads," I mused, feeling the familiar tug of indecision. The desire to believe in second chances warred with the need to protect the fragile pieces of myself.

"Crossroads lead somewhere. Where do you want ours to go?" Steve pressed, his voice a blend of desperation and determination.

"Forward," I breathed out, the word less a direction. "But I don't know if that's together or apart."

"Let's find that out together," he suggested, a plea wrapped in a vow.

"Maybe," I allowed, though the maybe tasted like bittersweet chocolate—rich with possibility but tinged with past pain.

I looked at him, really looked, seeing not just the man who had broken my trust but also the one who had once filled my world with laughter and love. Could we salvage the remnants of a bond frayed by cheating, or were we chasing the ghosts of a happiness long since past?

As I watched him retreat to the solitude of his study, a part of me wondered if hope was merely a prelude to greater heartache. The night whispered promises of revelations yet to come, starts symbolizing the countless possibilities that lay beyond the horizon.

CHAPTER 4

Digging Deep

THE EARLY EVENING sun threw a kaleidoscope of colors across my desk, the orange hues dancing over the scattered blueprints and fabric samples. The phone felt like a rock in my hand, almost like it knew I was about to ask for help, something that didn't come easy to me. I dialed Sofia's number, the beeps echoing my racing heart.

"What's up, girlie?" Sofia's voice was like a wave of comfort, washing over me.

I started fiddling with my pen. "I'm drowning in tulle and table settings here. I've got the Henderson birthday bash and the Daltons' wedding on my plate, and I—"

"Say no more," she cut in, her tone laced with enthusiasm. "I'm your girl. When do we start?"

Relief washed through me as I leaned back in my chair. Sofia's eagerness was like a life raft. "How soon can you get here?" I asked, not wanting to waste a single second now that I had her on board.

"Give me thirty minutes." The clacking of her keyboard filtered through the line as she spoke. "I've got ideas!"

"Thirty minutes," I said, grateful beyond words. As I hung up, my gaze drifted to the photographs lining my wall—events that were once just ideas in my head, brought to life with Sofia by my side. I let myself smile, feeling that rush of creative energy I always got before diving into a new project.

When Sofia arrived, she swept into the room like a whirlwind of inspiration. Her black hair cascaded over her shoulders, her hazel eyes sparkling with determination.

"Alright, let's brainstorm," she said, rolling out a whiteboard from the corner of the room. She grabbed a marker and started scribbling. "For the birthday party, what if we go with a vintage circus theme? Think big-top tents, acrobats, fire breathers!"

My mind raced with the possibilities. "That could be sensational. We can have popcorn stands, candy apple stations..." I trailed off, picturing the delight on the guests' faces. "I've changed my mind about the theme a hundred times."

"And for the Daltons' wedding?" Sofia tapped the marker against her chin. "I know Dylan's family is old money, so they'll want elegance. But we need to shake it up a bit. How about a garden soirée with a twist?"

"Perhaps an enchanted forest vibe?" I suggested, warming up to the idea. "Fairy lights woven through the trees, moss-covered centerpieces, ethereal music..."

"Perfect!" Sofia's excitement was infectious. "Mads, this is going to be epic. You've got the vision; you just needed a little push."

"Thanks, Sof," I murmured, feeling a surge of confidence. With her by my side, I suddenly believed we could pull off anything. "Seriously, Sof, I can't thank you enough," I said, perching on the edge of the coffee table. The words felt small compared to the swell of gratitude in my chest. "You swoop in like some kind of fairy godmother whenever I'm lost. I'd be floundering without you."

She looked up, her eyes glinting with warmth. "What are friends for? Besides, planning events with Madelyn Montgomery is hardly a hardship. It's thrilling, like diving headfirst into a masterpiece waiting to be painted. Speaking of masterpieces," she continued, a nostalgic smile playing on her lips, "it reminds me of my own wedding to Mark seven years ago, remember? It was something out of a fairy tale."

Sofia's wedding to Mark had been the talk of their circle, a lavish affair that was both elegant and deeply personal. As a stay-at-home wife, Sofia had devoted herself to planning every detail of their special day, working closely with event planners to ensure that their wedding was nothing short of spectacular. Mark, with his successful career in finance, had wanted to give Sofia the wedding of her dreams, sparing no expense. The venue was breathtaking, nestled in a luxurious estate with sprawling gardens that were in full bloom, creating a picturesque setting for their vows.

Mark's career had indeed afforded them a life of comfort and luxury, but Sofia needed him more; his career kept him away from home a lot. She always maintained that the true wealth was in their relationship and the life they were building together. Even now, as she helped me plan another event, her experiences from her own wedding brought a depth of understanding and creativity to the table, making her contributions invaluable.

"Every detail mattered to us," she mused, her eyes reflecting the joy of that day. "From the flowers that seemed to dance in the light to the music that filled the air with love. Mark and I wanted our wedding not just to be a celebration of our love, but a memory our friends and family would cherish as much as we do."

As Sofia reminisced on her memories, it was clear that her wedding to Mark wasn't just an event from the past; it was a cornerstone of her life's story, a moment when two paths entwined to create a joint journey forward. Her ability to bring such passion and attention to detail to the wedding planning she'd help me with was not just a skill, but a gift, born from the love and joy of her own experience.

I chuckled at her analogy, feeling a familiar affection thread itself around my heart. She always knew how to remind me that I was more than my insecurities whispered.

"Okay, brass tacks time." Sofia clapped her hands together, sending a shower of imaginary glitter through the air. "For the birthday bash, do we have a venue yet?"

"Thinking The Grandiose Room at the Pennington Hotel. It has that old-world charm that'll complement the vintage circus theme perfectly," I mused, envisioning trapeze artists swinging from the ornate ceilings. "Or we could do it in our backyard. There is plenty of space."

"Let's think about it," she said decisively. "It screams spectacle. And for the wedding?" Her gaze settled on a lace sample, hinting at the elegance required for such an affair.

"Rosewood Gardens," I breathed out. "It's as if the place were designed for fairytales. I can already see the string quartet nestled beneath the weeping willows."

"You're something else," Sofia praised, jotting down notes on her clipboard. "Decorations?"

"String lights, lanterns..." My voice trailed off as I visualized every detail. "And for the Daltons' wedding... oh, those centerpieces with greenery and crystals to catch the light."

"Genius." Her pen danced across the page. "Guest list management?"

"Digital RSVP system for the party," I proposed, the gears in my mind whirring. "As for the wedding, something more personal. Hand-delivered invitations, perhaps?"

"Classy touch, Mads." Sofia's approval was a the calm to my ever-present anxiety. "It says, 'Your presence is a gift' without uttering a word."

My lips curved into a smile, comforted by the knowledge that together, we were an unstoppable force. The doubts that so often clouded my judgment were slinking away, banished by the clarity of our joint vision.

The golden hour sunlight spilled through the bay window, igniting flecks of amber in Sofia's hazel eyes as she leaned forward, her enthusiasm a strong force. "And Dylan Dalton," I began hesitantly, my fingers tracing the edge of an ivory lace tablecloth sample, "What do we know about the groom himself?"

"Ah, the man of the hour." A sly grin played on Sofia's lips, and she lowered her voice conspiratorially. "He's like a novel with half the pages mysteriously missing. I've heard whispers about his philanthropy, seen glimpses of him at charity galas."

"Whispers and glimpses," the words rolling over in my mind like smooth pebbles in a stream. "But what lies beneath that polished veneer?" My curiosity was a live wire within me, electric and insistent.

"Curiosity killed the cat, but satisfaction brought it back," Sofia quipped, then softened. "But you're right. There's something mysterious about him. He's not just any wealthy bachelor; he's a puzzle waiting to be solved. His family, though—that's where the plot thickens."

My heart rate picked up—a combination of excitement and trepidation—as I imagined unearthing the layers of Dylan Dalton's life. "What about them?" I probed, leaning in closer, my event planner's precision giving way to intrigue.

"Old money," she offered with a twirl of her pen, "and it seems they guard their privacy like a dragon hoards gold. Dylan has no pictures of himself online. I checked. People say he is handsome. But I did overhear that his grandmother was quite the matriarch, a real steel magnolia."

"And what about his fiancée?" I pressed, my curiosity demanding more details.

"Well," she began, "her name is Eleanor. Apparently, she's from another old-money family. The match seems to be one of those arrangements made for the benefit of the families rather than the individuals involved. Rumor has it that the families have a long history of intertwining their interests, and this wedding is just another strategic move in their social chess game."

"Interesting..." Was it professional interest or something deeper driving my questions? Could it be because I was raised by my grandmother, Ann, who instilled in me a fondness for drama and gossip? I couldn't yet tell.

"Maybe we should dig a little deeper," Sofia suggested, tapping the eraser end of her pencil against her chin.

"Alright, let's strategize," I agreed, and Sofia's face lit up with a victorious smile. We were more than planners now; we were sleuths embarking on a clandestine quest. And despite the risks, I couldn't suppress the flutter of excitement that danced up my spine.

The glow from the laptop screen softened the gathering dusk in my cozy home office, casting a pale light on Sofia's intent features as she perched on the edge of her seat. The cursor blinked patiently in the search bar, awaiting our next move.

"Okay," I murmured, my fingers hovering over the keyboard. "Social media is usually a goldmine for personal details. Let's start with the basics—Facebook, Instagram, LinkedIn."

Sofia nodded, her eyes alight with a detective's fervor. "I bet a guy like Dylan has his profiles locked down tight, but there's always something that slips through."

"Sometimes it's the small things that speak volumes," I agreed, typing swiftly. As profiles loaded, we leaned in, scrutinizing every post, photo, shared article for hints of the man who remained enigmatic despite our frequent interactions.

"Look at this," Sofia pointed to a group photo on Dylan's LinkedIn page—not of himself of course; a charity event by the look of it. "He's quite the philanthropist. That could be an angle for the wedding theme—elegance with a heart?"

"Philanthropy... yes," I said, scribbling the thought down. "Elegance with a heart." A potential key to Dylan Dalton lay within the charity work he so publicly aligned himself with.

"Public records next?" Sofia suggested, switching tabs with practiced ease.

"Property holdings, business ventures, anything that's filed with the state," I directed, my pulse quickening. This was more than mere curiosity—it was an immersion into the web of another's life, yet somewhere in the back of my mind, Jake lingered, an unbidden thought amidst my focus. *Will I see him again?* I thought. My gaze met hers, and I snapped back to reality. I saw the reflection of my own intensity mirrored there.

"Let's set some boundaries," I suggested, pushing back from the computer. "We'll look, we'll note, but we won't overstep. Agreed?"

"Agreed," Sofia smiled, her hazel eyes earnest. "After all, you're the best at creating dreams out of details, Maddy. We're just making sure they're the right ones."

"Right," I breathed out, my mind swirling with ideas and ethical lines not to cross. As the room darkened around us, the screen's glow hummed with potential secrets and stories yet untold. I felt the thrill of the hunt tempered by the responsibility of my role—a wedding planner, not a sleuth. And in that moment, as the first stars pricked the twilight sky, I knew that navigating this path would require every ounce of my creativity and discretion.

A quickening pulse danced beneath my skin as I pored over the open tabs on my laptop promising a sliver of insight into Dylan Dalton's mysterious life. The cursor blinked impatiently on the screen, mirroring my own restless anticipation.

"Stay focused, babe." Sofia's voice cut through my reverie, sharp yet coated in warmth. "We've got two major events to pull off. Don't let your personal feelings for Jake sidetrack you."

"Jake?" I asked, startled by the sudden mention of him. My thoughts flickered to our last encounter, the way his laughter had filled the spaces between us, making everything seem lighter, easier. But this—this was work, and Sofia was right. "How do you know about Jake?"

"You better be careful when you go around town. Keystone is so small. Everyone knows everything and everybody here." She slightly raised her eyebrows—something she'd do whenever she'd get worried. "You are lucky it was my cousin Sara. She said you looked quite interested in the guy."

I shifted uncomfortably under Sofia's scrutinizing gaze. "We only exchanged a few words," I said, trying to downplay the impact Jake had on me.

"And phone numbers," Sofia interrupted with a smile, but her concern still evident in her eyes. "Why didn't you tell me about this gorgeous stranger?"

"Because I only just met him. I don't even know if I will see him again. But he is so freaking cute." I looked down in a shy smile, the makes-you-blush kind. Sofia had been my best friend and partner in crime since college, and she always knew how to get through to me.

I took a moment to compose myself before speaking again. "You're right, Sofia," I admitted, my voice filled with a mixture of determination and vulnerability. "This Jake guy got under my skin. I don't know what I want to do about Steve. As you know, we are going through a very rough time and meeting Jake was a breath of fresh air. I was unaware I could have some kind of feelings by talking to someone else."

"Good." Sofia nodded approvingly. "This means you are still you. You are a woman that hasn't felt loved and admired the right way for a long time. Don't feel guilty. Steve messed up and that's on him. He knew by doing what he did things would change between you two."

I took a sip of water. "If something else happens with Jake, I'll let you know. Promise."

"You better believe it! Throughout our fifteen-year friendship, we've shared everything, and we're certainly not about to change that now," Sofia asserted firmly.

"Fifteen years... Can you believe it? Do you remember how we first crossed paths? That bar adjacent to our college campus... what was its name again? And just like that we are thirty-four years old now."

"Underdog," Sofia replied with a laugh, the memory bringing a spark to her eyes.

"Ah, yes! Our second home every weekend during those wild partying days. Yet, amidst all that fun, we found something priceless—each other," I reminisced, a smile spreading across my face.

"That's the best takeaway," Sofia agreed, her eyes softening for a moment before she refocused on the task at hand. "Now, back to business. This wedding won't plan itself, and I need you fully engaged. Let's make it flawless."

"Always," I reassured her with a determined smile, though the flutter in my chest hadn't stilled. It wasn't just about organizing flower arrangements or selecting the perfect font for invitations. It was about creating a day that would echo through the lives of two people—a day that, somehow, now held a piece of me within it.

And as I sifted through the pixels and data, I allowed myself a momentary indulgence, imagining Jake's reaction to our little investigation. Would he find it thrilling? Irresponsible? I let out a silent sigh, banishing the thought once more. This wasn't about him. It was about Dylan, his bride, and the story they were about to tell.

"Okay, for the birthday party, I'm thinking a balloon arch over the entryway," I suggested, my finger tracing as if drawing the vision into reality. "And we can't forget a photo booth with props that scream 'over-the-hill' humor."

Sofia chuckled, her eyes sparkling with approval. "That'll be interesting! That'll get everyone laughing. And for the wedding? Are we settled on the classic theme?"

"Absolutely," I replied, feeling the familiar thrill of seeing an event come together in my mind's eye. "White wooden chairs, centerpieces featuring wildflowers... It's going to be like stepping into an enchanted forest clearing."

"Enchanting indeed." Sofia's voice carried a note of admiration. "Dylan's guests won't know what hit them."

With every suggestion and confirmation, my confidence grew. Despite my seasoned experience as a wedding planner, the flutter of nerves would stay unaltered when working on each event. This was more than planning; it was crafting memories, sculpting moments from the ether of imagination. As Sofia busily typed away, creating spreadsheets that would guide us through the chaos, I couldn't help but marvel at how our skills complemented each other. Her precision and my creativity—a perfect match.

"Wait until they see the cake designs," I said, flipping through a portfolio of past creations, my fingers brushing over glossy photographs. "I want the wedding cake to be a showstopper—five tiers, maybe, with sugar flowers that mimic the real ones in the bride's bouquet."

"Make it six tiers, darling. Go big or go home," Sofia teased.

I grinned, jotting down the idea. "Six tiers it is."

We leaned back, surveying our handiwork, a combination of plans and possibilities laid bare before us. Our eyes met, and there was a spark there—an unspoken acknowledgment of the adventure we were embarking on.

"Imagine what we'll find out about Dylan Dalton," I murmured, the name itself sending a shiver of curiosity down my spine. "Every detail could be a clue, a piece of his story that he's kept hidden."

"Or a piece of his heart," Sofia added thoughtfully. "People are like puzzles. You never know what secrets lie just beneath the surface until you start looking."

"Exactly." My heart hammered with anticipation. The mystery of Dylan Dalton beckoned, promising revelations that might change everything. The notion was exhilarating, the unknown a siren call to my soul.

"Next, we dive deep," I declared, my voice confident, getting ready for our newfound mission.

"Leave no stone unturned," Sofia agreed, her determination mirroring my own.

As the clock ticked on, heralding the late hour, I felt a surge of energy pulse through me. The events were coming together, but it was the enigma of Dylan Dalton that truly captured my imagination. What would we discover? Would it be a tale of romance, a family saga, or something entirely unexpected?

CHAPTER 5

The Spark

THE CHIME of my phone broke the silence of the afternoon, a sharp ping against the soft hum of the air conditioner. I reached for it not sure if I hoped or not to see Jake's name. The screen lit up, casting a pale glow on the patterned tablecloth.

"Meet me at Quill Haven?" Jake's words danced before my eyes, each letter etching a mixture of elation and anxiety in my body.

I bit my lip, tapping my fingers against the wooden edge of the kitchen table. The room seemed to close in around me, pictures of my husband and me smiling from frames, watching my every move.

"Madelyn, what are you doing?" I murmured to myself, the words a faint whisper lost among the echoes of my indecision. My marriage, though frayed with silences and sidelong glances, was still a commitment I wore like a second skin.

I pictured Jake, his tousled dark hair falling into those warm brown eyes that saw right through me. He had this way, a gentleness wrapped in strength, which unraveled the knots in my chest without even trying. That feeling I hadn't felt in so long.

"Should I?" My loyalty to my husband clutched at me, a reminder of vows and dreams, now dulled by the passage of time.

A sigh escaped my lips as I traced the rim of my coffee mug, the porcelain cool and smooth beneath my touch. My heart raced with the thrill of rebellion, yet ached with guilt.

"Jake," I finally typed out, my thumb hovering over the send button, lingering like my resolve. "Why now? Why stir these dormant embers?" I deleted the text, only to retype it again, caught in a loop of longing and duty.

"Can I really do this?" I asked the empty room, seeking counsel from the silent walls. There was comfort in Jake's understanding, a solace that my marriage had ceased to offer. But at what cost?

"Damn it, Madelyn." My voice was a half-hearted scold, laced with a yearning I couldn't suppress. The battle within rage, love and loyalty clashing like waves against a rocky shore.

"Fine," I breathed out, my finger pressing down, sending the word through the ether. As the message delivered, a sense of finality settled over me. I'd crossed an invisible line, driven by emotions I couldn't ignore.

"See you there," came Jake's immediate response, a simple affirmation that sent my heart into a fluttering frenzy. I stood, the chair scraping back with a sound that felt like a verdict. With every step towards the door, I could feel the threads of my old life fraying, giving way to something new.

The bookshop door heralded my arrival, slicing through the silence that had cocooned me during the drive over. The familiar scent of aged paper and worn leather wrapped around me like a comforting embrace, yet my stomach churned with a cocktail of nerves and excitement.

"Deep breaths," I muttered to myself, clutching the strap of my purse tighter as I ventured further into the labyrinth of towering shelves. My fingers grazed the spines of novels, a world I'd once escaped to, seeking refuge from the chaos of my own life. But now, the titles blurred together, a jumbled reflection of the storm inside me.

"Madelyn?" The voice, soft and tinged with a warmth I didn't know but knew too well at the same time, cut through my reverie. My heart skipped, then galloped—a wild thing within my chest. I composed my features, schooling them into a mask of casual ease I was far from feeling.

"Hey," I called back, feigning nonchalance. My eyes darted around, unable to settle on anything but the anticipation bubbling within me. I rounded a corner, my heart thudding against my ribcage, betraying my composed façade.

"Thanks for coming." His words were simple.

"Of course," I replied, though every fiber of my being screamed that it was anything but ordinary. "I've missed this place," I added, letting my gaze linger on a display of new releases, avoiding the intensity I feared I'd find in his eyes.

"Me too," he said, and I could hear the smile in his voice, gentle and inviting.

I glanced up, finally meeting his gaze. His brown eyes were pools of understanding, reflecting back my own tangled emotions. For a moment, we simply stood there, two souls caught in a silent conversation only we could comprehend.

"Seems quieter than usual," I observed, clinging to small talk. My hands fidgeted with the hem of my cardigan.

"Maybe it's just waiting for us to fill it with our stories," he suggested, his tone playful yet edged with something deeper, something unsaid.

"Maybe." My reply was a whisper, my thoughts drifting to the stories we'd shared, the chapters of our lives that had intertwined and diverged.

"Shall we?" He gestured towards the cozy reading nook nestled in the corner, its plush armchairs an invitation to lose oneself in a good book—or perhaps, in a conversation that might alter the course of one's story.

"Let's." My feet moved of their own accord, carrying me closer to him, to the precipice of decisions whose consequences I couldn't yet fathom. It felt like the turn of a page, the beginning of a new chapter that I wasn't sure I was ready to write. Yet I couldn't deny the pull, the desire to read on, to discover where this tale might lead.

As we settled into the armchairs, a comfortable silence enveloped us, a prelude to the confessions and revelations that awaited. The scent of books was grounding me, giving me the courage to face whatever came next.

"How have the event planning trials and tribulations been?" Jake asked, a playful note dancing beneath his words.

"Trials is an understatement." I chuckled, allowing the familiarity of our banter to ease the thundering of my heart. "Last week's wedding would've made War and Peace seem like light reading."

"Ah, but you're the master of ceremonies," he countered. "Orchestrating chaos into harmony."

"More like herding cats." I brushed a stray lock of hair behind my ear, feeling the tension begin to unwind just a fraction. "But enough about me. What do you do?"

"I'm a business owner. My new coffee shop should open in two months. The process was low but steady. We finally found the perfect espresso machine," Jake replied, his eyes lighting up.

"That is awesome. I always dreamed of having my own coffee shop. I'd sell coffee, books, and flowers," I murmured, my fingers grazing the spine of a poetry collection, drawing comfort from its embossed title. "I'm glad it's progressing and it'll open up soon. Can't wait to see."

"Progress," he said, watching me with an intensity that spoke volumes without uttering a single word. "That's what life's about, isn't it? Moving forward, one step at a time."

"Sometimes, it feels more like stumbling," I admitted, a thread of vulnerability weaving itself into our exchange.

"Perhaps," he mused, "but even a stumble can be part of the dance."

The scent of aged paper and leather-bound tomes mingled with the faint aroma of roasting coffee beans, creating a cocoon that insulated us from the world outside.

"Bookshops are timeless sanctuaries," Jake said, and as I glanced around at the towering shelves, I understood why.

"Have you read this one?" Jake reached for a novel adorned with an intricate cover, its edges worn from the affection of many readers. "It's about second chances. The kind life hardly gives."

I took the book from him, our fingers brushing in a whisper of contact. "Second chances." The phrase hung between us, laden with meaning yet as delicate as the dust motes dancing in the slanting light.

THE SPARK

"Life's generous sometimes," he said softly, his gaze not leaving mine.

"Or maybe we just become better at seizing moments." The words tumbled out before I could stop them, each syllable infused with a yearning I hadn't intended to reveal.

"Maybe." Jake's voice was low, a note of something more flickering within it.

"Do you ever think about what-ifs?" His question crowding the space.

"Sometimes," I confessed, tracing the embossed title with my thumb. "But thinking can be... dangerous."

"Perhaps," he agreed, taking a step closer. "But feeling, now that's something else entirely."

I glanced up, startled by the proximity of him, the way his presence enveloped me. There was a warmth there, a magnetic pull that I couldn't deny, even as it sent tremors of trepidation through me.

"Feeling is..." I started, but the sentence dangled unfinished, too freighted with implications.

"Real," he supplied, his eyes searching mine. "Raw. And sometimes, it leads us down paths we never expected to tread."

"Paths fraught with complication," I added, unable to look away despite the alarm bells clanging faintly in the back of my mind. My pulse quickened, beats drumrolls marking the precipice on which we teetered.

"Complication isn't necessarily a bad thing," he whispered, almost as if he feared the words would shatter the harmony we'd found.

"Isn't it?" My question was barely audible, my breath catching.

"Only if you let it be." His hand brushed against mine, sending a jolt of electricity up my arm. The touch was fleeting but laden with intent, stirring a maelstrom within me.

"Jake," I breathed out, my voice a mixture of warning and plea. "We shouldn't..."

"Maybe," he conceded, stepping back slightly but not breaking our connection. "But then again, sometimes 'shouldn't' is just another word for fear."

My heart thundered, echoing off the walls lined with stories of love, disloyalty, and impossible choices. The tension crackled between us, a tangible force that threatened to consume all reason.

"Are we just characters in someone else's narrative?" I asked, half-joking, half-desperate to lighten the gravity that pulled us inexorably together.

"Or are we writing our own story?" he countered, his smile tinged with melancholy.

The dim light in the room cast shadows on his face, accentuating the lines of conflict etched there. His gaze searching for answers within the depths of my own confusion.

THE SPARK

But the truth was a looming specter, threatening to shatter the fragile bubble we had created in that moment. I took a step back, attempting to create a physical distance that mirrored the emotional abyss I was struggling to bridge.

"Jake," I began, my voice faltering as I looked away, unable to meet his intense gaze. "There's something I need to tell you."

He waited, the anticipation in his eyes betraying a mixture of curiosity and trepidation. The room constricted, amplifying the gravity of the confession.

"I'm... I'm married," I confessed, the words escaping my lips with a heaviness that matched the one of my conscience. The admission brought a tension I could sense we both felt.

For a moment, there was silence. Jake's expression remained inscrutable, as if he were processing the revelation, deciphering the many layers of our connection. The air seemed to crackle with silent words, a storm of emotions brewing beneath the surface.

"Married," he repeated, his voice barely above a whisper. The single word held a myriad of emotions—surprise, disappointment, and perhaps a trace of understanding. His gaze finally met mine, and in that moment, I saw a flicker of something that resembled resignation.

"I should've known," he said, his tone a mix of bitterness and acceptance. "There's always a complication, isn't there?"

The room, once filled with the promise of something undefined, now echoed with our truths. The choice between the path we had started to tread and the obligations we carried seemed more daunting than ever.

The seconds stretched into an eternity as we stood there. The room, once a haven for clandestine possibilities, now held an undercurrent of regret and unfulfilled desire.

"Jake, I didn't plan for any of this," I confessed. "I never intended for our paths to intersect like this."

He remained silent, his eyes revealing a mixture of emotions that danced between frustration and a resigned understanding. The tension an acknowledgment of the invisible threads that had bound us together, only to be severed by the truth.

"Madelyn," he finally spoke, his voice low and measured, "life has a way of surprising us. Choices, consequences — they're all part of the story we're living. There must be a reason you gave me your number and decided to come today." His gaze straight into mine. "Do you want to talk about it?"

"Steve doesn't... he doesn't see me anymore." The confession slipped from my lips like a sigh, betraying the façade of composure I had meticulously constructed. "Not the real me, anyway."

Jake leaned in, elbows resting on the table scattered with antiquarian volumes and forgotten lore. "You're saying he looks at you but doesn't actually *see* you?" His voice was a gentle prod, inviting more than questioning, encouraging the walls I had built around my heart to crumble.

"Exactly," I whispered, tracing the spine of an aged novel beside me. My fingers stayed over the embossed title, drawing comfort from the solid presence of something so enduring. "It's as though I'm just a character in our married life—a role I play. But inside, where it counts, I'm invisible."

He nodded slowly. "That must feel incredibly lonely."

I met his eyes again, finding solace in their depths. "It does. But that's not all. Ten months ago I discovered he was cheating on me with his assistant." I took a deep breath.

As I spoke, memories of the confrontation with Steve played vividly in my mind, each word he uttered cutting deeper into the trust we had built over the years. "I thought I was in a happy marriage," I sighed, a mixture of sadness and anger lingering in my words. "No marriage is perfect, but I didn't think something like this would ever happen to me. But he chose to throw it all away for a fleeting affair. Now, standing here, I realize that I deserve more than a relationship built on lies and infidelity."

As I recounted the painful realization of my shattered marriage, my thoughts involuntarily drifted to the beginning — to the moments of joy, laughter, and love that once defined our relationship. It was a stark contrast to the somber reality that had unfolded.

Trying to push the hurt aside, I began to reminisce about how we first met. The memory offered a brief respite from the current confusion. It was a rainy evening in the cozy corner of a bustling coffee shop, where the air was filled with the comforting aroma of freshly brewed coffee and the gentle hum of conversations.

As I spoke, the vivid images of that fateful day unfolded in my mind. Our eyes met across the crowded room, and a subtle connection sparked instantly. There was an understanding between us, an attraction that transcended words. It wasn't long before we found ourselves engrossed in conversation, sharing stories and discovering common interests.

In those early days, our love blossomed like a delicate flower, with every moment deepening our connection. From stolen glances to heartfelt conversations, we navigated the journey of getting to know each other. The initial awkwardness transformed into a profound sense of comfort, and before we knew it, we were entwined in a love that felt unbreakable.

Reflecting on these memories, I couldn't help but contrast the purity of our beginnings with the pain of the present. The heartbreaking journey we had undertaken, from the innocence of newfound love to the heart-wrenching betrayal that now defined our history.

Jake's eyes mirrored a mix of empathy and understanding as he absorbed my unpleasant confession. In that moment, I felt a connection, a joint understanding that surpassed words. As we navigated the uncharted territory of healing, the solace found in his eyes became a beacon of hope, guiding me towards a future free from the shadows of deception.

"I'm so sorry. I truly am. Does he still live with you?" Jake asked, his brows furrowed in concern as he sought to understand the intricacies of my situation.

I sighed, reality settling in, "Yes, he still lives with me. Untangling our lives has proven to be a complicated process. It's challenging, to say the least, especially because of our daughter. We have an almost ten-year-old together, Lauren. She believes in us so much and she is such a daddy's girl. I don't want to keep her away from her dad."

Jake's expression shifted, registering the chaos of my circumstances. "I can't even imagine how challenging that must be for you. Having to share the same space with someone who betrayed you..."

"It's like walking on a tightrope," I admitted, "trying to maintain a semblance of normalcy while the wounds are still fresh. But I'm determined not to let his actions define my present or future. I'm actively working towards finding my own place and creating a space where I can rebuild without the constant reminder of the past."

Jake nodded in understanding, a supportive glint in his eyes, "That takes incredible strength. If there's anything I can do to help or support you through this, don't hesitate to let me know."

I appreciated his offer, sensing a genuine willingness to stand by me in the midst of my commotion. As we continued our conversation, I found solace not only in the depths of his eyes but also in the understanding that true healing often requires navigating through the intricacies of life with the support of those who genuinely care.

His hand moved across the table, palm up, an offer of solidarity rather than an invasion of space. "I want you to know that I see you. The passionate, vibrant woman who gets lost in the worlds between these covers." He gestured to the shelves, brimming with stories that mirrored our own situation. "And I'm so sorry you tasted unfaithfulness from the person you should trust the most."

My breath caught, and for a heartbeat, I allowed myself to imagine a different life—one where such understanding was the norm rather than the exception. "Thank you, Jake. That means more to me than you might realize."

"Everyone deserves to be seen, to be acknowledged for who they truly are. And not be cheated on."

"Sometimes," I started, "I wonder if I made the right choices. If the life I've built is really mine or just one I thought I should want." I took a deep breath. "The only thing I will never regret is my daughter. I love her to death."

"Choices can be daunting," he said, folding his hands atop the weathered wood. "But remember, Madelyn, it's never too late to choose differently. To choose for yourself." He placed his hand on my shoulder. "I bet you are a loving mother. I can see it." His tone of voice soft.

THE SPARK

The air between us hummed with the gravity of his words, laden with possibilities that both terrified and thrilled me. In that quiet bookshop, amidst the echoes of countless narratives, I found an unlikely confidant—an ally in my search for authenticity.

"Talking to you... it's like coming up to breathe after being underwater for too long," I admitted, allowing vulnerability to color my tone.

"Then breathe, Madelyn," he urged softly. "Just breathe."

"Jake..." The word was a whisper, a tentative step toward an unknown destination. "There's this part of me that's been asleep for so long. Talking to you, it's like I'm waking up, and it's both terrifying and exhilarating."

"Sometimes, waking up is exactly what we need," he said, reaching out to let his fingers graze mine—a feather-light touch that sent ripples across the still waters of my soul.

I watched our fingers tentatively explore the newfound territory, a silent dance of curiosity and caution. His hand was warm, the contact sending a cascade of unbidden emotions through me. It was the touch I hadn't realized I'd been craving, the connection that made the world outside fade into monochrome.

"Is this okay?" His voice was barely above a murmur, laced with concern.

"Yes," I breathed out, surprised at the certainty that anchored the word. "It's more than okay."

Our conversation had spiraled into a realm where words felt inadequate, where the language of touch spoke volumes more. I could see the reflection of my own confusion and longing mirrored in his eyes, which held me with a depth that suggested he saw past the façade I presented to the rest of the world.

The finality of the evening encroached upon us, the impending closure of another chapter in the day. Yet as we lingered in the silence, it was clear that something between us had irrevocably shifted. In the quiet sanctuary of the bookshop, we found solace in each other, a refuge from the tempest of our lives.

As the clock neared closing time, signaling the end of our interlude, I realized that the comfort I found in Jake's presence was akin to the solace I sought within the pages of a beloved book—familiar, yet exhilaratingly unpredictable. With a heavy heart, I knew that stepping out of the shop meant returning to reality, but the memory of this moment would linger, a bookmark holding our place until we could return once more. I wasn't ready to give up on this feeling.

The bell above the bookshop door jangled, a sound that often heralded the beginning or end of an unexpected journey. On this night, it marked an ending of sorts; the conclusion of our clandestine meeting, and maybe more.

"Take care," Jake said softly, his gaze lingering on mine as I stepped backward toward the door.

"Goodnight, Jake," I replied, my voice a mere whisper, betraying the tumult inside me. There were words we hadn't dared to speak, each syllable a brushstroke in the painting of our connection, a portrait not yet fully realized.

Outside, the city breathed a cool breeze that sent shivers down my spine as I wrapped my arms around myself. The cobblestone street, damp from an earlier drizzle, reflected the golden hues of the street lamps—a distorted mirror of the warmth I'd left behind.

The click-clack of my heels against the old buildings was a metronome to my racing thoughts. I was returning to my reality. My marriage, once a bastion of security, now felt like a fortress I had unknowingly built around my heart.

As memories of happy times with my husband mingled with the fresh imprints of tonight's revelations, I grappled with the juxtaposition. How could one heart house such discordant melodies—love and longing, contentment and curiosity?

Jake's understanding eyes haunted me, a silent plea for recognition in a world that often ignored the quiet truths of the soul. And yet, his touch—the simple comfort of his arm around me—had sparked a different kind of fire, one that threatened the very foundation of my vows.

"Am I being selfish?" I wondered aloud, my breath forming clouds in the chill air. The question hung there, unanswered, as if waiting for permission to dissolve into the night.

At home, the front door creaked open with a familiarity that spoke of years traversing its threshold. Inside, the soft hum of the refrigerator and the ticking of the hall clock were the only sounds that greeted me. They were the ambient noises of my life, so constant that I seldom noticed them anymore.

"Maddie? Is that you?" The voice of my husband, Steve, called from somewhere within the depths of the house, his tone a blend of concern and sleepiness.

"Yes, it's me," I answered, setting my keys on the entryway table, their metallic clink a punctuation in the stillness.

"Everything okay?" he asked, emerging from the hallway, his figure blurred by the absence of my glasses.

"Everything's fine," I assured him, though the word 'fine' felt like a costume too small to fit over the coatings I now wore. A smile, a nod, a kiss on the cheek—it was a dance of normalcy I performed with a grace born of practice. "I'm going to bed. Long day tomorrow with Lauren's birthday party preparations."

"Goodnight then," he said, retreating back to the couch he had been sleeping on for the past few weeks.

"Goodnight," I said, watching his shadow disappear, my heart waging a silent war within the confines of my ribcage.

In the solitude of the bedroom, I sank onto the soft bed, the sheets cool beneath my fingertips. I looked at the space around me, this room a reminder to the life I had chosen, the choices I had made. But now, another choice loomed

THE SPARK

before me—a crossroads where the heart's compass wavered between duty and desire.

I closed my eyes, envisioning Jake's warm smile, the refuge I found in his presence. It wasn't just about him, though; it was about the parts of myself that came alive when he was near. Parts long buried beneath compromise and routine.

CHAPTER 6

The Birthday

I CAREFULLY ARRANGED a collection of Lauren's favorite cookies into the shape of the number ten, hoping to see her face light up with joy at the sight. As I placed the cookies in its designated spots, memories of her laughter replayed in my mind, like a cherished melody that held my heart captive.

"Mommy, will there be chocolate chip cookies? They're my favorite," Lauren had asked earlier that week, her big brown eyes shimmering with the simple innocence of childhood expectations.

"Of course, sweetheart," I had promised, and here I was, keeping that promise. Each cookie was a pact between mother and daughter, to the love that swelled within me for her.

I stepped back, surveying the room with a critical eye. Balloons in shades of red and gold floated above, tethered to chairs and banisters. Streamers twisted elegantly from

LORAIN RIZK

one corner of the room to another, creating a canopy of festive cheer and circus mystery. The party games were set up outside, stations for pin the tail on the donkey, a bean bag toss, and a makeshift stage for karaoke—all chosen to spark joy in those eager little faces soon to fill the space.

Are there enough confetti for the table? I thought, as I sprinkled a handful of glimmering stars over the white tablecloth. The confetti caught the light, winking at me like tiny beacons of celebration.

Moving to the drinks station, I aligned the paper cups with military precision. Lemonade, iced tea, and fruit punch—each dispenser was labeled with curly handwriting that took me three tries to perfect. My fingers brushed against the glass, leaving fleeting smudges I quickly wiped away. Everything had to be perfect for her. Everything.

"Remember, it's not just about how things look, but how they make people feel," I reminded myself, exhaling a breath I didn't realize I'd been holding. Could I really create an atmosphere that wasn't just visually pleasing, but emotionally resonant too?

Lauren loves these colors, I thought, smiling faintly as I straightened a banner that read 'Happy Birthday' in bold, cheerful letters. I had chosen every hue with her in mind, hoping to reflect the brightness she brought into my life.

I moved through the motions, dipping into a dance of preparation I knew all too well. There was comfort in the ritual, in knowing that each task completed brought me closer to seeing her eyes light up with wonder and

THE BIRTHDAY

excitement. But beneath that comfort, a thread of anxiety wove through my thoughts, tugging at the edges of my consciousness.

Will everything go as planned?

Will she truly enjoy it?

Will Steve see how much effort I've put into making our daughter happy?

These questions fluttered around me like moths to a flame, relentless and unyielding. I pushed them aside, focusing instead on the tangible, on the joy I would bring to Lauren today. That was what mattered.

"Everything looks wonderful, Madelyn," I whispered to myself, allowing a small moment of pride to seep in. "Lauren will love it."

And with that final affirmation, I placed the last touches to the party set-up, stepping back to take in the panorama of my labor. It was a labor of love, a canvas painted with the deepest affections of a mother's heart, ready to be filled with the happy memories of a tenth birthday celebration.

"Lauren's going to flip when she sees this." I heard Sofia's voice. I turned around and saw her approaching me. "That popcorn machine is huge!"

The corners of my mouth quirked up at Sofia's comment, her enthusiasm infectious. Our friendship had always been like this—a seemingly effortless harmony of action and understanding.

"Wow!" Sofia's voice carried a tone of sympathy, her hazel eyes locking onto mine with a knowing intensity. "This is amazing. Truly."

"Thanks," I murmured, my gaze momentarily drifting away, cheeks warming under her praise. But Sofia's discerning eyes caught a hint of melancholy, and she seemed to sense the chaos within me.

"It's a shame your parents couldn't make it," she added, a real-check of my relationship with them. "I know how much their acceptance means to you."

Quietness settled between us, the absence of my parents casting a shadow over the vibrant celebration. Steve, a man of compassion, had won my heart a decade ago despite the reservations of my deeply religious parents. Their absence at Lauren's milestone birthday was a poignant reminder of their continued disapproval, a decision not to embrace the love and life Steve and I had built together.

Sofia's touch on my shoulder provided a comforting anchor as the first guests arrived, their arrival marked by the familiar sounds of car doors closing. I couldn't help but steal glances at the excited faces of Lauren's classmates, their joy contrasting with the ache in my heart.

"They're here!" Sofia nudged me gently, her voice snapping me out of my contemplation.

"Right, right," I said, exhaling slowly, determined to focus on the celebration at hand. "Time to play hostess. I wish Rebecca could be here," I confessed to Sofia, a wistful smile

THE BIRTHDAY

playing on my lips. "But she's caught up in the whirlwind of New York, you know how it is."

I found myself missing not only my parents but also my sister Rebecca, who had once been my closest confidante. The two of us used to share everything, but after my marriage to Steve, she had relocated to the bustling streets of New York City, chasing her own dreams and forging a bachelorette life. Our once inseparable bond had slowly unraveled, strained by the distance and the diverging paths we had chosen.

Being the youngest, she had a fire in her soul that couldn't be contained. She was always the life of the party, the one with the infectious laughter and the insatiable appetite for adventure. While I settled into the rhythm of married life, she sought out the excitement and unpredictability of city living, forging a bachelorette life that was as vibrant and dynamic as she was.

As the years passed and our paths diverged, our once inseparable bond began to slowly unravel, strained by the distance and the differing lifestyles we had chosen. Her late-night texts and spontaneous calls became fewer and farther between, replaced by the hustle and bustle of her new life in the city that never sleeps.

Sofia nodded, her expression understanding. "People change, and life takes them in different directions. But today is about Lauren, about the love and family you've built. Hold onto that. Don't think about it; you're better than that. Let's go get this party started."

We greeted the arrivals with smiles and pointed them towards the activities we'd set up in my backyard. The lush green grass transformed into a whimsical arena, hosting a menagerie of lawn games strategically scattered like the colorful pieces of a jigsaw puzzle. Laughter and excitement bubbled up, a harmonious prelude to the main act about to unfold under the imaginary circus big top.

"Fantastic party, Madelyn," one of the mothers commented, her eyes sweeping over the scene appreciatively. "You really have a knack for this."

"Thank you," I replied, feeling a swell of pride mixed with the ever-present fear of imperfection. "It's all for Lauren."

Sofia stayed close, her mere proximity a silent vow of solidarity. We moved together amongst our friends, some who had known Steve and me since our college days. Their familiar faces were like anchors in the sea of planning and performance.

"Hey, Madelyn, this is amazing!" one of Steve's buddies clapped his hand on my shoulder, his grin wide and genuine. "Lauren's a lucky kid to have a mom like you."

"Thanks, Mike," I said, tilting my head to acknowledge him, even as I scanned the crowd for any signs of distress or discomfort, ready to swoop in and smooth any ruffled feathers.

"Everything okay?" Sofia's voice cut through my internal monologue, pulling me back to the present.

THE BIRTHDAY

"Of course," I lied smoothly, my gaze darting to the entrance once more, anticipating Steve's arrival. "Just making sure everyone's having fun."

"Girl," she leaned in, lowering her voice, "you worry too much. Relax. It's a party, not a military operation."

"Maybe," I conceded with a small sigh, allowing the tightness in my chest to ease slightly. "But you know how important today is."

"Listen to me," she placed a reassuring hand on my arm, grounding me. "Lauren is going to remember the love you put into this, not whether the napkins matched the plates."

I wanted to believe her, to trust that my efforts were enough, that Steve would see them for what they were—an expression of love, not just for Lauren, but for our family —we had to show to everyone we had it all together, even if that wasn't the case behind closed doors. But doubt was a persistent whisper, threading its way through my thoughts, unsettling the fragile peace I tried to maintain.

Sofia handed me the plates for the food. "So... Any news about Jake?"

"Shhhh." I quickly shushed her. "You're so loud."

"Ops, sorry!" She whispered. She took a deep breath and kept whispering. "So...?"

"Alright, alright. I saw him again." I whispered back.

"You did what?" Sofia's voice raised again.

"Shhhhh. Yes, I saw him again. I don't know what to do." I quickly looked down.

Sofia's expression remained neutral as she processed the news. "It's your decision. I'll support you no matter what, you know that. But be cautious. Remember what's at stake."

Her words were measured, devoid of judgment or urgency, which surprised me. "I know it's complicated, Sofia. But every time I'm with Jake, I feel this... pull. It's like I'm caught in a whirlwind of emotions, and I can't seem to find my way out."

Sofia nodded, her gaze steady. "I understand. Just make sure you're considering all the consequences, Maddie. Your choices affect not just you, but Lauren and Steve too, and everyone who believed in your family."

Her statement reminded me of the tangled web of responsibilities I couldn't ignore. "I'll try, Sofia. I'll try to think things through before I act. But I think I'm going to end things with Jake. If I can even refer to them as 'things.' Really nothing happened."

"Well, something happened in your heart, and I can tell. I know you, and I know your eyes. Just think about it." Sofia put her hand on my shoulder. "We'll figure it out together," Sofia said, her tone neutral yet reassuring. "Just remember, you're not alone in this."

As Sofia's words replayed in my mind, clarity began to form within me. She was right; I had a lot at stake. Perhaps it was time to make a difficult decision, for the sake of my family

THE BIRTHDAY

and my own sanity. The thought of never seeing Jake again weighed on me, but I knew it might be necessary for the greater good.

With a newfound determination, I made a silent promise to myself: I would confront Jake and tell him that we could no longer see each other. It wouldn't be easy, but it was the right thing to do. And with Sofia's unwavering support, I knew I could find the strength to follow through.

"Where is Mark?" I asked in an attempt to change the conversation's direction.

"I don't think he can make it. You know, work. What's new?" Sofia shrugged her shoulder.

"I'm sorry. It must be hard having all the time in the world and a husband who works this much. You must miss him."

"Terribly. But it's fine, I get it. He should be getting a promotion soon and his schedule should be more stable. We're planning a small vacation to Jamaica."

"That sounds fun! We should have a date night soon. Let's go welcome the new arrivals," I suggested, plastering on a smile as fresh waves of guests poured in. "We can't keep the birthday girl waiting."

The hum of happy conversations put me as ease as I wove through clusters of guests. Lauren's laugh, a bright chime amidst the cacophony, anchored me. "Happy birthday, sweetheart!" I greeted her friends with warmth blossoming in my chest.

"Your mom is the coolest," one of her little friends gushed, eyes wide at the chocolate fountain cascading with liquid gold.

"Isn't she just?" I smiled, the compliment reaching deep, soothing frayed nerves. Their giggles helped calming my anxiety.

"These cupcakes are divine!" Mrs. Hatcher, clad in a pastel summer dress, praised, holding one aloft as if it were a rare gem.

"Thank you," I replied, watching her take a dainty bite, "Lavender and honey—a new recipe I tried."

"Delightful," she mused, and I tucked the word away, a small victory against the swell of doubts that threatened to capsize my composure.

"Everything looks wonderful," Mr. Davis, Steve's golf buddy, chimed in, his smile genuine. "Steve is a lucky man."

"Thank you," I said, though the words snagged on a thorn of unease—the feeling that luck had little to do with it.

Amidst the sea of approval, I noticed him—Steve, standing at the threshold, his presence commanding as always. With a broad smile, he handed Lauren a beautifully wrapped gift, his affection for her clear as day. My heart swelled seeing them together—their relationship was like two anchors in the unpredictable ocean of life.

THE BIRTHDAY

"Hey, Maddie," Steve greeted me after ruffling Lauren's hair, planting a kiss on my cheek, the stubble on his chin grazing my skin. "Looks great in here."

"Thanks," I murmured, leaning into his solid frame for a fleeting moment. But as I pulled back, I saw it—the flicker in his eyes, a spark of something dark that sent a chill down my spine. He was watching me, too closely, and my pulse quickened.

"Madelyn, this is great," Steve's interrupted, pulling me from the undercurrent of Steve's gaze.

"Lauren helped pick the theme," I deflected with a chuckle, the words light but my heart pounding a frantic rhythm. "I can't take all the credit."

"Mom's amazing," Lauren piped up, beaming, and I melted despite the tension coiling tighter within me.

"Absolutely," Steve agreed, but his mysterious stare didn't lift. I knew that look—it was the precursor to questions I wasn't sure I could answer.

"Go on, join the games," I encouraged Lauren, needing space to breathe, to think. She scampered off.

"Is everything okay?" Steve's question came softly, barely audible over the din.

"Perfect," I lied, the single word tasting like ashes. "Just perfect."

"Steve, have you seen the balloon arch by the garden? I had them match Lauren's favorite colors." My voice fluttered with feigned enthusiasm, hoping to steer his attention away from whatever he was thinking about.

He arched an eyebrow, curiosity momentarily overriding the intensity in his eyes. "No, I haven't," he conceded. "Let's check it out."

Walking alongside him, I could feel the tension winding around us like ivy, like a delicate dance on a spider's web, my heart flitting about like a trapped butterfly.

"By the way," he began casually, too casually, "who's Jake E.? I saw a message pop up on your phone earlier."

The question landed like a stone in a still pond, sending ripples through the façade I'd so carefully constructed. I swallowed hard, the taste of fear mixed with the faint sweetness of the buttercream frosting that scented the air.

"Jake E., oh—" A laugh escaped me, hollow and brittle. "He works at the bookshop downtown. We were discussing some new arrivals for the book club, that's all."

"Is that so?" His voice was level, but the blue of his eyes darkened like the sea during a storm. "Seems like he texts you quite often for just book recommendations."

"I'm telling you, honestly, it's nothing," I insisted, my fingers nervously adjusting a ribbon on the nearby gift table. "You know how passionate I am about our reading group. It's been such a great outlet for me."

"Right," he said, his smile not reaching his eyes. "Just seems odd, that's all."

THE BIRTHDAY

"Let's not do this here." I glanced around nervously; it felt as if our bubble of tension might burst and silence the joy of the event.

"Then where? When is a good time to talk about this?" His tone was sharp, controlled but slicing through the festive atmosphere.

I reached for a napkin, dabbing at a nonexistent spill on the table. My heart hammered against my ribcage, each beat echoing 'liar, liar.' I'd always been terrible at keeping things from him, but now the truth seemed more dangerous than the secret.

"Look at Lauren, she's having such a wonderful time," I deflected, gesturing to our daughter who was giggling with her friends, her innocent joy a stark contrast to our adult emotions.

"Lauren's happiness doesn't answer my question." He took a step closer, his presence commanding, even when laced with vulnerability. "Are you happy, Madelyn?"

I swallowed, feeling his gaze on me, the intensity of his blue eyes searching mine. "Of course, I am," I whispered, the words sounding hollow even to my own ears.

"Because I've been trying, you know? Really trying." His voice had softened, and it cut deeper than any accusation could. "But it feels like you're somewhere else these days."

"You're imagining things," I countered quickly, too quickly. I was a poor actress; my eyes couldn't hold his. "This is about Lauren, let's keep the focus on her today."

"Right." He nodded, but the nod was mechanical, void of agreement. "We'll talk later."

As he moved off to mingle, the mask of the congenial host settling back onto his features, I released a breath I hadn't known I was holding. But it did little to ease the tightness in my lungs. Steve's frustration, so strong, twisted like the ribbons above us. And beneath the surface of my crafted calm, the fear of what lay ahead churned like dark waters, threatening to pull me under. In moments like these I felt thankful to have someone like Sofia; a real friend I could trust.

As the last guest made his way out and Lauren fell into a deep sleep from post-party exhaustion, I stepped out onto the porch. The sun began its descent, painting the sky in strokes of orange and pink, a beautiful backdrop to an ugly tension.

"Steve," I called out, catching up to him near the punch bowl.

He came from inside the house, the edges of his frustration softening ever so slightly at my approach. "Madelyn."

"Can we talk? Just for a minute?" My voice was barely above the din, but he heard the urgency in it.

"Sure."

"Please." My hand found his arm, fingers gently pressing into the his shirt. "It's important."

THE BIRTHDAY

He stepped out onto the porch next to me.

"Hey, look at me." I waited until his blue eyes met mine, until I felt like he could see right into the corners of my soul. "What's going through your head?"

"I want to believe you. I do. But something feels off." His words were measured, and a muscle ticked in his jaw. "You never mentioned this Jake before."

"Because there's nothing to mention." My hands fluttered in the space between us, then settled on his chest, feeling the steady rhythm of his heart beneath my palms. *Why am I even trying so hard to explain? He is the one who cheated. Damn guilt.*

I hated Steve being mad at me. Although he was the cheater who ruined our relationship and the trust I had in him, I still caught myself seeking his approval. I wanted him to see me a certain way; the innocent, trustworthy and loyal Madelyn.

His eyes searched mine, looking for the reassurance that I willed them to convey. The seconds stretched taut, filled with silent pleas for understanding.

"Okay," he finally said.

"Okay?" A hesitant hope flickered within me.

"Okay." His nod this time carried more conviction, though shadows of doubt still haunted the depths of his gaze. "I believe you. But this still doesn't solve anything. We need to talk about us."

The relief that washed over me was palpable, sweet as the icing on Lauren's birthday cake. I stepped closer, wrapping my arms around him in a hug that I hoped conveyed all the words I couldn't say—guilt, confusion, love. Yes, because at the end I still loved him. He was my daughter's father.

"We will talk, I want to talk about us." I breathed against his shoulder, the tension in my body unwinding as he returned the embrace.

"Let's get back inside and finish cleaning up," Steve suggested after a moment, pulling away but keeping one arm draped over my shoulder.

"Sure." I nodded, allowing his warmth to seep into my skin. As we re-entered the living room, I tucked away the lingering traces of fear, choosing instead to hold onto this reprieve, however fragile it might be.

For now, it was enough. It had to be. Amid this emotional rollercoaster, a new character emerged—Jake. His presence, a contrast to the strained relationship with Steve, added an unexpected layer to my confusion.

Torn between the familiarity of my marriage and the allure of something new, I grappled with conflicting emotions. Could I rebuild trust with Steve, or was our foundation irreparably damaged? And what did Jake represent—a fresh start or a distraction?

As the night wore on, the internal debate intensified. The road ahead seemed murky, and the script of my life remained unwritten, awaiting the pen that would guide me toward resolution or further chaos.

THE BIRTHDAY

A chime from my phone distracted my thoughts. "I hope the birthday party was a success. I can't get you out of my thoughts. Sweet Dreams. J."

Exactly what I needed to confuse me even further.

As I was just digesting the text I had just received, with the phone still in my hands, a knock on the door interrupted. Startled, Steve and I both turned to look at each other. Steve raised an eyebrow, wondering who could be visiting us at this hour.

I made my way to the door, my heart racing with curiosity. Opening it slowly, I was met with a sight that warmed my heart. Standing on the doorstep was none other than my sister Rebecca, a wide grin on her face and a suitcase by her side.

"Surprise!" she exclaimed, stepping into our home. "I'm here for a few days! Mom said you could use some company."

I couldn't believe it. Rebecca lived halfway across the country, and her sudden appearance felt like a dream come true. Tears welled up in my eyes as I embraced her tightly, feeling a rush of love and gratitude for her presence.

Steve came up behind me, his expression shifting from confusion to warmth as he greeted my sister.

"Becca, what are you doing here?" Steve asked, pulling away from our hug and giving her a warm smile.

"I needed some time off and thought I'd surprise my favorite sister... and niece! Where is she?" Rebecca asked, hugging Steve briefly before stepping back to look at us both.

"She is already asleep. She had a blast at her party today," I replied.

"I tried to get here as soon as possible, but my flight got delayed. Everything seems to happen to me, hug? With my luck. Can I stay until Wednesday?"

"Are you kidding even asking? You can stay as long as you want." Steve placed his right hand on her shoulder. "You're always welcome here, without trouble following you, of course."

We all shared a laugh and made our way to the living room. Rebecca had always been the light in our family, her infectious energy and positive attitude always making things better.

"So..." she said as we settled down on the couches. "What's been going on with you guys? Mom mentioned something about a fight..."

Steve and I exchanged a glance before filling my sister in on everything that had happened between us. Well, almost everything. I did not share Steve's affair because I didn't want her to look at him differently, permanently.

Rebecca listened quietly, her expression shifting from shock to concern as we spoke. When we were done, she took a deep breath and looked at me with a determined expression.

THE BIRTHDAY

"I think it's great that you're still living together and giving your relationship a chance," she said, placing a hand on mine. "But I agree with you, Mad, therapy is necessary if you want this to work."

Steve's face twisted into a skeptical expression, as it often did when the topic of therapy came up. He never liked the idea and always tried to downplay its importance. But we had to keep up appearances and act like this was the right thing to do. The last thing I wanted was for my mother to get her hopes up about a potential breakup between Steve and me. I tried to maintain a calm facade, knowing that any slip-up could lead to disaster.

"Thank you for being here Becca," I said gratefully, feeling overwhelmed with emotion. "I really needed this."

"I figured it was time to bother you," she replied with a smile.

The rest of the evening was spent catching up and enjoying each other's company. It felt like old times again, when we were just carefree siblings without any worries or responsibilities.

As night fell and Rebecca retired to her guest room, Steve and I made our way to the bedroom.

"Can I sleep here tonight? I don't want Rebecca to see me on the couch."

I nodded, my heart racing. It had been weeks since we last shared a bed, and I couldn't wait to feel this warm body next to mine again. The thought alone sent shivers down my spine, igniting a fire within me that could only be quenched by the touch of his skin against mine in the darkness of night. But I had to keep this desire to myself, at least for now.

Steve then turned to me with a serious expression. "I'll make an appointment for therapy tomorrow if you really want me to go," he said firmly. "I want us to work through our issues and become a stronger couple."

I was surprised by Steve's words. Was Steve seriously considering therapy? Who was this person and what happened to my husband? Perhaps he was ready to finally make the change I'd been waiting for. I went to bed with a smile on my face, and for the first time in a very long time I felt hopeful.

Due to a lack of words, I nodded, and we drifted off to sleep.

CHAPTER 7

Conflicted Hearts

"MADDIE. What's going on? You called me ten times," Sofia asked as I greeted her at my door. "Is everything alright?"

"I'll get straight to the point. Steve wants to go to therapy."

Sofia stayed quiet for a few seconds, then she walked to my living room and sat on the couch.

"No way! Steve, like in Steve your husband Steve?" The tone of her voice shifted to concerned disbelief.

"Yeah, that Steve," I confirmed, feeling a knot tighten in my stomach as I braced myself for Sofia's reaction. Her incredulity mirrored my own initial shock when Steve had broached the subject earlier the night before.

"Do you think he can actually change?" Sofia's voice was laced with genuine concern, her words a reflection of the close bond we shared.

"That's the thing, Sofia. I'm not entirely sure," I admitted, a note of uncertainty creeping into my voice. "Steve didn't go into much detail, but he seemed convinced that therapy could help us work through some issues."

Sofia fell silent for a moment again. I could almost hear the gears turning in her mind as she processed the news, her thoughts racing to make sense of the unexpected turn of events.

"I mean, it's not necessarily a bad thing, right?" Sofia ventured cautiously, her tone a mixture of optimism and caution. "Maybe this could be an opportunity for both of you to address any underlying issues and strengthen your relationship. And go from there."

Her words offered a glimmer of hope amidst the uncertainty, a reminder that perhaps this unexpected detour on our journey could ultimately lead to a brighter destination. Yet, as I mulled over Sofia's words, a nagging sense of apprehension lingered in the back of my mind, reminding me that the road ahead would not be easy, but it was a journey we would navigate together, one step at a time.

"I just don't know if he is serious," I replied.

"Well, only one way to find out," she smirked. "So, what else is on your mind?"

"My sister is in town. She surprised us last night."

Sofia's eyes widened in surprise. "Becca? Your sister Becca?" she exclaimed.

CONFLICTED HEARTS

I nodded, a smile tugging at the corners of my lips as I thought about the unexpected but welcome reunion with my younger sister.

"I haven't seen her in ages," Sofia remarked, her tone taking on a wistful quality.

"Yeah, me too," I replied, my mind drifting back to our childhood memories of running around the backyard and playing pranks on unsuspecting neighbors.

"So how is she?" Sofia asked, breaking through my reverie.

"She seems good," I replied. "She's doing well in her new job and it seems like she's really happy."

"That's great to hear," Sofia said sincerely. "I've always liked Becca. Where is she now?

"Me too," I agreed with a smile. "It's so nice having her here. She" dropped Lauren off to school and then she went to get coffee. You know, she doesn't like staying home much."

I walked to the kitchen and grabbed two mugs for coffee.

"So, have you made a decision, then? Are you going to go to therapy with Steve?"

I knew what she was hinting at. Jake.

My mind churned with uncertainty. "I don't know, Sof. Part of me wants to believe that he can change, but another part of me is scared to trust him again after what happened. And then there is his jealousy…"

"It's a risk, but if you're willing to try, maybe there's hope. Maybe it's time to prioritize her and your family. See what happens. If it doesn't work out at least you tried. Have you talked to Jake about ending things?"

"Not yet, but I need to. I can't keep stringing him along while I figure out my own feelings. You're right, I need to give Steve and I a real shot." Tears welled up as gratitude flooded my heart. "Thank you. I don't know what I'd do without you."

"Anytime, Maddie. Now, let's figure out how to navigate this mess together."

We finished our coffee and Sofia stood up to leave. "I have to run some errands before heading home," she explained apologetically.

"That's okay, thank you for meeting up with me," I said gratefully as we hugged goodbye.

"Anytime," Sofia replied with a smile before heading out the door.

As I watched her walk away down the street, I couldn't help but think about how lucky I was to have such supportive friends in my life. With Rebecca's surprise visit and Steve's sudden willingness to seek therapy, it felt like things were finally looking up after weeks of tension and uncertainty.

I now had something else to deal with.

A plan began to form in my mind like the pieces of a puzzle finally clicking into place. It was time to face Jake, to confront the swirling emotions head-on, and put an end to our tumultuous "affair" once and for all. But where would I meet him? I had to be discreet this time.

A sudden realization dawned on me, and I pulled out my phone, fingers flying over the screen as I composed a text message to Jake.

"Hey Jake, can we meet somewhere intimate? There's something important I need to talk to you about."

I hit send, my heart pounding in my chest as I waited for his response. Moments later, my phone buzzed with his reply.

"Sure. How about the park behind the library? It's usually quiet there."

A sense of relief washed over me as I read his message. The park behind the library was perfect—secluded enough for a private conversation, yet not too far from civilization.

"Sounds good," I typed back, my fingers trembling slightly with anticipation. "Let's meet there in an hour."

I carefully stowed away my phone, a tangible reminder of the impending decision I was on the precipice of making.

The journey to the designated meeting spot felt like a pilgrimage through the depths of my disorder. I felt the gravity of what lay ahead, a weighty burden pressing against my every move.

Arriving at the appointed location, I settled onto a weathered bench nestled within the solitude of the park.

Nervous energy coursed through me, manifesting in the rhythmic drumming of my fingers against the wooden surface. The faint aroma of freshly brewed coffee wafting from the nearby store mingled with the scent of anticipation, creating a sensory backdrop to the impending encounter.

Minutes stretched into eternities as I waited, each passing second amplifying the cacophony of emotions roiling within me. My heart thrummed a rapid cadence against my ribcage, a mixture of apprehension and determination.

Then, like a beacon in the midst of uncertainty, I caught sight of Jake's familiar figure approaching through the park. Anticipation held me in its grip as he drew nearer, his presence a harbinger of the conversation that loomed on the horizon.

"Madelyn," his voice, a blend of warmth and concern, reached my ears as he settled onto the bench beside me. Relief flooded through me at the sight of him, his very presence offering solace in my me. "I'm so happy to see you."

I forced a small smile, masking the how I really felt beneath the surface. "I had to, Jake. We need to talk."

He nodded solemnly, his eyes searching mine for answers. "Is everything alright?"

His words cut through me like a knife, a painful reminder of the tangled web of emotions that had brought us to this moment. But I knew what needed to be done.

"Jake, I—" I began, but my words were abruptly cut off by a tap on my shoulder.

"Hello, Madelyn. What a pleasant surprise," came a deep voice from behind me.

My heart skipped a beat. *Oh no, not now. Who could it be?*

Turning around, I was met with the familiar face of Mr. Sally, one of my recent clients for whom I had organized a wedding. "Hello, Mr. Sally, how are you?" I stammered, my nerves getting the best of me.

Before I could compose myself, Jake stepped forward, extending his hand. "Hello, I'm Jake, nice to meet you, Mr. Sally."

"We are... We are discussing the wedding vision for Mr. Evans. He's considering getting married here in the park."

Mr. Sally smiled warmly, shaking Jake's hand. "Please, call me Paul. Nice to meet you, Jake. You won't regret working with this talented woman for your wedding. There is no one better than her. You'll see."

"Thank you, Mr. Sall— Uh, Paul," I managed to say, forcing a smile despite my anxiety.

"It's only the truth," Paul insisted. "And I meant to call the office to congratulate you. I heard you are working on Dylan Dalton's wedding. Did I hear correct?"

"Yes, thank you so much," I replied, feeling a surge of gratitude for his kind words. "It hasn't been the easiest task, but at WedLux we always try our best."

"I'm sure you'll do great," Paul said reassuringly. "Well, I'll leave you to your planning. Good luck to you, Jake, and talk to you soon, Madelyn."

With a nod of farewell, Paul walked away, leaving me and Jake standing there in awkward silence. As the tension eased, I couldn't help but feel a twinge of guilt for the fabricated excuse I had used to explain our meeting in the park. But for now, I pushed those thoughts aside, focusing on the task at hand: ending things with Jake once and for all. But, again, I found myself having a hard time getting the words out of my mouth.

And before I could start the conversation back, Jake spoke. "You never told me you're working on the Daltons' wedding."

I found myself sharing the peculiar tale of Dylan, the elusive multimillionaire for whom I was planning a wedding. The man I had never met, yet who managed to intrigue and frustrate me simultaneously.

"The town talks about him like he's some mysterious figure," I continued. "A man of mystery and excess, but without ever showing his face."

"Oh, everyone knows who he is around here. He is like a Hollywood celebrity in Keystone." Jake continued talking about Dylan as if he was describing a murder mystery. "The thing is... he is a very private person. He rarely shows face around town. He is like a ghost."

"Well, believe it or not I don't go out much. Between weddings I plan, and my daughter, I don't have much time for myself, so even if he was out often, I wouldn't know what he looked like anyway."

"Isn't he your client?" Jake asked in a perplexed look on his face.

"Yes, he is, but he must be an extremely busy man—he showed face in my office only once to sign his contract... and I wasn't even there. Go figure!" I shook my head.

Jake paused, his eyes fixed in the air. He glanced at me, a hesitancy in his gaze, as if weighing the burden of the revelation he held.

"Madelyn," he began, choosing his words with care, "Dylan's family—"

"They have a history." A voice interrupted. "A legacy that goes beyond the wealth and glamour. It's a story marked by shadows and secrets." The homeless man walking by whispered.

My curiosity heightened, I urged him to continue.

"The Daltons were prominent figures in the town for many years, revered and feared in equal measure," the man revealed. "But as the years passed, whispers of scandal and family feuds became the undercurrent of their legacy. There's a darkness veiled behind the glamour."

"I think it's all gossip," Jake said. "Dylan has carried the weight of his family's gossip or 'secrets' as others call it, choosing to remain hidden to shield himself from the scrutiny of the town," Jake explained. "His presence in the shadows is probably not just about privacy; it's a reflection of a past he's been trying to distance himself from."

I was finally learning more about the mysterious man; my client.

"So why have such a big wedding then?" I finally voiced the question.

Jake's gaze held a mix of understanding and empathy. "Sometimes, the grandeur is a shield, a distraction from the whispers and the prying eyes. It's a way to create a façade, to bury the past beneath layers of opulence."

I pondered his words, my mind weaving through the mix of motives and the intricate dance between secrecy and public spectacle. The upcoming wedding, designed to be a spectacle of wealth and extravagance, now bore the weight of a deeper narrative—a tale of a man trying to rewrite his family's history through the grandeur of the present.

"Dylan's desire for a lavish wedding might be his way of rewriting the story, of forging a new chapter that eclipses the shadows of the past," Jake continued, his words carrying a nuanced understanding of the dynamics at play.

"Is he even in love with his fiancée? Isn't she a super rich girl from Europe?"

Jake's thoughtful expression held a momentary pause, as if considering the intricacies of a delicate truth. "Their relationship, like everything with Dylan, is shrouded in layers. It's not just about love; it's about alliances, mergers of influence, and perhaps, an attempt to rewrite the Dalton legacy through a union of two powerful families."

I couldn't help but feel a twinge of sympathy for Dylan, trapped in a narrative not entirely of his own making.

"His fiancée, Victoria, comes from wealth, yes," Jake continued, breaking the silence. "Their union serves multiple purposes—societal standing, business connections, and, of course, the façade of a picture-perfect life. It's a delicate dance of expectations and obligations, a masquerade that both of them seem willing to participate in."

As Jake spoke, the image of the upcoming grand wedding transformed in my mind. No longer just a lavish celebration, it became a stage for a complex performance, a play where the actors navigated the expectations of their families and the scrutinizing gaze of the town.

"Love is a subjective term in their world," Jake added, his eyes revealing a hint of sadness. "For Dylan, it might be a silent rebellion against the predetermined path set by his family. A chance to reclaim a sliver of control over his destiny."

"How do you know about all this?" I asked, my voice a gentle yet probing inquiry.

Jake met my gaze with a thoughtful expression, as if carefully choosing his words. "I've been a part of this town for a long time. The Dalton legacy is woven into the very veins of Keystone, and over the years, I've become a repository of its stories."

He looked up in the sky and took a deep breath as if he was taking in all of Keystone. "People talk, especially in a close-knit community like ours. The whispers of the past linger in the air, and if you pay attention, you can catch fragments of the Dalton tale in hushed conversations, old records, and the collective memory of the town."

I nodded, absorbing the explanation. It made sense that someone like Jake, deeply rooted in the community, would hold fragments of the town's history.

Jake leaned back, his gaze thoughtful. "You're not just planning a wedding. You're stepping into a story that transcends the confines of celebration. The choices you make will echo through the Dalton legacy, shaping its narrative for generations to come. I believe you have the power to bring about change, to untangle the threads of secrecy that have bound this family."

The park, with its soft lighting and the gentle hum of small raindrops coming down, provided the perfect backdrop for an intimate exchange between Jake and me, making the hard conversation I needed to have with him even harder. As he spoke of the Dalton legacy, I couldn't help but feel the intricacy of the stories.

In a moment of vulnerability, Jake's gaze locked onto mine, and everything else faded into the background. The small rain, a silent witness to the brewing connection, echoed the emotions swirling within.

"I can't do this anymore," I began, my voice trembling with emotion.

CONFLICTED HEARTS

"We can stop talking about the Daltons if you wish."

"No, I mean *us*. Our connection, it's not fair to anyone involved. Not to Steve, not to Lauren, and certainly not to me." I found the courage to finally say it. And my tone sounded colder than I wanted to sound.

He reached out, his hand hovering over mine as if seeking reassurance. "I understand." Jake's hand was now over mine. "But please... Are you sure this is what you want? I know we basically just met, but I really, *really* enjoy you... Your company."

Jake's earnest plea sent a pang through my heart, his vulnerability mirroring my own. I wrestled with conflicting emotions, torn between the pull of our undeniable chemistry and the responsibility to those we might hurt in the process.

"I... I don't know, Jake," I confessed, my voice barely above a whisper. "But I do know that what we have is complicated, and I can't ignore the consequences of our actions."

His hand retreated, and I felt the loss keenly. "I understand," he said softly, his expression a mix of resignation and longing. "If this is what you want..."

Silence stretched between us. The rain intensified, its rhythmic patter adding to the melancholy atmosphere.

Finally, I met Jake's gaze with determination. "I think we both need some time to figure things out," I said, forcing myself to keep my tone steady. "I'm sorry, Jake."

Jake nodded, a flicker of sadness crossing his features. "Of course," he agreed, though I could sense the disappointment lurking beneath his acquiescence.

As we rose to leave the park, I could feel his eyes on me even as I was walking away in the opposite direction. A sense of inevitability settled over me. Our connection, though undeniable, was fraught with complications we couldn't afford to ignore. But even as I grew distance from him, I couldn't shake the feeling that our story was far from over.

CHAPTER 8

More Secrets

I PUSHED OPEN the door to the little café called Cool Beans that had become a sanctuary for Sofia and me, and the coffee aroma enveloped me right away. My eyes scanned the familiar setting, past the baristas steaming milk and crafting lattes, to find her waving from our usual spot in the back—a quiet corner shielded by a tall ficus with twisted limbs.

"Hey," I greeted, my voice barely a whisper above the clinking of cups. The wavy tendrils of my chestnut hair fell forward as I settled into the chair across from her, tucking them behind my ears.

Sofia's hazel eyes studied me, a silent recognition of the storm brewing within me. She knew me well enough to see through the façade I often presented to the outside world.

I wrapped my fingers around the warm ceramic mug she had ordered for me, peppermint tea—I couldn't stomach coffee today. "I've made a decision," I started, tracing the rim of the mug with my thumb. A decision that felt like stitching a wound with a thread made of doubts.

"About Jake?" Sofia prompted gently.

Nodding, I let out a slow breath in anticipation of what I was about to confess. "I've ended things with him." The words felt foreign, even as they left my lips, like a sentence handed down by a judge rather than a choice made by a woman torn between two men.

"Really? That's... big." Her voice was a mix of surprise and concern, a mirror to the tumult inside me.

"Is it?" I questioned."Or is it just me returning to where I started? To Steve..."

"Does he know?"

"Jake? Yes, I told him. I met him." My gaze dropped to the liquid warmth in my hands, seeking comfort in its simple presence. "But I can't keep living in limbo, caught between who I am with Jake and who I was with Steve."

"My girl..." Sofia reached out, her touch grounding. "It sounds like you decided, but you have to be sure it's what you want. Not because it's easy or familiar, but because it's right for you."

"Steve deserves a second chance," I said, more to convince myself than to inform her. "And I... I need closure, one way or another. Isn't this what you suggested I'd do?"

MORE SECRETS

"Yes, but you need to be happy as well. That's what I want for you, first of all." Sofia's gaze held mine, unflinching and sincere.

"I will be. I need to open my heart to Steve again, trust him, and believe it'll work." I admitted, the emotions swirling within, eager to break free yet afraid of the unknown. "Maybe I still love him."

"Then that's where you start," she said softly. "With love."

The steam from my cup curled into the air, a silent witness to the storm brewing in my heart. Sofia's eyes held mine, offering a harbor in their hazel depths.

"Follow your heart," she said gently, her voice a lighthouse piercing through the fog of my indecision. "It knows the way, even when the path seems dark."

She was right, of course. My heart had been whispering its truths all along, but I'd muffled its cries with doubt and fear.

"Tonight," I began, the word coming out as a shaky exhale, "I'm going to talk to Steve. Face to face about giving him another chance. " The thought alone set butterflies loose in my stomach, their wings brushing against my insides with wild abandon.

"Are you scared?" Sofia asked, her tone not one of judgment, but of understanding.

"Terrified," I confessed, tracing the rim of my cup with a fingertip, finding solace in the small, mindless action. "I don't know how he'll react. How I'll react... What if he changed his mind now?"

"Steve loves you. That much has always been clear," Sofia reminded me, grounding me back to the present with the honesty that underpinned our friendship.

"Love can be a complicated beast, though," I countered with a wry smile, knowing all too well the labyrinth of emotions love could entangle one within.

"Complicated or not, it's worth navigating for the chance at happiness," she said, her belief in love unwavering, a beacon in my twilight.

Tonight, under the soft glow of lamplight and amidst the vulnerability of dusk, I would lay bare my heart to Steve, come what may.

Gripping my cup, I watched the steam twist like a dancer into the air—a silent ballet that somehow steadied my nerves. "I've been thinking... When I talk to Steve, I need to just lay it all out there. The fears, the hopes, everything."

"Exactly," Sofia's voice was like a warm blanket, enveloping me in comfort. "Whatever you're feeling, Maddie, he needs to hear it. Keeping things inside never did anyone any good."

"Open communication..." I mumbled, more to myself than to her.

"Is the only way forward." She leaned closer, her hazel eyes locking onto mine with an intensity that seared away falsehoods. "It's not about accusations or blame. It's about expressing what lives in your heart."

"Right." I nodded slowly, feeling the truth of her words anchor within me. My heart, for so long shrouded in silence, yearned to beat out its rhythm, loud and clear for once.

The conversation shifted then, as if the confessional had opened a door to matters equally pressing but cloaked in mystery rather than emotion. "There's something else..." I hesitated, wondering how to unwrap the twists of intrigue that had entangled me.

Her brows lifted, curiosity igniting in her gaze. "What is it?"

"About Dylan..." I began, lowering my voice despite our secluded corner. "I found something odd when digging through his family history, trying to tie up loose ends for the wedding. There are gaps, Sofia. Puzzling ones. Addresses that don't exist, years with no records, pictures where faces are always turned away..."

"Sounds like they've got secrets," she whispered back, her love for a good mystery evident in the slight tilt of her head.

"More than just secrets, I think. I heard stories from Jake the other day. He knew about Dylan's life so much." The discoveries strong yet thrilling. "And now it's as if they've been deliberately erasing their tracks, but why?"

"Could be anything from scandal to protection. Maybe they're not who they say they are?" Sofia offered, her mind already racing ahead.

"Or maybe," I paused, my own thoughts spiraling, "it's something even deeper. I have no idea what it could be. I just have a feeling."

"This is important." Sofia reached across the table, her hand briefly covering mine. "You need to tread carefully. If there's something more to this, you don't want to get caught in the crossfire without knowing exactly what you're dealing with."

"Of course." A small smile crossed my lips at her fierce protectiveness. "But isn't it strange? To find such a tangle right when I'm trying to untie knots in other parts of my life?"

"Life has a weird sense of timing," she agreed with a soft chuckle. "Just promise me you'll be careful."

"Always am." But even as I said it, my pulse quickened with intrigue. The mysteries surrounding Dylan and his enigmatic family were pulling me in, and I knew that untangling them would be irresistible.

Sofia's hazel eyes were wide, her coffee cup paused halfway to her lips as I laid out the labyrinthine details I'd uncovered. "So, you're saying that Dylan's family might have aliases? That his past could be a carefully constructed façade?"

Her intrigue was evident. The cozy corner of the coffee shop a bubble of conspiracy in the midst of frothy cappuccinos and the dull murmur of other patrons.

MORE SECRETS

"Exactly," I whispered, leaning closer. "It's like peeling back layers of an onion—each piece more pungent than the last. There are property records that don't add up, photos that seem staged, even scrubbed social media profiles." My fingertips traced the rim of my own cup, the ceramic cool and smooth under my touch. "It's all too perfect, too deliberate."

"God, it's like something straight out of a mystery novel," Sofia breathed out, her voice tinged with awe and concern. "But why would they go through all that trouble?"

"I wish I knew," I replied, my brows knotting together as I considered the enigmatic puzzle before me. "There's a missing piece somewhere, and I can't help but feel it's important."

The intensity of our discussion faded as I glanced down at my planner, the scribbled notes and checklists a stark reminder of the reality waiting for me. "And speaking of important," I continued, my tone shifting from speculative to determined, "there's the wedding in one month."

"Right, the Dalton extravaganza," Sofia said, her posture readjusting as she settled back into her seat, her curiosity now mixed with professionalism.

I nodded. "I need to finalize everything with the WedLux team. Despite this... investigation, I can't let it derail the plans. The flowers, the catering, the music—it all needs to be perfect."

"Of course," Sofia agreed, her gaze acknowledging the gravity of the event we were orchestrating. "Dylan's depending on you, and I know you won't let him down, despite all these mysteries he and his family may be holding."

"Thanks, Sof," I murmured, the warmth in her eyes making me feel better. "I need to make sure every detail is accounted for. It's not just another job—it's probably the biggest event of my career. And if there's one thing I'm certain of, it's my ability to throw an unforgettable wedding."

"Nobody does it better," she said with a supportive smile, and I felt a flicker of pride amidst the chaos of my personal life and newfound mysteries.

With that, our conversation turned from the shadows of uncertainty to the tangible tasks at hand. As we discussed timelines and vendors, I couldn't help but feel a thread of excitement weave through my apprehension. The upcoming wedding wasn't just a professional milestone—it was a beacon, guiding me through the fog of doubt and towards a future where perhaps all would be revealed.

As we delved deeper into the final logistics of the wedding, a sudden shift in Sofia's demeanor caught my attention. There was a subtle tension in her posture, a veil of unease that belied her usual composure.

"Maddie," Sofia began, her voice tinged with a quiet vulnerability, "there's something I need to talk to you about."

I paused. "Of course. What's on your mind?"

MORE SECRETS

Sofia hesitated for a moment, her gaze momentarily faltering before meeting mine. "It's about Mark," she admitted, her voice barely above a whisper. "His work, it's consuming him. He's hardly ever home, and when he is, he's... distant. I feel like we're drifting apart, and it scares me."

My heart ached for Sofia, the depth of her pain mirroring my own. "I had no idea, Sof," I murmured, reaching out to grasp her hand in a gesture of solidarity. "You shouldn't have to go through this alone."

Tears welled in Sofia's eyes; I could clearly feel the hurt she was feeling. "And there's something else," she continued, her voice trembling with emotion. "We've been trying to get pregnant for over a year now, but... nothing. It's like another piece of our happiness slipping through our fingers."

The revelation hit me like a blow to the chest, the magnitude of Sofia's suffering nearly overwhelming. "Oh, Sofia," I breathed, my own eyes filling with tears. "I had no idea you were going through all of this."

Sofia offered me a sad smile, her vulnerability laid bare before me. "I didn't want to burden you with my problems, especially with everything you're dealing with," she admitted, her voice thick with emotion.

But I shook my head, squeezing her hand gently. "You're not a burden. You're my best friend, and I'm here for you, no matter what. We'll get through this together, I promise."

I let out a shaky laugh, the sound tinged with nerves yet buoyant with gratitude. It was easy to lose myself in the whirlwind of personal dilemmas, but Sofia's unwavering belief in my abilities acted as an anchor amidst the storm. And I hoped I had the same effect on her

"Thank you, Sof," I said, my heart swelling in my chest. The words felt small compared to the enormity of my appreciation, but they carried our history together—from late-night planning sessions, emergency flower runs, and moments just like this one. "You mean so much to me. Without you I don't know where I'd be." My throat tightened as I spoke, a result of the sincerity of my sentiment.

Sofia squeezed my hand, her hazel eyes sparkling with emotion. "We're a team, Maddy. And there's not a single curveball life can throw at us that we can't handle —together."

Her confidence was contagious, and for a moment, I allowed myself to bask in it, letting her words chase away the shadows of doubt. With Sofia by my side, perhaps the path forward wasn't as daunting as it seemed.

I leaned back, taking a slow, measured breath. Oxygen filled my lungs, cool and invigorating.

I would speak to Steve about starting fresh. The thought sent a shiver of nerves dancing across my skin, but beneath that, there was a burgeoning sense of hope. Our future—a panorama of possibilities—spread out before me, daunting yet bright.

CHAPTER 9
The Decision

I BROUGHT Becca at work with me. We hovered over the blueprint of the venue, my fingers tracing the fine outlines of tables set for the Daltons' guests. Every placement was a strategic decision, designed to foster comfortable conversation and avoid age-old family rifts. I murmured names under my breath, envisioning faces as I arranged and rearranged the seating cards with purposeful attention.

"Uncle John cannot be near the bar," I muttered, sliding his card further down the long, imperial table. "And the Hendersons should be in view of the sweetheart table—they adore pomp and pageantry."

Satisfied, I took a step back, allowing myself a brief moment of pride. Every detail, from the crisp fold of the napkins to the gentle curve of the calligraphy on place cards, bore the marks of my dedication.

I turned my focus to the floral arrangements laid out across my workspace. "What do you think of this, Becca?"

"I love it. The colors are perfect."

With a discerning eye, I compared swatches of fabric to blooms, ensuring continuity in the color palette—a perfect combination of blush and cream with whispers of sage green. The fragrance of peonies and garden roses remained in the air, promising an ethereal atmosphere for the ceremony.

"More greenery here," I said, plucking at the leaves, "less symmetry, more romance."

"Agreed," Becca said. "I still don't know how you can put all this together. It's incredible."

"It certainly isn't easy. Do you want coffee? We have a great machine. I'll be right back."

I walked to the lunch room, and made coffee for us. As I returned to my office with the freshly brewed coffee, I heard Rebecca's voice drifting from within, engaged in a conversation that piqued my interest.

"...I know, Mom," Rebecca's voice carried a mixture of apprehension and determination. "I just don't want to keep it from her anymore. It's time Maddie knows the truth. I'll talk to her about it when she gets back."

My heart skipped a beat, the words sending a jolt of confusion through me. Mom? Why would Rebecca be talking to Mom about something she wanted to discuss with me? And what truth was she referring to?

Suppressing the urge to burst into the room and demand answers, I strained to catch the rest of the conversation.

THE DECISION

"Yes, I met him yesterday," Rebecca continued, her voice trembling ever so slightly. "It was... overwhelming, to say the least. But I need to tell her. She deserves to know."

A sinking feeling started settling in the pit of my stomach. Met him yesterday? Who could this mysterious man be? And why was Rebecca so hesitant to tell me about him? The more I thought about it, the more I realized that there were a lot of things I didn't know about my family.

My thoughts were interrupted by the sound of footsteps approaching. Panicking, I quickly made my way back inside the office and pretended I didn't hear anything.

"I gotta go," Rebecca quickly told my mother. "Hey Maddie," she then said as I entered the room, her expression guarded. "Thank you for the coffee."

"No problem," I replied, trying to appear nonchalant.

Rebecca nodded and started sorting through some files on my desk, clearly avoiding eye contact. After a few moments of tense silence, she finally looked up at me.

"There's something I need to talk to you about," she began hesitantly. "It's about our family."

My heart rate spiked as a million different scenarios raced through my mind. Had someone passed away? Was there a family secret that had been kept from me all these years?

"What is it?" I asked, trying to keep my voice steady.

"I... I met someone yesterday," Rebecca said in a small voice, her eyes downcast.

"Okay," I said slowly, not sure where this was going.

"His name is Sebastian... Sebastian Jones." She took a deep breath. "He... he claims to be our biological father," she blurted out.

I felt like the wind had been knocked out of me. Our biological father? So who was the man who raised us?

"That's impossible," I whispered hoarsely, feeling tears prick at the back of my eyes. "Why do you even think this? And how long have you known?"

"I know," Rebecca said with a sad look in her face. "But... there is evidence that proves otherwise."

Rebecca hesitantly handed me a folder, her hands shaking slightly. I took it from her and opened it, my heart pounding with anticipation and fear.

Inside were documents and photos that seemed to confirm what Rebecca was saying. A DNA test confirming he was indeed her biological father. Photos of a man who looked surprisingly like both Rebecca and I.

"This can't be real," I said, my voice trembling. "And the DNA test is between you and him. Why do you believe he is also my father?"

"I know it's hard," Rebecca replied, tears welling up in her eyes. "But he says that mom had an affair with him before she met our dad. And it continued for a few years... even after Dad was in the picture. And Dad was sterile, so we Dad can't be our real father."

THE DECISION

I sat down heavily in my chair, trying to process the information. My mind felt clouded, my heart heavy with confusion and betrayal.

"But... why would Mom keep this from us?" I asked, trying to understand.

Rebecca shrugged, her expression defeated. "I don't know. Maybe she wanted to protect us from the truth. He—Sebastian—contacted me. He is the one who told me the truth, said he couldn't keep the lie anymore. I then confronted Mom about it, and came here to Keystone for a DNA test, and well, to meet him..."

Tears streamed down my face as I thought about our childhood memories and the man we called Dad. How could he not be our biological father? And if this was true, what did that make us? Suddenly everything I thought I knew about myself and my family was thrown into question.

"Does Dad know?" I asked.

"No, he doesn't know. And I think we should keep it this way. He thinks we were his two miracles that came despite his diagnosis. Why shatter his heart now? It'd only bring him pain." Rebecca held my hand and looked me straight in the eyes. "Maddie, please, I need you to be on board with this."

"What are we going to do?" I whispered, feeling lost and overwhelmed.

"We need to talk to Mom, together," Rebecca said firmly. "We deserve to know everything. Exactly how everything happened."

But before we could even begin to think about how we were going to approach our mother about this bombshell revelation, there was a knock on the door.

"Come in," I called out, wiping away my tears as best as I could.

The door opened and Mom walked in, wearing a concerned expression on her face. She frowned when she saw our tear-stained faces.

"Mom," I called out.

"We need to talk," she said and softly closed the door behind her.

Tears spilled down my cheeks as it all started making sense now. The hushed conversations, the secrecy, the photos and letters that Mom had always kept in a secret box.

Mom sat down across from us, her eyes flickering between us with worry. "Did you tell her already?" she asked looking at Rebecca, her voice shaky.

"Yes." Rebecca took a deep breath and explained everything that Sebastian had told us. Mom's face turned pale as she listened, her hands clasped tightly in her lap.

"I never meant for any of this to happen," she said, her voice barely above a whisper.

THE DECISION

"Why didn't you tell us the truth?" I demanded, my hurt and anger bubbling to the surface.

"I was scared," Mom admitted, tears now streaming down her face. "I didn't want to lose you both."

"Lose us? What do you mean?" Rebecca asked, confusion written all over her face.

"I was young and foolish. I had an affair with Sebastian while I was married to your father," Mom said, her shoulders trembling with emotion. "When I found out I was pregnant with him, I knew it would destroy our family if anyone found out."

"So you kept it a secret all these years?" I asked incredulously.

"Yes," Mom replied, hanging her head in shame. "A few times I thought maybe it was time for the truth to come out, but I never found the courage."

Silence filled the room as we all struggled to process what had just been revealed. My heart felt heavy with conflicting emotions—anger towards my mother for keeping such a huge secret from us, but also empathy for the difficult position she must have been in.

"We have another brother out there," Rebecca said softly, breaking the silence.

"Yes," Mom whispered.

"What are we supposed to do now?" I asked, feeling lost and unsure of what to do next.

"It's up to you both," Mom said. "But please, let's keep this from Dad. His health is deteriorating and this will only cause him more pain."

"I want to meet him. I want to know my real father... the person I share genes with. Dad will always be my daddy, of course." I sat down. "But I don't think I can meet Sebastian now nor his son... my new brother. I need time to process all of this."

"I understand if you both need some time to process all of this," she said, her voice shaky. "But please know that I never meant to hurt anyone."

"How can you say that?" Rebecca snapped. "Do you have any idea what this means for us?"

"I know, and I am so sorry," Mom said, tears streaming down her face.

"Why did Sebastian show up now?" I asked, my own anger still simmering beneath the surface.

"It's complicated," Mom replied evasively. "He has always wanted to meet you, be a father to you, but I stopped him. I didn't want to complicate things by bringing Sebastian into the picture."

"So you just... ignored him?" Rebecca said, her voice full of disbelief.

"I thought it was for the best," Mom replied, tears still streaming down her face. "But now I see that I made a mistake."

THE DECISION

The room fell into a heavy silence, punctuated only by the sound of our collective breaths and the occasional sniffle as tears continued to flow freely. It was as if the weight of years of secrets and lies had finally come crashing down upon us, leaving us to sift through the wreckage of our shattered trust and fractured family bonds.

As I sat there, grappling with the enormity of what had just been revealed, I couldn't help but feel a sense of profound loss. The idyllic image of our family that I had clung to for so long now lay in ruins, replaced by the harsh reality of betrayal and deceit.

And yet, amidst the chaos and confusion, a small glimmer of hope flickered to life within me. Despite the pain and uncertainty that lay ahead, I knew that we were not alone —that we had each other to lean on as we navigated the stormy waters of our newfound truth.

Taking a deep breath, I met my mother's tear-filled gaze with a mixture of sadness and forgiveness. "We'll get through this," I said softly, reaching out to squeeze her hand in a gesture of solidarity.

Rebecca nodded, her expression softening as she reached out to clasp our hands together in a silent vow of unity. "We're in this together," she said, her voice steady despite the tears that still streamed down her cheeks.

And as we sat there, bound together by the ties of blood and shared experience, I knew that no matter what the future held, we would face it with courage and resilience, drawing strength from the unbreakable bonds of family that had endured despite the secrets and lies that threatened to tear us apart.

The sky was now painted in hues of fiery orange and soft lavender when I finally allowed myself to step away from the office: burgeoning files, spreadsheets and a new family secret that had consumed my day. The Daltons' wedding was shaping into a masterpiece of meticulous planning, but now it was time to address a few different sorts of unfinished business.

"Hi," Steve's voice broke through the silence as I stepped in the house, "How was your day? Where is Becca?"

"She went out to dinner with some friends." I sat down on the plush sofa that had become more of a storage space for samples and vendor catalogs than a place of rest. Steve took my hands in his, his blue eyes searching mine with an intensity that was both familiar and unsettling.

"Look, I know things haven't been right between us," he began, his voice steady with a practiced sincerity. "But I'm here, really here this time. I've been working on myself, on us. Can we give it another shot?"

His words were like rays of hope piercing through the overcast sky of our strained relationship. It would have been so easy to bask in that warmth, to forget the cold shadows of doubt that loomed just beyond. And yet...

"Steve," I started, my voice betraying the tempest of emotions swirling within me, "I meant to talk to you about this, and I want to believe that. More than anything, I do. But..." My heart ached with skepticism. "How can we just pick up the pieces as if they weren't scattered everywhere? I want to start again, fresh."

He squeezed my hands, a gesture meant to reassure. "We rebuild, together. Trust me."

Perhaps there was a sliver of possibility worth exploring, after all.

"There is something I need to tell you." I sighed. "It's about my family."

"What's going on?"

I took a deep breath, steeling myself for what I was about to reveal. "My mother just dropped a bombshell on us today," I said, looking at Steve with a mix of apprehension and disbelief.

"What kind of bombshell?" he asked, his expression turning serious.

"She told us that our father isn't really our father," I said, my voice shaking as the words left my mouth. "She had an affair with a man named Sebastian before and while she was with Dad."

Steve's eyes widened in shock. "Are you serious?" he asked.

I nodded solemnly. "She kept it a secret from us all these years. I found out from Rebecca first, and Rebecca found out from this man, Sebastian."

"Wow. I can't believe it. Are you sure he is your father? That must have been quite a shock for all of you," Steve said, reaching over to squeeze my hand in comfort.

"Yes, he is." I admitted. "I'm still trying to process everything. He wants a relationship with Becca and I."

"How do you feel about it?" he asked gently.

"I don't know," I replied honestly. "I need time before I meet him. Oh, and I also have a brother... I mean, half brother; his son. I feel angry and betrayed by my mother for keeping such a huge secret from us. And then there's this whole new family dynamic that I have to wrap my head around, not to talk about how guilty I feel about Daddy."

"I can imagine it's overwhelming," Steve said sympathetically. "But remember, this doesn't change who you are or where you come from."

"I know," I sighed. "But it's still hard to wrap my head around."

We sat in silence for a few moments, lost in our thoughts and emotions.

"Do you want to talk more about it?" Steve finally broke the silence.

"Not really," I admitted. "I just wanted to let you know what was going on."

THE DECISION

"Well, thank you for trusting me enough to share this with me," Steve said sincerely.

"I trust you more than anyone else," I replied with a small smile.

"And I'll always be here for you, no matter what happens with your family," he said, leaning in to give me a gentle kiss.

Before I could gather my thoughts into coherent words, Steve stood up, a playful spark lighting up his features. "Come with me," he said, extending a hand to help me up. "Let's go somewhere special."

"What, where?"

"It'll be good for you... for us. We haven't been out in forever."

"And Lauren?" I asked.

"I'll ask my mom if she can stay over tonight. I'll call her right now."

Confused but curious, he instructed me to change into nicer clothes while he made the phone call, and when his mother, Allie, arrived, I let him lead me outside. Once parked, we walked in companionable silence until we reached the entrance of 'La Belle Époque,' a restaurant renowned for its exquisite French cuisine and enchanting atmosphere.

"This place is impossible to get into without reservations months in advance," I murmured, my surprise evident as we were greeted by the maître d'. "One rule tonight. Let's leave all the drama out the door. No negative talk. Deal?"

"Deal. And nothing but the best for you," he replied with a grin. "One of my clients works here; he owes me."

I smirked and nodded while my mind kept reassuring me I was making the right decision.

The dining room enveloped us in its timeless elegance; crystal chandeliers cast a golden glow over tables draped in white linen, while the murmur of hushed conversations and the gentle clinking of fine china created a melody of sophistication.

"Wow," I breathed, taking in the details—the fragrant bouquet of roses on every table, the impeccable attire of the staff, the soft melody of a piano playing in the background.

"Happy?" Steve asked, watching me with an expectant shine in his eyes.

"Very," I admitted, allowing myself a moment to appreciate the gesture. There was no denying the effort he had put into this surprise, the lengths he had gone to in order to make this evening memorable.

Yet, even as we were led to our secluded table, the flicker of candlelight casting dancing shadows on the tablecloth, the doubts remained like uninvited guests, whispering questions that I wasn't sure I was ready to answer. Could one romantic dinner truly mend the cracks in our foundation? Could I let go of the past and move forward

THE DECISION

with Steve, or was I clinging to a love that had already slipped through my fingers?

"Thank you for this," I said, my voice soft but genuine, "It really is beautiful."

"Only the best," he repeated, reaching across the table to gently touch my hand, "for us."

The chime of my fork against the plate punctuated a silence that had settled between us, as if every bite were an attempt to anchor myself in the now, with Steve. The rich aroma of the truffle risotto before me was intoxicating, yet even the decadence of each mouthful couldn't fully command my attention.

"Everything tastes incredible," I offered, glancing up at Steve, who seemed pleased with my approval. His eyes held mine, and for a moment, the world felt small and intimate.

Then, laughter erupted from a nearby table, pulling my gaze away. The sound was lively, a stark contrast to the careful choreography of our own interactions. And there he was—Jake, his dark hair tousled just so, a careless smile lighting up his face as he animatedly recounted a story to his friends. A pang of something complex twisted inside me, an emotional cocktail of surprise, guilt, and an undeniable pull towards the man whose presence suddenly filled the room.

"Madelyn?" Steve's voice cut through my trance, but I was too caught in the undertow of conflicting emotions to respond immediately.

"Sorry, what?" I murmured, feeling as though I'd been dragged back onto the shore from a deep sea of thought.

"Is the risotto to your liking?" he repeated, unaware of the storm raging within me.

"Um, yes, it's delicious," I said, forcing a smile as I turned back to my plate. But my appetite had waned, the creamy dish now just a mass on my tongue.

I stole another glance at Jake, watching him throw his head back in laughter, the ease of his joy a stark reminder of what entangled Steve and me. The sight of him made my heart skip a beat, every interaction we had replaying itself like a highlight reel in my mind. It was a dangerous game, letting my thoughts drift to Jake, when I was here trying to rebuild something with Steve.

"You seem distant," Steve observed, a frown creasing his brow. "Are you still thinking about what happened today?"

"A bit," I lied. "Also... thinking about the wedding plans."

"Ah," he nodded, accepting the excuse. Yet I knew, in the quiet recesses of my heart, that the distance between us was more than just the span of a table—it was a rift filled with unspoken words and lingering doubts.

As I sipped my wine, its velvety warmth slid down my throat, failing to thaw the chill of indecision that had settled within me. The romantic ambiance, once comforting, now felt like a stage set for a play where I had forgotten my lines. Every time I laughed or touched Steve's

THE DECISION

hand, part of me retreated, scared of making a promise my heart wasn't sure it could keep.

"Excuse me for a moment," I whispered, pushing back my chair. The need to breathe, to be alone with my turbulent thoughts, was overwhelming. I didn't dare look at Jake again as I stood; I feared that one more glimpse would shatter the graceful veneer I struggled to maintain.

Alone in the restroom, I leaned against the cool marble of the countertop trying to steady the storm within. My reflection stared back at me, green eyes searching for answers that refused to come. What did I want? Who did my heart yearn for in the silent spaces between beats?

I turned the faucet, letting the cool water cascade over my trembling hands. The chill was a temporary balm, a momentary anchor in the storm of my thoughts. I lifted my gaze to the mirror, staring into eyes that felt like belonged to someone else—green pools reflecting a trouble I could no longer name.

"Get it together, Madelyn," I whispered to my own image. I smoothed down my dress and prepared to return to the table, to Steve, to the night that was supposed to be about us—yet felt haunted by the ghosts others.

Once visibly back together, I headed back to the table. Steve's jokes barely registered over the clatter of my own discordant thoughts. He was recounting an anecdote, something about his latest business venture, but every word seemed to dissolve before it reached me, like sugar in a stormy sea.

"Sorry about that," I slid into the booth across from Steve, offering a smile that didn't quite reach my eyes. "Just needed a moment. Oh, the crème brûlée is here."

"Hello?" His voice broke through, tinged with concern. I blinked, refocusing on his deep-set blue eyes that sought mine with an intensity that demanded attention. "You seem miles away. Do you prefer if we call it a night?"

I offered him a tight smile, the kind you give when you're trying not to fracture. "No, I'm fine." I tucked a stray wavy chestnut lock behind my ear. The gesture betrayed my unease; I knew he noticed. "I'm sorry."

"Hey," Steve reached across the table, covering my hand with his—firm and reassuring. "I know you're going through a lot with the wedding planning and with today's news." His thumb brushed my skin in an attempt to ground me, to bring me back from wherever my mind had wandered. "I'm here."

"Thanks," I murmured, but the warmth from his touch couldn't thaw the chill of apprehension that coiled within me. I glanced away, feeling as though I were teetering on the edge of a precipice, one wrong step from tumbling into an abyss of indecision.

"Is there something else?" His tone of voice was soft. There was a note of something else too—jealousy, perhaps? A reminder that Steve could sense when my heart strayed before my feet ever did.

"No, not at all." I picked at the remains of the crème brûlée, the spoon's clink against porcelain sounding far too

THE DECISION

loud in the strained silence. Steve's attempts at conversation, once a comforting cadence, now felt like ragged stitches trying to hold together the frayed edges of our relationship.

"Did you see the Johnsons are expecting again?" he asked, his eyes scanning my face for a reaction.

"Third time's the charm," I replied, my voice flat, the words not quite meeting his gaze that sought assurance, warmth—anything that resembled the Madelyn he knew.

He leaned back in his chair, running a hand through his short-cropped hair—a gesture of defeat, perhaps, or simply resignation. His broad shoulders, usually squared with confidence, now seemed to bear the weight of our dwindling connection.

Jake's smiles were rich and sure as he regaled his business partner with stories I couldn't decipher. I tried to focus on my husband, to be present in this celebration of his success, but my senses were betrayingly attuned to another presence.

And then, Jake's eyes found mine—an electric charge in the glance that passed between us. His warm brown eyes held a depth I could easily see, a narrative in a language only we seemed to understand. My breath hitched, a shiver running up my spine despite the warmth of the crowded restaurant. I could feel Steve next to me, oblivious, his hand casually resting on his wine glass, unaware of the storm brewing within me.

The merlot swirled in my glass. With every sip, the connection amplified, the tension between Jake and me. The wine was starting to weave its way into my bloodstream, each beat of my heart sending it coursing quicker, bringing a flush to my cheeks.

"Are you tired? Should we go?" Steve's voice broke through my reverie, his deep-set blue eyes searching mine with a mixture of concern and something else—was it suspicion? I nodded, forcing a smile, and turned to him, letting the moment with Jake slip away like a shadow at dusk.

"I'm a bit tired," I said, my voice steadier than I felt. "Just lost in thought about how cute it was for you to bring me here. This place is so charming."

Steve's face softened, the charismatic smile that had first drawn me to him playing on his lips. He reached across the table, enveloping my hand in his larger, athletic one, and I was reminded of the strength and safety those hands had once represented.

"Let's get out of here," he murmured, his blue eyes now alight with a different kind of ambition. "I want to spend this night with you... alone."

My heart wavered, guilt and desire intertwining like thorns. But as the wine's influence grew, so did my longing for intimacy, a craving not entirely for the man before me but stoked by the silent exchange with another. Yet I allowed myself to be swept up in the moment, in Steve's eagerness, as if his passion could somehow anchor me back to him.

THE DECISION

"Let's do it," I whispered back, feeling reckless, romantic, and terribly conflicted.

With a conspiratorial grin, Steve stood, offering his hand to help me up. We made our way to the foyer, Steve's arm possessively around my waist. As we stepped outside, I glanced back through the restaurant's window, catching Jake watching us leave.

"Come on," Steve said, eager, pulling me gently toward the hotel across the street, his energy infectious. "Let's forget everything else. Tonight's just for us."

And yet, as we crossed the threshold of the hotel lobby, my mind couldn't help but wander back to the intensity of Jake's gaze, burning into memory the silent promise of what could never be.

We slipped through the revolving doors of the hotel, a barrier between the reality of candlelit dinners and the whispered promise of silk sheets. The lobby was grandiose, marble floors reflecting the soft glow of chandeliers, but it was Steve's insistent tug on my hand that drew me forward, not the opulence.

"Good evening," he said to the receptionist, his words laced with an undertone of urgency that matched the rapid beating of my heart. "We'd like a room for the night."

As he handled the formalities, I stood there. My body thrummed with anticipation, yet each heartbeat reminded me of a name that wasn't his.

The keycard felt like ice against my palm as Steve guided me toward the elevator. His touch was familiar, comforting, but it was Jake's phantom fingers I felt interlacing with mine, sending shivers up my spine.

"Are you alright, Maddie?" Steve asked, concern flickering across his face as we ascended.

"Never better," I didn't totally lie, my voice a soft melody concealing the discord within.

Entering the suite, Steve wasted no time in dimming the lights, casting the room into a seductive twilight. The cityscape outside painted streaks of light across the walls, a silent witness to our impending communion.

His hands were eager as they found the curve of my waist, pulling me close. Our lips met in a kiss that was meant to sear away doubt, to tether me to the here and now. But behind closed eyelids, it was Jake's dark eyes that burned into me, igniting a fire Steve believed was his.

Steve's lips grazed my skin, igniting a fire within me that only he could quench. My body melted into his as he carried me to the bed, the sheets already tangled in anticipation.

With his touch of hands, caress of his tongue, I couldn't help but repeating Jake's name in my head, the forbidden desire burning within me.

Our bodies moved together in a primal dance, fueled by desire and fueled by lies. Every kiss felt like a façade, every whisper a deception. But in that moment, none of it mattered as we surrendered to each other, our bodies entwined in ecstasy.

But even as I cried out Steve's name in pleasure, my heart still longed for Jake's touch, unable to let go of the connection we once had. And in the midst of our wild night, I knew that no matter how much satisfaction Steve could offer, at that moment my mind and body were dancing with someone else.

CHAPTER 10

Pure Passion

I LAY THERE, my chest rising and falling in sync with Steve's steady breaths, struggling to shake off the haze of last night's passion. Guilt settled upon me, suffocating, as I watched him stir from his slumber.

Steve's eyes fluttered open, his gaze landing upon me with a mixture of contentment and longing. He reached out to brush a stray strand of hair from my face, tenderly tracing the curve of my cheek with his fingertips. But even in that gentle touch, I felt the absence of something more, something intangible.

A sigh escaped my lips as I propped myself up on one elbow, staring at the sunlight dancing across his face. Questions swirled within me like a tempestuous storm, threatening to untangle the fragile threads that still held our marriage together. How could I have surrendered myself so easily to Steve's touch? And most of all, how could I continue this charade of a happy marriage while my heart was still consumed by longing for another man?

Steve stirred again, his eyes meeting mine with understanding. He knew these thoughts were consuming me—well, not the exact ones—but he also knew that neither of us were willing to confront them.

I couldn't help but wonder if there was a part of Steve that also yearned for someone else, someone who wasn't his wife. But we both knew it was easier to keep up this façade than to admit the truth and face the consequences. This time I knew it was me who had another man in mind, and not Steve, or at least I didn't think so. The story was now flipped.

I found myself sinking deeper into the sheets, lost in my own thoughts. I couldn't shake off the feeling of guilt and shame, knowing that while what had happened between us last night my mind wasn't all there, and that hadn't happened before.

But as much as I wanted to bury these feelings and move on with our lives, they continued to gnaw at my consciousness.

I need time alone to sort through these emotions and make sense of them, I thought.

"Good morning," he whispered, his voice a soft caress against my ear. "Last night was... incredible."

I forced a smile. "Yes, it was," I replied, my voice lacking the enthusiasm he expected. I tried to be normal, sweet even, as we basked in the afterglow of our passion. But behind my façade, my mind was still consumed by thoughts of Jake.

The hotel room was filled with the smell of coffee as Steve prepared some for us both. He moved around the hotel room trying to find his shirt to put on, and called the front desk for room service. I loved breakfast in bed and he knew it. That was the thing; nobody knew me better than Steve. We shared many years together and a beautiful daughter. He knew how to win my heart back if he truly wanted to.

"Here you go," he said, placing a cup of coffee in front of me.

Steve's eyes searched mine, searching for reassurance that I struggled to offer. "You know, Maddie," he began, his voice hesitant, "I've missed this. I've missed us." There was a note of vulnerability in his voice that tugged at my heartstrings.

"I've missed it too," I replied softly, meeting his gaze briefly before looking away.

"But something's different," Steve continued, sounding almost accusing.

I froze, my heart racing as I tried to come up with a believable explanation. But before I could speak, Steve placed a gentle hand on mine.

"I'm not upset or angry," he said earnestly. "I just want to understand what's going on with you. I hope it's everything else that's being going on... and nothing to do with me."

"I don't know," I finally admitted, my voice barely above a whisper. "It'll take some time for me to go back to the way

I was. I'm sure I'm a bit stressed about everything. It'll pass."

Steve's expression softened as he took in my words. He pulled me into a comforting embrace and held me close.

"We'll figure it out together," he promised. "I'm just so happy you're giving us another chance. You won't regret it."

Once back to reality, a heavy unease settled in my chest. The nagging feeling that I was heading down the wrong path consumed my thoughts. Jake's face kept appearing in my mind, haunting me with doubts about the decision I had made. A decision that would impact my entire life. My heart twisted with fear and regret, wondering if I had made the wrong choice. Was this truly the optimal route for my happiness? Or was I merely extending a lifeline to Steve in a bid to salvage my family? I dreaded mirroring my parents' plight. Did my mother stay with my father out of love or obligation? What if her heart yearned for Sebastian, leaving her to endure a lifetime of unfulfilled longing?

I had to find a distraction. I wanted to bring Rebecca out for lunch before her departure to New York later today.

We sat at The Elm, a small restaurant near my house; Rebecca looked at me with concern, her hazel eyes reflecting a mix of empathy and curiosity.

"Madelyn, you seem lost in thought. Is everything alright?" she asked, her voice laced with genuine care.

I let out a sigh, setting down the spoon as I met her gaze. "Steve betrayed me," I whispered, my voice barely audible over the ambient noise of the restaurant.

Rebecca's eyes widened in surprise, her hand reaching out to cover mine in a gesture of support. "Oh, Madelyn, I'm so sorry. What happened?" she asked softly.

"It was months ago. He cheated on me with his assistant," I blurted out, the words feeling heavy and unfamiliar on my tongue.

Rebecca's eyes widened in shock, her hand dropping from mine. "Why didn't you tell me?" she asked, her voice filled with confusion.

"Because I didn't want you to look at him differently. We're working on things, you know," I said. "But I learned it's better to be honest from the get-go."

I then went on to explain everything that happened. I felt a sense of relief as I poured out all my emotions and frustrations to Rebecca. She listened patiently, offering me comforting words and gentle touches.

"I can't believe it," she said, shaking her head in disbelief once I finished. "Are you going to stay with him?" she asked cautiously.

"I don't know," I repeated, feeling uncertain. "Part of me wants to forgive him and try to make things work. But another part of me is still reeling from the betrayal."

"It's a tough decision," Rebecca said sympathetically. "But ultimately, it's good that you're trying. I believe in second chances... and most importantly therapy."

We fell into a comfortable silence, lost in our own thoughts. After a few minutes, I started talking.

"Becca, can I ask you something?" I asked hesitantly.

"Of course," she replied.

"Do you think Mom and Dad's relationship was only founded on obligation? Or did they truly love each other at one point?" I asked softly.

She thought about it for a moment before answering. "I'm not sure," she said. "They never really talked about their relationship or showed much affection towards each other."

"I always thought they were together for our sake," I replied. "And after finding out of Mom's infidelity, I'm convinced of this."

"Who knows. Now you know why I don't want to get married. It's messy."

I nodded in understanding, knowing that whatever happened in the past couldn't be changed. But still, the idea of our family being different lingered in my mind.

We finished lunch and walked back to my house. Rebecca and I talked about other things—work, gossiping about mutual friends, and even discussing our future career goals.

PURE PASSION

But when we reached the house, a taxi was already waiting to bring Rebecca to the airport.

"I guess this is it, huh?" I hugged her and she squeezed me back. "When am I going to see you again?"

"We need some girls time alone. Come to visit me in New York. It'd be so much fun."

"I agree. Once I get some of these life dilemmas figured out, I'll plan it. Pinky promise." I caressed Becca's hair.

She walked backwards toward the taxi and waved at me one last time before getting inside. "Give Lauren one last hug for me when she gets home for school. I miss her already."

And off she went.

I walked into the house and immediately collapsed onto my couch, feeling exhausted both physically and emotionally. Part of me wished that I could just turn off my brain for a while and escape from all of this chaos.

But amidst the storm, one thought was constant on my mind.

I reached for my phone, fingers trembling slightly as I scrolled through my contacts. There it was, Jake's name, buried amidst a sea of other names, but it stood out like a beacon calling to me. With a deep breath, I pressed the call button and brought the phone to my ear, heart pounding with anticipation. I knew I had to call him, but I didn't know why nor what to say.

It rang once, twice, and then I heard his voice on the other end, warm and familiar, sending shivers down my spine. "Hello?"

"Jake," I murmured, my voice barely audible, as if I were afraid of the weight of my own words. "Can we meet?"

There was a pause on the other end, a pregnant moment filled with uncertainty. "Madelyn," he said finally, his voice tinged with a mixture of surprise and caution. "Is everything okay?"

I hesitated, unsure of how to answer that question. Was everything okay? No, far from it. But did I have the courage to admit that to Jake, to confront the tangled mess of emotions that swirled within me? "I... I just need to talk," I managed to say, my voice cracking slightly.

There was another pause, and then Jake sighed softly. "Of course," he replied, his voice gentle and understanding. "Where do you want to meet?"

I glanced around my home, suddenly feeling suffocated by the walls closing in on me. "There's a café near my office called Sweetwaters," I said. "Can we meet there in an hour?"

"Sure," Jake replied, his voice tinged with concern. "I'll see you then."

As I ended the call, both relief and anxiety attacked me. I knew that meeting Jake meant confronting the truth, facing the reality of my feelings and the consequences of my actions. But I also knew that it was a necessary step, a chance to finally untangle the web of lies and deceit that had ensnared me for far too long.

I used to never believe people who said hard times cause recklessness, but I now understood more than ever. These bold decisions came from a place of deep introspection and a desire for transformation.

With a heavy heart, I rose from my couch, feeling the weight of my decisions bearing down on me like a burden too heavy to bear. But deep down, beneath the layers of guilt and shame, there was a glimmer of hope, a flicker of possibility that maybe, just maybe, I could find the clarity and resolution I so desperately sought. And as I stepped out into the sunlight, ready to face whatever lay ahead, I knew that no matter how difficult the journey may be, it was a journey I had to take.

Sweetwaters was a cute little place tucked away on a side street, its windows adorned with delicate lace curtains that billowed gently in the breeze. As I walked through the door, a rush of warmth enveloped me, mingling with the fragrant aroma of freshly brewed coffee and baked goods. The soft murmur of voices and the clinking of cups filled the air, creating a soothing backdrop to the storm of emotions raging within me.

I scanned the room anxiously, heart pounding in my chest as I searched for Jake. And then, there he was, sitting at a small table by the window, bathed in the golden light of the setting sun. His warm brown eyes met mine, sending a jolt of electricity through me, as if our gaze had ignited a spark that danced between us.

I made my way towards him, each step heavy with anticipation and trepidation. As I sat down opposite him, I was acutely aware of every little detail — the flickering candle casting dancing shadows on his face, the soft strains of a jazz melody playing in the background, the gentle hum of conversation around us. Jake's warm brown eyes met mine, and I saw a flicker of concern mixed with longing in them.

"You looked so happy at dinner last night with your husband," Jake began softly, his voice filled with an unspoken question.

I swallowed hard, feeling a lump form in my throat. How could I explain the truth to him? How could I tell him that my happiness was a façade, a carefully constructed illusion that I had been living for years?

"I was," I said finally, my voice barely above a whisper. "I mean... I am. It's complicated."

Jake nodded, his expression understanding yet guarded. He knew there was more to the story, but he also knew not to push me too far.

"I'm sorry," he said sincerely. "I didn't mean to pry."

"It's okay," I replied with a faint smile.

For a moment, we sat in silence, each lost in our own thoughts.

"I know we said we would end things," Jake began tentatively, breaking the silence. "But I can't help but feel that there's something more going on with you."

My heart skipped a beat at his words."I... I don't know where to begin," I stammered, my voice thick with emotion.

"Maybe you can start by telling me why you're not happy," Jake suggested gently. "I saw you looking at me last night. You looked so damn beautiful."

A blush crept up my cheeks as memories of our past flooded my mind.

Jake's warm hand reached up to caress my face gently, his touch sending shivers down my spine. The way his eyes bore into mine with such intensity made my breath catch in my throat. In that moment, the bustling bookstore around us seemed to fade away, leaving just the two of us in a world of our own.

"I... I never imagined things would turn out like this," I whispered, my gaze locked with his. His thumb brushed softly against my cheek, wiping away a stray tear that had escaped down my face. I closed my eyes briefly, savoring the sensation of his touch against my skin, relishing the way his presence enveloped me in a cocoon of warmth and safety. When I opened them again, I found myself lost in the depths of his warm brown eyes.

"Madelyn," Jake's voice was strained, his emotions bubbling just beneath the surface. "We need to leave. Find somewhere away from everyone else."

The sound of Jake's voice made my heart skip a beat. I wanted to follow him, to get lost in his embrace and forget about everything else. But at the same time, I knew that this decision would complicate things further.

"Please, come with me." Jake got up and extended his hand towards me.

With a heavy heart, I reluctantly followed Jake out of the bookstore and into the busy streets of the city. We walked in silence for a few blocks, our hands brushing against each other every now and then.

As we turned down a quieter side street, Jake finally spoke up. "I know I promised to stay away from you, Madelyn," he began, his voice filled with regret. "But seeing you last night... it brought back all these feelings that I thought I had buried."

His words pierced my heart like sharp daggers. I knew exactly how he felt because I too had been struggling with my own buried emotions.

"I shouldn't have come," I said softly, feeling an overwhelming sense of guilt towards Steve. "I should have stayed away from you..."

Jake stopped in his tracks and turned to face me, his eyes pleading for me to understand.

"But you did come, Madelyn," Jake said firmly, his voice tinged with frustration. "And I couldn't stay away either. I only kept my distance because you asked me to."

PURE PASSION

"I never stopped thinking about you," Jake continued, his voice softening. "Every day since we last saw each other, you've been on my mind."

Tears threatened to spill from my eyes as I took in his words. Despite everything that had happened between us, he still felt the same way.

His warm breath brushed against my cheek as he leaned in closer, his eyes searching mine for any sign of hesitation. His lips, soft and tender, pressed against mine in a gentle caress that ignited a fire deep within me.

In that moment, every doubt and fear dissipated as we clung to each other, lost in the whirlwind of emotions. As we pulled apart slightly, our gaze locked once again, and without words, an unspoken understanding passed between us.

As we pulled apart slightly, our eyes met again, and an unspoken agreement passed between us. Without a word, Jake reached into his pocket and retrieved a sleek key fob emblazoned with the Ferrari logo. With a flick of his wrist, the car lights blinked in response, beckoning us towards the luxurious vehicle parked nearby.

He opened the passenger door for me and I climbed into the luxurious red Ferrari, taking in every detail of the interior. The leather seats were soft and comfortable, and the scent of expensive cologne lingered in the air.

Once we were both seated, Jake revved up the engine and we sped off into the night. The city lights blurred past us as we drove through empty streets, lost in our own world.

"Where are we going?" I asked.

Jake turned to me with a mischievous smile playing on his lips, his warm brown eyes reflecting the glow of the dashboard lights. "It's a surprise," he replied cryptically, his voice tinged with excitement.

The car hummed softly as we navigated through the quiet streets, the only sound accompanying us was the gentle purr of the engine and the soft rustle of the night breeze. After what felt like an eternity, we arrived at our destination—a secluded beach by the ocean. The moonlight illuminated the sandy shore, casting a magical glow over everything. I stepped out of the Ferrari in awe, gazing at the vastness of the sea before us.

Jake took my hand and led me towards a cozy bonfire that he had set up earlier. The flames danced in front of us, casting shadows on his face as he turned to look at me.

"I used to come here when I needed to clear my head," he said softly, his gaze never leaving mine. "It's my special place."

I smiled at him, touched that he would share this intimate part of himself with me. We sat down by the fire and watched as it crackled and flickered in front of us.

"Thank you for bringing me here," I said sincerely, feeling a sense of calm wash over me.

"This place wouldn't be complete without you," Jake replied with a crooked grin.

As I looked into Jake's warm brown eyes, my heart swelled with a mixture of emotions—desire, gratitude, and a profound connection that seemed to transcend words. Without breaking eye contact, he reached out a hand to cup my cheek, his touch sending shivers down my spine.

All the tension and uncertainty melted away, leaving only a raw and unspoken yearning between us. Without a word, our lips met in a tender and passionate kiss, igniting a fire within me that matched the one blazing before us.

His lips were soft yet firm against mine, moving in perfect harmony as if they were meant to be together.

I wrapped my arms around his neck, pulling him closer as our bodies pressed against each other. His hands caressed my back, sending shivers down my spine and igniting a fire within me.

Lost in the moment, we moved closer to the fire, the warmth only intensifying our passion. As we broke apart for air, Jake rested his forehead against mine and whispered, "I've been wanting to do that since I first saw you."

A surge of emotions washed over me—desire, longing, and a sense of belonging that I had never felt before. In that moment, I knew that what we had was special and worth fighting for.

Jake's lips traced a path along my jawline, down my neck, leaving a trail of kisses that seared my skin with their tenderness. His whispers were like silk against my ear, promising a world of ecstasy and love that I never knew existed.

As we stood there, I couldn't help but marvel at the beauty of the moment—the stars twinkling above us, the soft sand between my toes, and Jake's hand intertwined with mine.

"I never want this moment to end," I whispered, my heart overflowing with emotion.

Jake turned to me with a gentle smile and pulled me closer. "Then let's make it last forever."

His strong hands held me tightly as we kissed, the passion consuming us, the moonlight shining down on us like a spotlight. It felt like time had stopped, just for this moment, and we were the only two people in the world.

Slowly, Jake broke the kiss and gazed into my eyes, his warm brown irises radiating with desire. "I want to make love to you right here," he whispered, his voice hoarse with passion.

I looked into his eyes and saw the same longing and desire reflected back at me. There was no turning back now.

We started to undress each other, the fire dancing in the background, illuminating our bodies as we revealed ourselves to each other.

Every touch, every kiss felt like an eternity as we explored each other's bodies with a hunger that could not be satisfied. Our hands were everywhere, caressing and exploring every inch of skin.

Jake's lips traced a path from my neck down to my chest, leaving a trail of fiery kisses in their wake. I couldn't contain my moans as his lips met my skin, sending waves of pleasure throughout my body.

As he continued his journey downwards, I could feel the heat radiating from his body against mine. My heart was racing with anticipation and desire.

I reached for his shirt and pulled it off him, desperate to feel his bare skin against mine. His muscles rippled beneath my fingertips, making me crave him even more.

With trembling hands, Jake unbuttoned my dress and let it fall to the ground. He took a step back to admire me in all my nakedness before pulling me into another passionate kiss.

Our bodies moved together in perfect sync as we made love on the sand under the stars. Every forceful thrust sent us careening towards the brink of overwhelming pleasure, our bodies intertwined in a frenzy of desire. As our moans and gasps grew louder, we reached the pinnacle of ecstasy simultaneously, our bodies trembling and quivering in perfect synchrony.

The waves crashed against the shore as we lay on the soft sand, our breathing heavy and our bodies still intertwined. The moon shone down on us, creating a beautiful glow that surrounded us.

I couldn't believe how amazing it felt to be with Jake in this moment. Every touch, every kiss, every forceful thrust had taken us both to the brink of overwhelming pleasure.

As we caught our breath, I looked into Jake's eyes and saw an expression of pure lust and adoration. I knew in that moment that I was exactly where I was meant to be —with him.

We stayed there for a while, wrapped up in each other's arms and listening to the sounds of the ocean. It was like time had stopped just for us, allowing us to bask in the afterglow of our lovemaking.

Finally, Jake broke the silence. "That was... incredible," he said, a smile spreading across his face.

I couldn't agree more. "It was," I replied breathlessly.

But what did this mean? Was it pure lust or something more? Was this a rebellious act or real feelings?

He leaned in for a sweet kiss before helping me up from the sand. We gathered our clothes and made our way back towards Jake's car.

As Jake and I sat in his Ferrari, our bodies still tingling from the passionate encounter on the beach, he turned to me with a serious expression.

"I'd love it if you could come back to my home and sleep with me," he said, his voice low and full of desire.

I couldn't help but feel a pang of guilt at the thought. As much as I wanted to spend the night with him, I knew I couldn't. Lauren was waiting for me at home, and Steve. Even though we were going through a rough patch, I couldn't.

"I know, but I can't.. .Lauren..." I started to explain.

"Steve," Jake interrupted, his voice firm. "I understand that you're in a relationship, but let's not pretend like there's real love there. You're unhappy and unfulfilled."

His words hit me hard. He was right.

"I can't just leave him like that," I said with a heavy heart.

"I don't want to pressure you. But what harm would one night do? Just one night where you let yourself be completely free and happy."

His words were tempting, but my conscience wouldn't let me give in so easily. "I'm sorry, Jake. I just can't."

Jake let out a sigh and ran a hand through his hair before turning back to me. "I understand," he said, disappointment evident in his voice. "But I want you for myself."

My heart ached at the sincerity in his words. I couldn't help but wonder if things would have been different if I had met him before Steve.

"I'll drive you home. I'll make sure to leave you a block away so no one sees you." Jake placed his hand on my thigh.

As we drove back to my house, the atmosphere in the car was different. It wasn't tense or awkward, but there was a sense of sadness between us. I felt overwhelmed with emotions—the high of our lovemaking, the thrill of being

LORAIN RIZK

together, and the fear of what could happen if Steve found out.

"Thank you for understanding," I said softly, breaking the silence.

Jake nodded and gave me a small smile. "Of course. I just want you to know that I'll always be here for you, no matter what."

I felt a lump forming in my throat and quickly turned away, trying to hide the tears threatening to spill from my eyes. This situation with Jake was complicated and I didn't know how to navigate it without hurting someone. I decided I'd deal with it the next day.

We arrived near my house and before I could even unbuckle my seat belt, Jake leaned over and planted a gentle kiss on my lips.

"Goodnight," he whispered before pulling away. He then walked out of the car to open my door and help me out.

As I stepped out of the car, my eyes immediately fell upon Steve. He stood there, tall and confident, his dark hair ruffled by a light breeze. His knowing gaze locked onto mine, as if he could see into my soul. He looked furious, his blue eyes burning with anger.

"What the hell is going on here?" he snapped, his voice shaking with rage.

I stumbled back, clutching at Jake's arm for support. "Steve, it's not what you think," I pleaded, my voice shaking.

Steve's anger turned to disbelief as he looked between the two of us. "Not what I think? You're cheating on me with him? Let me guess... Is this that Jake?"

I could feel the tears starting to form in my eyes as guilt and shame washed over me. I had never intended for things to get this complicated.

"No, it's not like that," I tried to explain.

"Now I know why you've been acting weird," Steve continued. "I knew it, I fucking knew there was someone else."

"Steve, calm down." I implored.

But Steve didn't listen. He lunged forward, his fists clenched, and I could see the familiar anger that he always struggled to keep in check.

"Get your hands off my wife!" he roared, and I flinched as he struck out at Jake with a blow that I never expected.

Everything seemed to happen in slow motion. I watched as Steve's fist connected with Jake's jaw, sending him staggering back. I could feel the panic rising in my chest as I tried to process what was happening.

"Steve, stop!" I shouted, trying to intervene.

But he ignored me and continued to attack Jake, his rage evident in every punch and kick. Jake did his best to defend himself, but he was clearly caught off guard and overwhelmed by Steve's sudden violence.

I could hear people shouting and cars honking their horns as they drove past, but it all felt distant and unimportant. All that mattered to me was stopping Steve from hurting Jake.

I ran towards them and tried to pull Steve away, but he pushed me roughly aside. Tears were streaming down my face now as I watched the two men—one who had been my husband for years, the other who had quickly become so important to me—fight each other like animals.

"Stop it! Please stop!" I cried out desperately.

And then suddenly, everything went black. The last thing I remembered was a loud thud before everything faded away into darkness.

CHAPTER 11

Consequences

I WAS LYING on a hospital bed with bright lights shining down on me. My head was throbbing and my body ached all over. It took me a few moments to remember what had happened before everything went black.

"I see you're finally awake," a nurse said kindly as she noticed me stirring.

"What happened?" I asked groggily.

"You were brought in after passing out at the scene of a fight," she explained. "Do you remember anything?"

I nodded slowly, images of Steve attacking Jake flashing through my mind. "Is... Is Jake okay?" I asked with concern.

The nurse hesitated before answering. "He's okay, don't you worry about any of that right now. How are you feeling? You have a minor concussion."

I tried to sit up, but my head began to spin and I quickly lay back down.

"I have a headache," I muttered, rubbing my temples. "But I'll be fine."

The nurse gave me a sympathetic smile. "We'll keep an eye on you for a little while, just to be safe."

As she left the room, I closed my eyes and took deep breaths, trying to calm my racing thoughts. Everything had spiraled out of control so quickly. How did things get so messed up?

A few minutes later, the doctor came in and did some check-ups on me. He asked me questions about what happened and I reluctantly told him about the fight between Steve and Jake.

"You're lucky it wasn't more serious," he said sternly. "Fighting is never the answer."

Tears welled up in my eyes again as I thought about how much pain and hurt I had caused everyone involved.

"I know," I whispered, feeling guilty and ashamed.

The doctor must have noticed how upset I was because he softened his tone. "It's alright. You're going through a lot right now. Just try to rest and take care of yourself."

After he left, I couldn't help but think about everything that had led up to this moment. My marriage with Steve was falling apart, yet I couldn't bring myself to leave him for Jake. And now everything was even more complicated.

CONSEQUENCES

I knew that it was time for me to make a decision—whether it was staying with Steve or leaving him for Jake. But with both men in the hospital because of me, it felt impossible to make such a life-changing choice.

I closed my eyes and tried to push away my thoughts, but they continued to haunt me.

Suddenly, there was a knock on the door and before I could respond, Jake walked in with flowers in his hand, a bruised eye, and a couple of band-aids on his foreheads.

"Hey," he said softly as he approached my bed. "How are you feeling?"

"I'll live," I replied. "I'm happy you're okay. Where is Steve?"

"He went home to Lauren," Jake said. "He was in the room with you until a few minuted before you woke up. I refused to leave until I saw you."

"I'm sorry," was all I could manage to say.

"It's okay," Jake replied, setting the flowers down on the bedside table. "I know this is hard for you."

I couldn't believe how understanding he was being, especially after everything that had happened between us.

"I need to talk to you," he said, pulling up a chair next to my bed.

I braced myself for what was about to come. I knew that our conversation would determine the future of our relationship.

"I want to be with you," he said, looking me straight in the eye. "But we can't keep doing this anymore. I need to take a step back."

My heart dropped as his words sank in. Was giving me an ultimatum? Choose him or lose him forever?

"I know I messed up," I pleaded with tear-filled eyes. "I need to make a decision."

Jake looked at me with a mix of sadness. "I want you to focus on feeling better. I hope you understand why I need to take a step back. Steve is right."

Tears streamed down my face as the realization hit me—I had pushed away the two people who cared about me the most because of my own indecisiveness and selfishness.

"I don't know what to do," I cried, feeling lost and alone.

"You need to figure it out," Jake said firmly before getting up from his chair. "For the good of us all. Until then, goodbye, Mad." He leaned closer, kissed my forehead with a small and soft touch, smiled, and walked out of my hospital room.

As I sat alone in my room, I couldn't stop thinking about the choice I had to make. On one hand, there was Steve— my husband who knew me like no other; a beautiful relationship that turned sour after his betrayal. On the other hand, there was Jake—someone who I had just met but that I had strong feelings for.

I knew that whichever decision I made would have consequences. But as much as it scared me, I also knew that I couldn't keep stringing both of them along any longer.

I took a deep breath and picked up my phone, scrolling through my contacts until I found Steve's number. My hands were shaking as I pressed call, unsure of what his reaction would be.

"Hey," he answered after a few rings. "You worried me sick. How are you feeling?"

"Just... tired, I guess," I muttered, trying to sound more composed than I actually felt. "But, I wanted to talk about what happened."

He fell silent for a moment, and I could almost see him running his fingers through his hair in frustration. "I want you to rest, Madelyn," he finally replied. "All I can say is I was just trying to protect our family, to keep us together. Seeing you with him drove me crazy." He let out a sigh. "We'll talk about it when you get better. I'll come by later with Lauren."

As soon as Steve said he would come by later with our daughter, Lauren, I felt a wave of relief wash over me. I missed her so much and having her around would make everything feel just a little bit better.

But as the hours passed and I waited for them to arrive, my anxiety started to creep back in. I kept replaying the conversation I had with Jake.

I heard a knock at the door, and before I could see who it was Lauren ran into my arms and hugged me tightly. Her presence immediately lifted my spirits.

"I'm so glad you're here," I said, tears welling up in my eyes. "I've missed you so much."

"I missed you too, Mommy," she replied with a smile.

Steve gave me a warm hug as well before sitting down next to me on the couch. We spent some time catching up and Lauren excitedly told me all about her adventures at school.

But eventually, we couldn't avoid the elephant in the room any longer. When Lauren went out to find a bathroom, Steve looked at me with concern in his eyes. "Do you love him?" he asked softly.

I shifted uncomfortably on the hospital bed, not sure how to answer. How could I possibly know who I loved when my heart felt so torn between two men?

"I... I don't know," I finally admitted, feeling guilty for not having a clear answer.

Before I could say anything else, Lauren came back into the room and happily chattered on about her friends and school. It was a welcome distraction from the heavy conversation we were just about to have.

I was finally back home and it felt like nothing had changed between Steve and I, but deep down, everything had changed. Our relationship was hanging by a thread and I didn't know if we could ever repair it.

As evening approached, Lauren went to bed early while Steve and I stayed up to talk. We sat on opposite ends of the couch in silence for a few minutes before Steve finally broke it.

"How are you feeling?" he asked tentatively.

"Physically or emotionally?" I replied with a small smile.

"Both."

"I'm physically exhausted but emotionally... I don't even know where to begin," I admitted truthfully. "I feel like everything has been turned upside down."

"I know what you mean," Steve sighed. "But maybe this is a chance for us to start fresh."

I looked at him skeptically. "Do you really think we can do that after everything that's happened?"

"You slept with him, didn't you?"

I was taken aback by Steve's question. It had been lingering between us ever since that night, but this was the first time he had actually said it out loud.

"I did," I said quietly, my heart sinking at the hurt in his eyes.

"And you still can't tell me who you love?" he asked, his voice was strained and low, barely masking the hurt and frustration radiating off of him. He clenched his fists at his sides. The tension in the room was palpable as I remained silent, my eyes avoiding his gaze.

"I'm sorry," I replied, feeling tears welling up in my eyes. "I just don't know."

Steve slumped forward in his chair, letting out a deep sigh as he ran his fingers through his disheveled hair. His voice was heavy with sadness as he spoke, "I never imagined we would end up in a situation like this."

I stared at the ground. "I know," I said, my voice barely above a whisper. My fingers fiddled with the hem of my shirt, and I couldn't shake off the guilt that consumed me.

"You know, we both fucked up. I just hope this is a revengeful act. The Madelyn I know would've never done something like this."

"It was a mistake."

"A mistake?" he scoffed. "Sleeping with someone else is not a mistake. And who knows this more than me."

"I'm aware," I replied, feeling the weight of my actions on my shoulders. "But it wasn't planned or intentional."

"Then why did you do it?" he asked, his voice filled with pain and confusion.

I took a deep breath before answering honestly. "I don't know. Maybe... maybe it was because things between us were falling apart and I felt neglected. Or with everything going on I just lost it."

"The thought of someone else touching you drives me mad." His fists were now closing tight.

The weight of everything hit me all at once. The guilt of hurting Steve, the confusion over my feelings for both him and Jake, and the fear of losing either one of them.

"Do you want me to leave?" Steve asked softly, seeing how emotional I was getting.

"No... please stay," I whispered, not wanting to be alone with my thoughts.

He wrapped his arms around me and pulled me close as we both sat there crying silently together. In that moment, despite everything that had happened between us, I knew that Steve was still someone special to me and a part of me still loved him.

CHAPTER 12

Reality Check

THE OFFICE FELT like a second home, its walls adorned with sketches of table layouts and other things that mapped out dreams and desires. That day, the Daltons' wedding preparations commanded my full attention, and every detail had to be perfect—even if I was still on the mend.

"Morning, and welcome back," greeted Jenna, her fingers dancing across a keyboard, eyes scanning the screen for any discrepancies in the seating chart. She was the anchor of my team, her organizational skills rivaling even my own meticulous nature. "How are you feeling?"

"Good morning," I replied, offering a smile while shrugging off my coat and rolling up my sleeves. "I feel brand new." My team didn't know the real reason being my hospitalization. "It's nice to be back, thank you! Let's ensure those vendor confirmations are all on schedule."

Nods and hums of agreement rippled through the small cadre of planners who orbited around clusters of paperwork and phones. Their dedication was evident, each one invested in the tiny miracles that transformed mere spaces into realms of romance.

As the whirr of printers and the tap-tap-tapping of keys filled the room, the door opened again, and a breeze of indecision wafted in with Eleanor. Dylan's fiancée—usually so poised—stood in the threshold, her brow creased ever so slightly, her lips pressed into a thin line.

"Ah, Eleanor," I said, stepping toward her with practiced warmth, noting the way her hands fidgeted at the hem of her tailored blazer. "Come inside, let's talk in my office."

"Thank you," she murmured, allowing me to guide her past the organized chaos of my domain.

Once we were ensconced in the relative calm of my office, I gestured towards the plush chair opposite my desk, a silent invitation to unload whatever she was holding back. As she settled, I perched on the edge of my desk, close enough to offer comfort, yet far enough to give her space to breathe.

"Can I get you anything? Water? Coffee?" I asked, though my real intention was to give her a moment to compose her thoughts. I could tell by the slight tremor in her hand as she declined that whatever had brought her here this early wasn't just last-minute jitters. Something deeper troubled the surface of her usually serene demeanor, and my heart tightened with both concern and curiosity. What could possibly unsettle a woman like

Eleanor, on the brink of marrying into the enigmatic Dalton family?

"Everything's going to be beautiful, Eleanor," I reassured her, though my own insecurities flickered behind my composed façade. "You're in good hands."

She offered me a smile, but it didn't quite reach her eyes, and I braced myself for the storm beneath the calm.

I noticed the way Eleanor's fingers twisted in her lap, a ballet of anxiety. "Dylan couldn't be here," she said, her voice tinged with an apology that wasn't hers to give. "His work... There's so much demanding his attention right now."

"Of course," I responded with a nod, reaching for my notepad and pen. The early sunlight cast long shadows across my desk, mirroring the situation. "It's quite common for work to ramp up at inconvenient times. But I assure you, we can go over everything together."

Eleanor's grateful glance was fleeting, masked quickly by the return of her concern. "He's been so preoccupied lately," she continued, a crease forming between her brows. "Most of the wedding planning has fallen on me."

My pen paused against the paper as I looked up, my eyes locking onto hers. I wanted to offer more than just platitudes; I wanted to provide solace. "I understand. Planning a wedding is a significant undertaking," I said softly, my tone imbued with empathy born from personal experience. "But remember, Eleanor, you're not alone in this. We're here to shoulder this with you."

"Thank you." She released a breath she seemed to have been holding since she walked in, and I felt a small victory in offering her that sliver of relief.

"Let's focus on what we can control," I suggested, shifting into the practicality that underpinned my creativity. "What details are you most concerned about? Let's tackle those head-on."

As I jotted down her responses, my questions aimed to distill her vague unease into actionable items. My mind, always searching for order amidst chaos, began to form a checklist that would bridge the gap between Eleanor's vision and reality. I was determined to weave the scattered threads of this wedding into a tapestry worthy of the Dalton name, even if it meant stitching some of the pieces together myself.

I tilted my head, studying the way Eleanor's fingers traced the edge of her engagement ring—twisting it round and round. "Eleanor," I began gently, setting my pen aside to give her my undivided attention. "Is there anything else, any other concerns that might be troubling you? It's important that we address everything to make your day perfect."

Her eyes darted away for a moment, seeking refuge in the mundane details of my office: the neatly arranged bouquets, the stacks of menus, the framed thank-you notes from past clients that adorned the walls.

When she spoke, her voice was a hushed confessional, weighed down by a truth she'd been carrying alone. "It's just... Dylan and I have had some disagreements about the wedding," she admitted, her gaze finally meeting mine, revealing a sea of worry in her eyes.

"Disagreements?" I asked, keeping my tone graceful, non-judgmental. "It's normal for couples to have different visions. What matters is finding a compromise."

She nodded, but there was a hesitation that told me this was more than a simple clash of preferences. "It's not just about the choices for the reception or the guest list," Eleanor continued, her hands now still in her lap. "Lately, he's been so distant, almost like he's not really present. He doesn't talk to me about his thoughts, his feelings... I'm starting to feel like I don't know the man I'm about to marry."

My heart tightened at her words, empathy coloring my thoughts. Distance—the kind that seeps into relationships, leaving cold, empty spaces where warmth used to reside—was a familiar pain. "Uncertainty can be frightening," I acknowledged, my voice barely above a whisper, as if speaking louder might fracture the fragile moment.

"Especially with so much at stake," she whispered back, a lone tear betraying her composed façade.

"Have you tried reaching out to him?" I asked, the planner in me wanting to fix, to mend, to make whole again.

"Many times. But it feels like he's locked himself away, somewhere I can't reach." Her shoulders slumped, and in that instant, she seemed smaller, vulnerable under her confession.

"Communication can sometimes bridge the gap," I said, though I was aware that such bridges were not easily built. "But it takes both sides to build it."

Eleanor nodded, a tired soldier bracing for another battle. My mind raced with the realization that there was much more work to be done than just finalizing the seating chart. There were hearts to heal. I made a silent vow to guide her through this, even as questions about Dylan's absence began to form shadows on the edges of my own understanding.

Leaning forward, I reached across the mahogany desk to lightly touch Eleanor's folded hands. My touch was tentative, an offered anchor in the storm of her emotions. "Eleanor," I began, my voice a soft but steady beacon, "it's natural to feel overwhelmed before your wedding. Pre-wedding jitters are more common than you think."

She looked up, her eyes searching for reassurance in mine. The vulnerability there tugged at something deep within me, a resonance with my own familiar dance with doubt. I recognized the tremor of a heart teetering on the precipice of change.

"Openness with Dylan now," I continued, "might pave the way for a deeper connection later. Remember, love isn't just about the grand gestures; it's built on understanding."

A sigh escaped her, a mixture of relief and lingering trepidation. "But what if he's not open to talking?" she asked, biting her lower lip in anxiety.

"Then you start the conversation," I replied. "Be the advocate for your future happiness. You both deserve that chance."

Her gaze drifted past me, perhaps picturing the difficult discussion ahead. I could almost see the cogs turning as she contemplated the possible outcomes. It was a critical juncture, not just for the wedding but for their lives together.

"Take some time for yourself too," I suggested softly, breaking through her introspection. "Reflect on what you truly want from this marriage, beyond the flowers and the music. It's important to be honest with yourself first."

Eleanor nodded, absorbing my words. "And then talk to Dylan," I added with emphasis. "Lay everything out on the table—fears, hopes, the whole spectrum. Honesty is the bedrock of trust, and trust is what will carry you both through life's challenges."

The determination flickered in her eyes, igniting a flame that had dimmed under the weight of her concerns. She gave me a warm smile, and I could tell she was fortified by our exchange.

"Thank you, Madelyn," she said, standing up with newfound purpose. "I needed to hear that."

"Anytime, Eleanor." I returned her smile. As she exited my office, a sense of accomplishment filled me—for potentially bridging a gap in a relationship. And yet, beneath the satisfaction, a whisper of curiosity fluttered in my chest, a silent question about the man who had become a mystery even to his bride-to-be.

I settled into the groove of my chair, the leather familiar against the curve of my back. My hands danced across the keyboard, a rhythmic tapping that filled the semi-silence of my office. One by one, I summoned the list of vendors on my screen, their names and numbers lining up like soldiers ready for roll call. The phone felt cool and solid in my grip as I dialed the first number, the ringtone chirping expectantly into my ear.

"Good morning, Petal Pushers Floristry," chirped a voice, sunny as the daffodils they so often wove into bridal bouquets.

"Hi, Lila, it's Madelyn Montgomery. Just checking in for the Dalton wedding in a few—"

"Everything's on schedule," she cut in, her confidence soothing my frayed nerves. "The roses are looking particularly vibrant. Dylan's going to be thrilled."

"Thank you, Lila," I replied, the corners of my mouth tipping upward. It was a small victory, but even the smallest victories stacked up against the tide of uncertainty that came with event planning.

I hung up, a checkmark flourishing beside Petal Pushers on my list. Next, the caterers, the string quartet, the cake artist —each call was a step closer to perfection, a lullaby to the part of me that craved order in the chaos of tulle and satin.

REALITY CHECK

But as I confirmed the last of the seating arrangements, ensuring that Aunt Mary wasn't seated anywhere near the open bar, my mind began to drift, pulled along by a current of thought that centered around one person: Dylan.

Dylan Dalton, whose name had been etched into my schedule for months, yet whose presence had been nothing more than a whisper through phone calls and secondhand messages. The man was a puzzle, and all pieces locked tight, leaving me to wonder about the image they'd form if only he'd let me in.

What could be so important that it kept him from being a part of this, his own wedding? Was it truly just business, or was there more beneath the surface? My gaze persisted on the empty chair across from me. It was where he should be sitting, discussing floral accents and song choices, not leaving Eleanor to shoulder it all alone.

I leaned back, my eyes tracing the lines of the ceiling as if they might reveal the secrets hidden behind Dylan's absence. A frown etched itself between my brows. It wasn't just professional curiosity that gnawed at me—it was something deeper, something personal. The compassion in me, the part that connected with clients beyond contracts and invoices, yearned to understand what was at the heart of his retreat.

I shook my head, dispelling the intrusive musings. There was no time for such distractions; there was a wedding to be orchestrated to symphonic perfection. With a determined sigh, I focused back on the spreadsheets before me, the guest lists and timelines that demanded my attention.

Yet, as I reviewed every detail, triple-checking every entry, Dylan Dalton remained there, a silent enigma hovering at my thoughts, a mystery that begged to be discovered.

I opened a new tab on my laptop, the cursor blinking like a beacon of possibility against the stark white search field. A moment's hesitation, and then I typed in "Dalton family" followed by "Stowe" —Dylan's hometown. The page refreshed, flooding with links to articles, socialite pages, and old money directories. It felt intrusive, this digital prying, but my instincts compelled me forward.

The first click brought up an archived article from a local paper, detailing the philanthropic endeavors of the Dalton dynasty; foundations and charities bearing their name like medals of honor. But as I scrolled, it wasn't the public accolades that caught my eye—it was the subtle hints of discord woven into the narrative, the faint shadows that clung to the corners of their gilded image.

An obituary for Dylan's grandfather revealed a legacy of strict expectations and rigid control. He was a titan of industry, yes, but also a patriarch who wielded his influence like a scepter. I imagined Dylan, a young man in the shadow of such a towering figure.

Further searches unearthed society gossip columns, brimming with rumors and whispers of the Dalton's internal conflicts. There was talk of estranged relatives, of fierce battles over the family estate, and through it all,

REALITY CHECK

Dylan's name appeared again and again—as if he were both participant and prize in some high-stakes familial game.

My heart clenched with sympathy, empathy threading through the confusion. This wasn't just about a wedding; it was about a life lived under scrutiny and expectation. Every small information added depth to Dylan's character, painting him not as a wealthy enigma, but as a man ensnared by his lineage.

The screen blurred slightly as I leaned in closer, devouring the details that suggested why he might keep his true self hidden, why he might stand at arm's length even from those he intended to marry. With each revelation, the pieces clicked together, illuminating the puzzle of Dylan Dalton's distant behavior.

"Madelyn?" The gentle voice of Jenna cut through the silence, pulling me back from the rabbit hole of the Dalton drama.

"Sorry," I murmured, snapping the laptop shut with more force than necessary. "Just lost in some research."

But the truth was, I wasn't just lost; I was found. I had uncovered enough of Dylan's world to glimpse the labyrinth within, and with this knowledge, I felt armed to navigate the twists behind the man behind the Dalton name.

I tucked the last file into its drawer, my fingers lingering on the cool metal. The office was hushed, the dusk casting long shadows across the room that mirrored the ones I'd chased all day in Dylan's past.

What must it be like to live in such a tangled web? A life where you were but a pawn in a game played by those who shared your blood? My mind whirled with the implications of my discoveries, Would this insight bridge the gap between us, or would it carve a deeper space?

I pushed back from my desk, a soft exhale carrying away some of the day's heaviness. As I shrugged into my coat, I couldn't help but wonder how much of the man I'd been planning a wedding for was real and how much was a façade built out of necessity.

"Goodnight," called one of my team members from across the now-dim office.

"Goodnight," I replied, my voice tinged with distraction.

Closing the door behind me, the anticipation for the upcoming nuptials mingled with a thread of tension so evident I could almost taste it. Every single step I took towards the exit felt like a step closer to an invisible precipice. What awaited on the other side remained shrouded in mystery—a mystery as compelling and intricate as the man who would stand at the altar.

I paused, hand on the cold glass of the door, and allowed myself a moment to acknowledge the thrill that pricked at my skin. A piece of me feared what lay ahead, yet another part—the part that thrived on complications—couldn't wait to discover the truth hidden within the ornate tapestry of the Dalton legacy.

As I walked to my car, the scattered pieces of today's news coalesced into a solution. I would approach Dylan with

REALITY CHECK

both the delicacy and the forthrightness these new insights demanded.

For now, though, I left the office and its whispered secrets behind, stepping into the quiet promise of a starry evening where my own thoughts were the only company I kept.

The key turned with a muted click, sealing the office and its day's burdens behind me. I stepped into the solitude of my car, the silence thickening around my thoughts. I rested my forehead against the cool steering wheel, allowing the remnants of Eleanor's troubled expression to wash over me once more.

I needed to see them together—Dylan and Eleanor. The image of their intertwined hands, the subtle exchanges that spoke volumes, could tell me more than any words they might offer separately. It was in the silent language of lovers where truth often hid, nestled between gestures and glances.

My fingers tapped a staccato rhythm on the leather-wrapped wheel, plotting my next move. A meeting with both Dylan and Eleanor was imperative. The wedding hinged not just on flowers, music, and a perfectly executed schedule, but on the harmony of two hearts pledging their tomorrows to each other. And if there was discord, it was my role to sense it, to smooth it before it could crescendo into something uncontrollable.

"Madelyn," I whispered to myself, "you've got this." The affirmation didn't quite banish the doubts lurking beneath the surface, but it bolstered me enough to reach for my phone. With care, I crafted an email meant to bridge gaps and heal unseen wounds.

'Dear Dylan and Eleanor,' I typed, each letter etched with intention, 'I hope this email finds you both well. As we approach your special day, I'd like to invite you to a final meeting. It would be wonderful to touch base on the last details and ensure everything is as perfect as you envisioned. Please let me know a time that suits you both.'

Sent. The word appeared on the screen, a small echo of finality. Now, all I could do was wait, poised on the edge of the precipice that was the unknown. My grip loosened on the phone; its glow faded as I slipped it back into my bag. Another deep breath, and I started the engine—the low hum a comforting reminder that life moved forward, relentlessly, towards moments of joy, of union, and sometimes, of revelation.

Headlights pierced the darkness, carving a path through the night as I drove away, leaving behind the Dalton mystery for the promise of tomorrow's clarity.

CHAPTER 13

New Beginnings

I DECIDED to take some time to myself. I needed to clear my head and figure out what I truly wanted. So, for the next few days, although Steve was still under my same roof, I went on long walks, spent hours journaling and reflecting on my thoughts and emotions.

As the days passed by, I realized that I had been living my life for others. My parents, Steve, Lauren, even Jake— everyone's expectations weighed heavily on me. But what about my own expectations? What did I want?

I allowed myself to think about Steve and our relationship. We had been through so much together and he had always been there for me. Maybe it was worth giving him another chance.

As I was leaving work, I texted him. "Hi, what time will you be home? I want to talk."

A few seconds like, my phone chimed with his reply. "I'll be home in 20. See you soon!"

Once home, I started preparing dinner while waiting his arrival. My heart raced with anticipation, unsure of how the conversation would go.

Suddenly, I heard his familiar voice calling out from the kitchen. "I'm home," he announced.

"I'm preparing dinner. Should be ready in ten. Where is Lauren?" I asked, expecting to hear her excited footsteps following behind him.

"She wanted to stay the night at mom's," Steve replied as he walked towards the bedroom to change out of his work clothes.

It's probably for the best, I thought. Although I always missed her when she slept away from home.

Dinner was now ready and we sat across from each other at the kitchen table. I could feel the tension between us but this time it felt different. It wasn't filled with resentment or anger, but rather a sense of understanding.

"I'm sorry," Steve said softly as he took my hand in his.

"Sorry for what?" I asked.

"For become a monster that night." Steve reached for my hand across the table. "No matter what the reason might be, I never want you to see me that way. It's not okay. Violence is never the answer. I got blinded by jealousy."

I looked into Steve's eyes and saw the sincerity in his words. He truly regretted what had happened that night and I could see how much he wanted to make things right.

NEW BEGINNINGS

"I know," I said, squeezing his hand gently. "And I'm sorry too, for not giving a real chance to our relationship. But all this opened my eyes, and I think we should give it another chance."

"Are you serious?" Steve's happiness showed in his eyes.

"Yes, but one condition. We go to therapy."

Steve's smile faltered for a moment, replaced by a flicker of uncertainty. "Therapy?" he echoed, his voice tinged with a hint of apprehension because he knew I was serious this time.

I nodded, my resolve firm. "Yes, therapy," I affirmed, meeting his gaze with unwavering determination. "We need help, Steve. We can't keep pretending that everything's fine when it's not. We need to confront the issues that have been festering beneath the surface for far too long."

Steve's expression softened, his eyes filled with a mixture of relief and gratitude. "I agree," he said quietly, his voice barely above a whisper. "I'll do whatever it takes to make things right, to earn you back."

"Thank you," I whispered, my voice choked with emotion. "For being willing to try, for not giving up on us."

I understood that we had a long road ahead of us, and progress would come in small, measured steps.

Becca had been gone for over a week. I hadn't informed her about the triangle mess, nor about my hospital trip. I didn't want to stress her or our parents, or reveal the reason for my concussion. Sofia was my only trusted confidante who could grasp the situation fully. During my hospital stay, I updated her on the news regarding my real father, the Jake situation, and all the other chaos going on in my life.

"Madelyn!" Her voice, infused with an energy that could brighten even the dreariest of days, cut through the collage of clinking cups and low murmurs of our favorite café, Cool Beans.

I weaved through the maze of tables, my heart skipping in sync with the jazzy undercurrent that lilted from the speakers. The soft cushion of the chair welcomed me as I settled across from her, the world outside the fog-kissed windows fading away.

"Look at you, all radiant," Sofia said, her hazel eyes crinkling with genuine delight. I couldn't help but mirror her smile, feeling the fluttering excitement in my chest spill into my eyes.

"Can you believe it?" I started, fidgeting with the hem of my sweater. "Steve and I, we're... We've turned a corner, I think."

"Tell me everything." Sofia leaned forward, her attention as intoxicating as the espresso shot I knew she would have ordered.

NEW BEGINNINGS

"We talked last night and we decided to give it another chance." I took a breath, ready to dive into the heart of it. "He agreed to go to therapy. For real this time. We need it."

"Wow, that's huge!" Sofia's hands enveloped mine on the table. "How do you feel about it?"

"Like I can finally exhale," I confessed, the words tumbling out with a weightlessness that surprised even me. "It's like we're rediscovering us, willing to find the reasons we fell in love all over again."

"Cheers to communication, rediscovery, and therapy," Sofia said, lifting her cup in a toast to the newfound hope that shimmered between us, as tangible as the steam rising from our drinks.

"Cheers," I said, the harmonious clink of porcelain against porcelain sealing the sentiment. In the comfort of our corner, with the symphony of scents and sounds, the future seemed filled with promise.

"So... No more Jake?"

"Nope. And I don't intend to think about that anymore. I am ready to give this marriage my one hundred percent. If it doesn't work out, at least I know I tried."

"That's my girl." Sofia winked.

The clatter of cups and the murmur of conversations faded to a hush as I leaned forward, urgency threading my words. "Eleanor stopped by the office the other day," I began, the anticipation prickling through me like a static charge. "She wanted to nail down the last of the wedding details—you know, the final touches that make everything perfect."

Sofia's gaze locked onto mine, her espresso forgotten, its steam curling untasted into the air. Her eyes, those pools of hazel that could so often read my thoughts, darkened with concern.

"Go on," she urged, her voice a low hum that only I was privy to in our cozy corner of the world.

I hesitated, not wanting to let the tremor in my voice betray the unease that had crept over me since Eleanor's visit. "Dylan was supposed to be there. But he wasn't. He didn't show up at all."

Sofia's nod was slow, deliberate, her empathy a tangible thing. She knew what these meetings meant to me, how each one was a stepping stone to proving my worth—not just as an event planner but as someone who could manage the chaos of life's unexpected turns.

"He didn't send any message? Nothing?"

"Nothing," I confirmed, and for a moment, I let myself float in the silence that followed, adrift in the sea of my own thoughts.

The warmth from the ceramic cup seeped into my palms, but the comfort it offered couldn't quell the fluttering anxiety in my chest. I found myself tracing the rim with a shaky finger, my gaze lost somewhere in the swirl of dark liquid.

NEW BEGINNINGS

"I just don't understand," I murmured, my voice barely rising above the cozy din of the café. The wisp of steam from my coffee carried my worries upward, dissipating into nothingness. "Could he have lost interest in his own wedding? Or maybe something came up, something urgent..."

My thoughts teetered on the edge of reason, threatening to spiral. I pictured Dylan's face, his usual composed expression now clouded in my mind with ambiguity. Was it disinterest that shadowed those eyes I thought I knew, or was it something else, something hidden?

"Hey," Sofia's voice sliced through my tangled musings, pulling me back to the safety of our corner table. I looked up to find her reaching out, her hand warm and steady on my arm. Her touch grounded me, an anchor amidst the storm of insecurities.

"Listen to me," she said, her gaze locking with mine, fierce and unwavering. "You know Dylan. He wouldn't just walk away from all this, not without a word. Maybe there's a complication we don't know about."

Each word spoken with such conviction that it felt like she was willing the truth into existence. Even in the face of my doubts, Sofia's faith never wavered.

"Think about every detail you've put your heart into," she continued, her voice laced with an encouraging strength. "The venue, the music, the way the light will hit just right during the ceremony. You've orchestrated a day that will be remembered forever. That's not something Dylan would take lightly."

I let her reassurance wash over me, absorbing the certainty that radiated from her. Sofia had always been the beacon that guided me back when I strayed too far into the fog of my fears. With her beside me, perhaps I could navigate through this, too.

"Thank you," I whispered, allowing myself a small smile. Her confidence in me, in us, was a balm to the worry-lines etched across my thoughts.

"Anytime," she replied, squeezing my arm gently before letting go. "That's what I'm here for."

In the simple gesture of her hand returning to her own cup, I found solace. The chaos within quieted, feeling the beginnings of determination stir within me once more.

A spark ignited within me, chasing away the shadows of doubt that had gathered like storm clouds. Memories of my tireless efforts unfurled before me—relentless days and sleepless nights. My lips curved into a smile as I recounted the countless hours dedicated to handpicking each bloom for the bouquets. "The flowers," I began, excitement threading through my words, "I remember standing in the middle of the florist's, surrounded by peonies and roses, and thinking how Dylan would appreciate their elegance."

The meticulous coordination with caterers, musicians, and decorators danced at the forefront of my mind. Every phone call, every meeting, every decision I made was imbued with purpose. The precision of it all brought a

NEW BEGINNINGS

sense of pride swelling in my chest. "I've had these vendors lined up for months, ensuring everything will launch without a hitch." My confidence grew louder, even if Dylan's shadow still lingered at the edge of my thoughts.

Sofia's hazel eyes were alight with affirmation, reflecting back the conviction I felt bubbling within me. She leaned forward slightly, her posture mirroring the support her presence always provided. "You," she said, her voice rich with sincerity, "have this incredible talent for making dreams tangible. Remember the Harrows' anniversary party? People are still talking about it. And they'll be talking about this wedding for years to come."

Her words were pulling me towards the harbor of my own abilities. I could hear the praise we'd received from past clients in my ears, a chorus of satisfaction and delight. Sofia's words were reinforcing the structure I had built against uncertainty.

"Right," I agreed, nodding along with her. "Every element has been so carefully crafted. The guests... they're excited, aren't they?" It was more than seeking confirmation—it was an affirmation of my dedication to Dylan and Eleanor's day.

"Absolutely," she replied, her tone leaving no room for argument. "They can't wait to see what magic you've spun this time. You've set the bar high, and everyone knows it."

Her faith in me was unwavering, a lighthouse cutting through any fog of hesitation that dared approach. I let out a breath I didn't realize I had been holding, allowing her certainty to anchor me. Yes, despite Dylan's mysterious absence, the celebration would be nothing short of spectacular. And it was my creation—reminding me of the love I poured into every detail, the silent promise I made to everyone who trusted me with their special moments.

The doubts that had clawed at me, seeking to undermine the foundation I had built, crumbled. I was Madelyn Montgomery, the architect of unforgettable moments. Let come what may, I would stand firm amidst the turbulence, my spirit unyielding.

"Babe?" Sofia's gentle voice pulled me back to the present, her hazel eyes gleaming with anticipation.

"Everything is going to be perfect," I told her, more to myself than to her, my voice threaded with a confidence that felt as integral to me as my own heartbeat. "No matter what happens, I'm ready."

And I believed it, wholly, as if those words were the very essence of the strength I carried within.

Sofia's hand, a graceful silhouette against the steam wafting from our cups, elevated her own with reverence. Her eyes sparkled with pride as she held my gaze, a sign reminding me of the journey we had embarked upon together.

"To the artist whose medium is moments," she declared, her voice a melody of warmth and admiration. "To Madelyn, who sculpts dreams into reality."

Our cups met in a gentle clink—a sound that sealed our bond as much as it did our mutual excitement for what was

NEW BEGINNINGS

to come. The porcelain was cool against my lips, but the coffee pooled into me like liquid courage, every single sip an affirmation of the faith Sofia had in me.

As the conversation unfurled, tendrils of worry about Dylan's absence began to dissipate, like morning fog surrendering to the sun's insistence. My thoughts drifted to the positive forces in my life—my family's unwavering support, the love that infused my every endeavor, the joy that blossomed whenever I saw my plans take shape.

"Can you imagine what they'll say when they see the lanterns go up?" I mused, a smile tugging at my lips as I envisioned the soft glow that would bathe the reception in warmth.

"Knowing you, it'll be nothing short of enchanting," Sofia replied, her hazel eyes alight with confidence in me that I was only beginning to fully embrace.

My heart swelled, buoyed by her belief, and something shifted within me. The lingering threads of doubt began to uncover, spun away by the strength of the bond we had.

I gazed out of the café window, watching as leaves danced on the breeze—a silent ballet choreographed by nature. It reminded me of how, despite any fear, life had a way of moving gracefully forward. And like those leaves, I too could find my rhythm, twirling through challenges with a poise born from years of quietly cultivated resilience.

"Life throws us curves, but we're the ones who shape them into something beautiful," I said, more to myself than to Sofia, but she nodded, her agreement a gentle affirmation.

"Exactly, Maddie. You've always had the knack for bending the world into wonder," she chuckled, and there was truth —my truth—in her words.

We embraced briefly, a tangible reminder of the solidarity in our friendship. As we parted, the outside coolness greeted me, a stark contrast to the warmth of the café. It sliced through the fog of doubts that had once clouded my thoughts, the breaths I took now sharpening my focus.

I watched as people passed by in a blur of motion, their lives unfolding in directions unknown, and it stroked me how much we both felt this dance of uncertainty. Yet here I was, amidst the flow of the city, anchored by a certainty that surged from somewhere deep—a wellspring fueled by the countless hours of meticulous planning, the myriad decisions made with care and consideration.

I could almost hear the music that will fill the wedding venue, see the arrangements of flowers that will grace the tables—each petal symbolized an effort to the creativity and dedication I'd poured into Dylan and Eleanor's special day. The image solidified my intent; I crafted those details with love, sculpting fragments of dreams into reality.

My phone rested in my pocket, a lifeline to the vendors, the schedules, the ever-ticking clock counting down to the ceremony. But its weight was no burden; it was a reminder of the role I play, the conductor of a symphony of celebration that awaited only my cue to begin.

With every step I took away from the café, the future beckoned—a canvas stretched taut, ready for the

NEW BEGINNINGS

brushstrokes of tomorrow's joys and challenges. The faintest hint of jasmine wafted from a nearby flower shop, intertwining with the smell of roasting coffee beans still clinging to my clothes, and I smile.

"Bring it on," I whispered to the city, to the universe, to myself. And in that moment, with determination my steadfast companion, I knew I was ready to weave the threads of Dylan and Eleanor's love story into a day they'll never forget.

CHAPTER 14

The Wedding

THE HEELS of my shoes clicked a determined rhythm against the polished floor as I pushed through the glass doors of the office. The scent of lilies and roses, carefully arranged for tomorrow's wedding, failed to soothe the anxiety churning within me. My expressive green eyes scanned the room, seeking out the familiar faces of my team. They were the architects of dreams, the weavers of matrimonial magic, yet today, their usual buzz of activity had been replaced by an unsettling hush.

"Has anyone heard from Dylan or Eleanor?" My voice cut through the silence like a knife, sharp with an urgency that betrayed my composed exterior. I watched their faces, searching for a flicker of knowledge, a clue to the whereabouts of the couple whose nuptials were the talk of Velvet Shadows.

"Madelyn," Jenna, my right hand with her no-nonsense efficiency, approached hesitantly. "There's been no word from either of them since yesterday."

A frown creased my brow, and I felt the cool grip of worry tighten around my heart. It was unlike Dylan to go silent, especially with the wedding so close. The man carried himself with such sophistication, always ensuring that every detail was accounted for. His absence was a puzzle piece askew in a picture I had painstakingly put together.

"Keep trying their phones," I instructed, brushing a stray wavy chestnut lock behind my ear. "And check-in with the vendors, make sure everything is proceeding as planned."

"Of course," Jenna nodded, turning back to her desk with a swiftness that mirrored my own concern.

I let out a slow breath, trying to still the rapid drumming of my heart. This was not the time for self-doubt to creep in, not when there was a wedding hanging in the balance. I needed to trust my instincts, to rely on the creativity and passion that had turned my event planning dreams into a successful reality.

"Everyone," I called out to the rest of the team, gathering their attention. "We are professionals. We've handled bigger crises before. Let's make sure that we're prepared for anything. Dylan and Eleanor are counting on us."

As they dispersed, I couldn't shake the image of Dylan's enigmatic smile from my mind. There was a depth to him that I hadn't quite deciphered. My intuition whispered that there was more to Dylan Dalton than met the eye, a thought I tucked away for another moment.

For now, the wedding awaited, and it was my mission to bring it to life, come what may.

THE WEDDING

The glow of the computer screen cast a pale light across my desk as I clicked through my inbox, each email subject scrutinized with a mix of hope and trepidation. My cursor hovered over the refresh button, willing new correspondence to appear from Dylan or Eleanor, but the digital silence was deafening.

"Nothing," I muttered under my breath, the word tasting like disappointment on my lips. My fingers tapped an impatient rhythm on the edge of the keyboard, echoing the anxious beat of my heart. Their absence from my messages was out of character, especially this close to the wedding day. I had half-expected to find a flurry of last-minute requests or jitters poured out in text form, not this void that expanded with every passing minute.

With a sigh, I swiped at my phone, scrolling through texts and missed calls, searching for a clue that might dissolve the knot of worry tightening in my stomach. But there was nothing—no cheerful emojis from Eleanor discussing floral arrangements, no curt updates from Dylan about the guest list. Just echoes of past conversations growing fainter with time.

"Come on," I whispered, a plea to the universe—or perhaps to them. My fingers persisted over the picture of Dylan that I had saved from one of our meetings, his eyes holding a story yet untold. He was more than the wealthy bachelor he presented to the world; I could see it whenever his gaze lingered just a moment too long, whenever his laughter didn't quite reach those deep-set eyes. The man named Dylan Dalton was a mystery wrapped in a tailored suit, and I ached to get to know him.

But uncovering mysteries wasn't why I was here. I needed answers, and if they wouldn't come to me, I'd have to seek them out myself.

Steadying my breath, I reached for the phone once more, this time with purpose. My fingers dialed a familiar number, one that belonged to the elegant matriarch of the Dalton family. Mrs. Dalton—Dylan's mother—would know something, anything that could shine a light on the situation.

"Please pick up," I murmured, the phone pressed against my ear. The first ring felt like an eternity, the second a millennium stretched thin. By the third, I could almost hear the quiet hum of anticipation that filled the room, as if the walls themselves were leaning in, waiting.

"Hello?" The voice on the other end cut through the tension, and I nearly sagged with relief at the sound of Mrs. Dalton's measured tones.

"Mrs. Dalton, it's Madelyn Montgomery." My voice, a tremulous thread, betrayed the anxiety I'd tried so hard to tame. "I apologize for any inconvenience, but I'm just following up on the details for Dylan and Eleanor's wedding day tomorrow."

"Of course," she responded, her voice a soft patina of calm that sought to smooth over the creases of my worry. "Everything is proceeding as planned. The bride and groom have been extremely preoccupied with some personal issues, but tomorrow is the big day. It'll be perfect." Her words were poised, a practiced waltz of reassurance that should have soothed the disquiet that had taken root deep within me.

"Thank you," I managed, the word a small vessel carrying a sea of unvoiced concerns. "I appreciate your confirmation." My grip on the phone loosened as I absorbed the import of her affirmation, yet the echo of my racing pulse lingered, a quiet reminder of the unease that had yet to be quelled.

The wedding was still on track, according to Mrs. Dalton. But where was Dylan? And why did my intuition scream that something was amiss?

A shiver of relief cascaded down my spine as I replaced the receiver, the cold plastic a stark contrast to the warmth Mrs. Dalton's assurances had attempted to wrap around my doubts. I leaned back against my desk, the knots in my stomach loosening, yet not quite undone. "Thank you," I whispered into the now silent room, a prayer of gratitude to an absent deity that all would unfold without hitch. *I can't believe I'll finally get to meet Dylan Dalton tomorrow.*

The day dawned with a rosy blush, the first rays of sunlight casting long shadows across the meticulously arranged flowers and satin ribbons. I stood amidst the burgeoning chaos, clipboard in hand, my eyes skimming over every detail with practiced precision. The wavy tendrils of my chestnut hair fell loose, framing my face as I bent to adjust a wayward floral arrangement, the fragrance of peonies infusing my senses with the promise of celebration.

"Everything must be perfect," I murmured, more to myself than to the bustling figures flitting around me. My green eyes, mirrors to the dedication etched into my soul, reflected back the cascading tiers of white frosting on the towering wedding cake, the glint of crystal stemware, and the soft glow of fairy lights woven through the boughs of surrounding trees.

My hands, steady and sure, fluttered over place settings, smoothed out linens, and straightened chairs. A symphony of impending nuptials played out before me, reminding me of the creativity and passion I poured into my work. Yet beneath the harmonious surface, questions buzzed like bees around a bloom, incessant and probing. Why had Dylan been so elusive? What was the measure of the silence that hung between our exchanges?

"Focus," I chided softly, directing my attention to the sea of white petals that carpeted the aisle. I crouched, aligning the last few roses that had dared to stray from their intended path. The guests would soon sweep through this place, their steps unaware of the undercurrent of concern that threatened to pull me under.

As the final hour drew near, I stepped back, a conductor surveying her orchestra. Every element was poised, waiting for the cue to breathe life into the vision I had so carefully orchestrated. This was the culmination of countless hours

THE WEDDING

and whispered secrets, a canvas painted with the hues of love and commitment. And yet, the artist within me trembled, the brush of doubt leaving unseen strokes upon the scene I had set.

"Let it be enough," I found myself wishing to the wind, a silent spectator to the beauty I had crafted. Today, I would watch two souls intertwine their destinies, and I would do so with the quiet hope that my own uncertainties would find their resolution in the echo of their vows.

The first of the guests fluttered in like the early petals of spring, their smiles as bright as the afternoon sun. I stood at the threshold of the grand hall, a sentinel guarding the gateway to nuptial bliss, my own smile stitched carefully onto my lips. "Welcome," I murmured, my voice a practiced melody of warmth and hospitality. Each handshake, each air-kiss was an exercise in poise, but beneath the surface, my heart drummed a staccato beat of worry.

"Beautiful venue," cooed Mrs. Hargreaves, her eyes twinkling behind pearl-rimmed glasses. "You've done an outstanding job."

"Thank you," I replied, the compliment washing over me, yet failing to penetrate the armor of my growing anxiety. The hall filled, the murmur of excited conversation blossoming into anticipation, and with every new arrival, my gaze flickered to the entrance.

I checked my watch for the umpteenth time, the minutes cascading away like grains of sand in an hourglass too eager to empty itself. Where was he? The question gnawed at me, a persistent whisper that refused silence. With each glance that came up empty, the tightrope of composure I walked frayed ever so slightly, threatening to send me plummeting into the abyss of fear.

"Everything alright?" Mr. Sullivan's voice cut through the haze of my thoughts.

"Of course," I lied smoothly, tucking a stray wavy chestnut lock behind my ear. "Just ensuring the groom makes his grand entrance."

He chuckled, unaware of the sincerity veiled within my jest. And as the clock's hands converged upon the appointed hour, my smile became a mask, my eyes sentinels fixed upon that door, praying for it to swing wide and reveal Dylan to dispel the disquiet of his own making.

The hushed whispers of the guests coalesced into a single, thrumming pulse that played my racing heartbeat. Every glance held a question, every furrowed brow mirrored my own concern. The grand clock, previously an adornment, now felt like an overseer marking time with relentless precision. Dylan's chair—empty, adorned in satin and hope—stood as symbol of the void we all felt but dared not acknowledge.

A light scent of peonies threaded through the air, the floral arrangements a silent witness to the growing unease that draped over the venue like velvet. I caught myself smoothing down my dress, an attempt to iron out the creases in time and expectation.

THE WEDDING

Then, a shift. The string quartet, sensing the need for a change in the atmosphere, began their rendition of Pachelbel's Canon. All eyes turned to the back of the hall, hearts hitching on the notes that should have heralded joy and union.

Eleanor appeared, a vision in the soft glow of the aisle lights. Her dress, pristine and elegant, whispered along the floor with every measured step. Yet her face, usually alight with happiness, was a canvas of confusion. The slight tremble of her bouquet's white roses betrayed the disappointment she gripped as firmly as the stems in her hands.

My throat tightened at the sight of her solitary figure, the embodiment of grace under distress. Eleanor's eyes, searching the sea of faces for one that should have been there to meet hers, found mine instead. In that gaze, I read a silent plea, a call for reassurance I wasn't certain I could provide. But I nodded subtly, willing my expression to convey a fortress of support and certainty amidst the storm of doubts.

Before drew nearer, the murmurs died away, leaving a space filled only by the music. We were all bound by an invisible thread of empathy and suspense, collectively holding our breath for a resolution that seemed to drift further away with each second that passed.

And there, in the midst of a moment that should have been written with beginnings, I found myself surrounded by unfinished sentences, my mind grasping for words that would soothe, explain, justify. The tale of this day had taken an unforeseen detour, and I, the orchestrator of celebrations, stood mute before the unfolding narrative of human emotion and unpredictability.

The final notes of the bridal march had an expectancy that would go unmet. My pulse hammered at my temples as I stepped towards her, the polished floor beneath my heels feeling like a precarious tightrope between poise and panic. In the periphery of my vision, I could see the guests exchanging bewildered glances, their whispers now silenced by a collective breath held too long.

"Madelyn?" Eleanor's voice wavered, barely audible over the hum of disquietude.

I reached her side in what seemed like a single heartbeat, my hand instinctively finding hers—an anchor in the sudden chaos of uncertainty. Her fingers trembled within my grasp, and I squeezed them gently.

"Where is he?" she asked, the words breaking through her lips like fragile shards of glass.

"I don't know," I admitted, my voice a hushed echo of her vulnerability.

I felt the raw ache of empathy tighten around my chest. I saw the confusion etched on Eleanor's face, giving me the stress that I fought to conceal behind a façade of composure. The room suddenly started to tilt, reality skewing as the seconds ticked by, each one devoid of Dylan's presence.

THE WEDDING

"Let's step aside for a moment," I suggested, guiding Eleanor towards the seclusion of a nearby alcove. The guests' eyes followed us, a silent procession of concern and curiosity, but I held my head high, deflecting their scrutiny with a calm I scarcely felt.

In the alcove's shadowed embrace, Eleanor's resilience faltered, a solitary tear escaping the confines of her will. I reached out, thumb brushing away the salty traitor with a tenderness that surprised even me. Here was a woman facing her worst nightmare, draped in lace and love, left standing alone at the altar.

The hushed whispers of the guests reverberated through the grand hall, like the soft fluttering of moth wings. Eleanor's heartbreak echoed in the oppressive silence, fractured beats carrying shattered dreams. Many emotions played across her face: a look of confusion, hurt, and disbelief. Her trembling lips struggled to form words as her tear-filled eyes searched mine, seeking solace, seeking answers.

I held Eleanor's gaze and took a steadying breath, my mind racing to find the right words, words that could somehow ease her pain. But in that moment, all I had were fragments of understanding and a profound sadness.

"We don't know what happened," I finally whispered, my voice barely audible above the whispers. "But you deserve more than this. You deserve someone who will cherish you and show up when it matters most."

Eleanor's fingers clutched at her chest, as if trying to hold together the pieces of her shattered heart. Her eyes were glistened with unshed tears.

"But why?" she pleaded, her voice trembling with emotion. "Why would he do this? Everything was perfect between us."

I shook my head, wishing I had an answer that could offer some semblance of closure. But the truth was, we may never understand Dylan's sudden disappearance.

"We may never know," I said softly, placing a comforting hand on Eleanor's shoulder. "But what matters now is how you choose to move forward."

Eleanor nodded, her gaze shifting towards the grand hall where their wedding reception was supposed to be taking place. The music still played and empty champagne glasses still on tables, an eerie reminder of the celebration that was now tainted with sorrow.

"I can't go out there," she said, her voice laced with anguish.

"You don't have to," I reassured her. "Let's get you somewhere safe and away from all of this."

Together, we made our way through the sea of guests until we reached the entrance of the mansion. I hailed a taxi and helped Eleanor into the backseat before climbing in myself.

As the car pulled away from the mansion and towards Eleanor's house, I couldn't help but feel a sense of guilt

THE WEDDING

wash over me. Guilt for not being able to stop Dylan from disappearing and causing Eleanor so much pain.

But as I glanced over at her tear-stained face and saw a glimmer of determination in her eyes, I knew that she would survive this. She would pick herself up and move on, stronger than ever before.

CHAPTER 15

The Secret

THE SHINY WOOD of Eleanor's front door swung open, and I stepped over the threshold. The familiar fragrance of lavender and vanilla reached out to me, a gentle reminder of the comfort and warmth that awaited inside. But despite the inviting smell, my heart still raced with anticipation and nerves.

As we made our way through the hallway, I couldn't help but notice the details that made Eleanor's home feel like a hotel. The soft lighting, the plush rug under my feet, the carefully placed trinkets and photographs that lined the walls. Everything seemed to exude a sense of calm and tranquility, and I found myself longing to stay forever in this peaceful haven.

"Make yourself at home," Eleanor called from somewhere beyond my sight, her voice broken. Tears still coming down her face.

I nodded, even though she couldn't see me, and my gaze drifted across the elegant living room. The meticulous order of Eleanor's house fascinated me, each piece of furniture and decor chosen with an eye for harmony and sophistication. My own place, cluttered with half-finished projects and stacks of books, seemed chaotic in comparison.

"Thank you again for coming with me." Eleanor's tone of voice sounded sorrowful as expected. "I have no idea where Dylan is. Nobody has heard from him since yesterday."

"Do you know what may have happened?" I asked, careful with my words trying not to upset her further.

"We've been having some issues. But I didn't think it was this bad." Eleanor walked away to the kitchen.

As I moved closer to the marble fireplace, my attention was snared by a picture frame on the mantel. The silver edges gleamed against the flickering light of the candles arranged nearby, but it wasn't the frame that caught my eye—it was the photograph it held. *Am I having a vision?*

There they were, Eleanor and Jake, his arm looped casually around her shoulders, their smiles bright and carefree. My breath hitched, and I felt as if someone had just spun me around too quickly; the room tilted, my vision blurred. Confusion clouded my mind like a sudden fog rolling in from the sea. *Is she Jake's sister? Cousin? Family friend?*

Jake's dark hair was tousled in that effortlessly charming way, a style that I had playfully ruffled just weeks before.

THE SECRET

And those warm brown eyes, which had looked into mine with what I believed to be genuine affection, now mocked me from the frozen moment within the frame.

A tumultuous wave of emotions threatened to sweep me away. How could this be? What did this mean? I wanted to reach out, to trace the curve of Jake's jaw in the photo as I had done a few times in person, searching for some clue, some slip-up in the image that would explain everything. But my hands were trembling, and I clenched them into fists at my sides instead.

Silence enveloped me, punctuated only by the soft ticking of a grandfather clock in the corner. The anticipation that had once fluttered within me like a moth now felt more like a trapped bird, frantic and desperate in its need to escape.

I swallowed hard, the taste of confusion bitter on my tongue, and forced myself to look away from the picture. The heat of embarrassment flushed my cheeks, and I willed myself to breathe, to steady the storm of questions raging inside me. I needed answers, but the truth was a puzzle where I hadn't even begun to fit the pieces together.

Eleanor's voice drifted from the kitchen, a soft melody against the clink of porcelain. "Can I get you anything to drink?" Her words were casual, an everyday courtesy, but they anchored me enough to find my voice.

"Actually, Eleanor," I began, turning towards her with a carefully measured step. "There's something... about that picture." My finger hovered in the air, pointing at the mantel, as if the mere act might shatter the glass and the illusion within it.

She appeared in the doorway, wiping her hands on a dish towel, her brow arching in curiosity. "Oh? What about it?"

My heart was a traitor, beating a rapid tattoo against my ribs, threatening to break free. But this was the moment to seek the truth. "It's Jake," I said, the name tasting strange under the circumstances. "How do you know him?"

For a second, a frown flickered across Eleanor's face, but it was gone so quickly I wondered if I'd imagined it. She glanced back at the photo as if seeing it for the first time. "Jake?" she repeated, her tone light, almost amused. "Madelyn, there must be some confusion. That's Dylan."

I felt a cold draft snake its way down my spine, even though the room was warm and inviting. "Dylan?" The name came out as a whisper, a prayer for this to be a mistake.

"Yes, Dylan, my fiancée," Eleanor said with a chuckle, as if we were discussing a trivial mix-up over a dinner reservation. "You've been planning our wedding, after all."

The room spun, a carousel of disbelief, and I gripped the back of a chair to steady myself. Dylan, the enigmatic figure whose wedding details I had orchestrated with such care, was Jake? The conversations, the stolen moments, the gentle brushes of hand against hand—they belonged not just to a man named Jake, but to Dylan, Eleanor's future husband.

THE SECRET

"Are you alright?" Eleanor's voice pierced the haze of my shock, and I realized I was holding my breath, waiting for the ground to stop shifting beneath me.

I tried forcing my racing heart to slow down as I straightened up and met Eleanor's gaze. "I... I must be mistaken," I said, the words feeling hollow and false.

Eleanor's eyes searched mine, her expression full of concern. "Is everything okay?"

I wanted to tell her the truth, that everything was far from okay. But how could I explain it all?

"I'm fine," I managed to say, my voice trembling slightly.

Eleanor's brow creased with worry, but she let the subject drop. "Well, if you're sure..."

"Yes," I said with more conviction this time. "I'm sure."

She nodded slowly before turning back towards the kitchen. "Alright then. Let me get you a drink."

As she disappeared into the kitchen, I sank into a chair at the dining table and ran a hand through my hair. This was all too much to process. Dylan... or Jake... whoever he was had been right in front of me this whole time, and I hadn't even realized it.

A glass clinked against the counter as Eleanor poured some water into it before placing it in front of me. "Here you go."

"Thank you," I murmured, taking a sip to moisten my dry throat.

Eleanor leaned against the counter, studying me closely. "You know," she began carefully. "You've been acting strange."

I swallowed hard, trying to keep my composure as I looked up at her with feigned confusion.

"It's nothing," I said dismissively. "Just... wedding planning stress."

Dylan—Jake—flashes of our time spent together flickered through my mind like old film snippets, disjointed and now tainted with deception. How could I have been so blind?

"Madelyn?" Eleanor's voice was tinged with concern, but my ears registered it as distant thunder, overshadowed by the storm raging within me. My hands, once steady and sure as they crafted centerpieces and sketched seating charts, now trembled uncontrollably, betraying the tempest of emotions that I fought to keep at bay.

"Excuse me," I managed to murmur, not trusting my voice with more. I turned away from the mantel, away from the smiling faces frozen in time, their secret mocking me from behind glass. The urge to confront Eleanor was a living thing inside me, clawing its way up my throat, desperate for release. But what good would it do? To expose the truth would mess with what bounded us all together, leaving nothing but tattered remnants of relationships and trust.

As I stood there, enveloped by the silence, I realized that exposing the lie would serve only to hurt Eleanor even more, who appeared oblivious to the duplicity of the man she intended to marry. And what of me? What would I gain but the confirmation of my own foolishness, the acknowledgment that I had allowed myself to fall for someone who was never truly within my reach?

A pang of sadness laced with anger settled in my chest, hard as stone. I looked back at Eleanor, her brow now creased with worry, and offered a weak smile. "I'm fine," I lied, feeling anything but. "Just remembered something I need to take care of."

With every ounce of willpower I possessed, I edged towards the door, the walls closing in around me. In my solitude, I would allow myself to crumble; but here, under Eleanor's watchful gaze, I held myself together with fraying strings of composure.

"Call if you need anything," I said, trying to make my voice sound as soft and genuine as possible.

"Thank you," she whispered.

I stepped out into the cool embrace of the evening air. It was a reprieve, however fleeting, from the suffocating warmth of the house that now housed too many secrets. A sanctuary where I could let the tears fall, the sobs come, and the world turn upside down as I grappled with the reality that the man I thought I knew was a stranger after all.

The door clicked shut behind me, the sound a final note to the chaos that now raged in my mind. I stood there for a moment, lost, the coolness of the night seeping into my skin, but not quite reaching the feverish heat of my thoughts. I felt as though I was inhaling shards of the life I thought I'd known, sharp and bitter.

The secret I harbored was now a physical burden that slowed my steps as I walked down Eleanor's front path. My hand grazed the wrought iron gate, fingers tracing the cold, intricate patterns as if seeking solace in their familiarity. But nothing could ease the tremble that had taken residence in my limbs.

I paused at the curb, the orange glow of the streetlamp casting long shadows across the pavement. The night was quiet, too quiet, as though it held its breath, waiting for me to shatter the silence with the scream that teetered on the edge of my lips.

Instead, I fumbled with my phone, the device feeling foreign and clumsy in my shaking hands. The screen lit up, a harsh contrast to the gentle darkness around me, and I blinked away the tears that threatened to fall as I struggled to summon the Uber app.

"Come on, Madelyn," I murmured to myself, the words a lifeline amidst the storm of emotions. Sofia's address, I needed to input Sofia's address. The numbers and letters blurred together, a jumble of meaningless symbols, until finally, with painstaking care, I managed to enter the information.

"Come on, come on," I whispered, urging the little car icon on the screen to move faster towards me. Relief, an emotion so distant just moments ago, began to trickle in as I saw the estimated arrival time count down.

Two minutes.

One minute.

My breath hitched as headlights rounded the corner, the vehicle pulling up to where I stood, a lone figure under the amber haze of the lamp. I glanced back at Eleanor's house, a shape against the dark sky, the windows now just rectangles of black, keeping their secrets from the world outside.

"Madelyn Montgomery?" the driver called out, and I nodded, voice lodged somewhere deep within me, unable to make its way past the tightness in my throat.

Slipping into the backseat, I closed the door with a soft click, sealing myself away from the night, from the revelation that had torn through my existence like a sudden squall. As the car pulled away, the distance was growing, and I leaned my head back against the seat.

"Are you okay?" the driver asked, glancing at me through the rearview mirror. His eyes were kind, but they held questions I wasn't ready to answer.

"Fine," I lied again, the word tasting of ash. "Just tired."

He nodded, accepting my half-truth and turning his attention back to the road. The city lights blurred as we moved through the streets, a kaleidoscope of color that matched the chaos of my thoughts.

Sofia's house. A place where I could let the dam break, where the secret could spill forth without fear of judgment or repercussion. The thought of her waiting presence, a beacon in the turmoil, coaxed a ragged sigh from my lips.

"Almost there," the driver announced, and I nodded, bracing myself for the next wave, for the inevitable deluge that would come when I crossed yet another threshold and into the arms of understanding.

Sofia would know what to do. She always did.

The Uber's headlights flashed against the familiar façade of Sofia's house, a silent herald to the end of my solitary ordeal. I stepped out, my legs still quivering like reeds in a strong current. The cool evening breeze brushed past, offering no solace to the feverish tumult within.

I barely registered the path to the door accompanied by relentless pounding in my chest. My hand, unsteady and hesitant, barely managed to press the doorbell before impatience took hold. The chime resonated with my pulse, a consonance of anxiety and relief vying for dominance.

The door swung open, and there stood Sofia, her hazel eyes instantly locking onto mine, a question forming in their depths. She didn't have to speak; our years of confidences had honed an unspoken language between us.

"Maddie?" she said, her voice laced with concern as she stepped aside, ushering me into the sanctuary of her home.

THE SECRET

I staggered past the threshold, my breaths shallow and rapid. The walls of her entryway, adorned with vibrant paintings and framed photographs, closed in around me— silent witnesses to the what was about to unfold.

"Sofia," my voice broke, a fragile whisper betraying the chaos of my emotions. "It was Dylan. Jake... he's Dylan. Eleanor's fiancée."

The words tumbled out in a rush, tripping over each other, as if desperate to escape the confines of my shattered heart. My vision blurred, tears welling up and spilling over in an uncontested flow. The pain and disbelief that clawed at my insides was hard to tame.

Sofia moved closer, her presence a solid force amid the storm raging within me. She reached out, her touch light on my arm, grounding me as I fought to stay afloat in the sea of deception.

"Slow down. Breathe," she urged softly, her voice the anchor I needed.

But the dam had burst, and with it came a deluge of grief and confusion, washing over us both as I surrendered to the truth I could no longer bear alone.

I sank into the plush embrace of Sofia's couch. She settled beside me, her warmth a counterpoint to the chill of dread that had taken up residence in my bones. Her gaze never wavered, hazel eyes reflecting a storm of empathy.

"Tell me everything," she urged, her voice a soft command that welcomed confession.

Piece by fragmented piece, I laid bare the mosaic of my heartache. The wedding fiasco, the picture on Eleanor's mantel, Dylan's smile beside her—a smile that had once promised something just to me.

Sofia's hand found mine, fingers intertwining in silent solidarity. Her touch was steady, unwavering, a lifeline cast across the waters of my sorrow. In her eyes, there was no judgment, only the quiet resolve of a friend who had seen me through the darkest of times and stood ready to do so again.

"Madelyn, you're not alone in this." Her voice wrapped around me, a cloak woven from threads of assurance. "It all makes sense now."

The dam inside me broke anew, but this time it wasn't just pain that poured forth. Gratitude mixed with the salt of my tears as I leaned into her side, allowing myself to be held. The simple act of sharing my burden with Sofia imbued me with a sense of relief that had seemed impossible mere moments ago.

Her support was a relief to my trust, frayed by deception. Here, in the refuge of our friendship, I found the strength to face the tangled web of lies and love that awaited resolution. Sofia's unwavering presence reminded me that while the path ahead was uncertain, I would not have to tread it alone.

"Thank you," I whispered, the words catching in my throat. But Sofia understood—all the things I couldn't yet express—and her nod was all the answer I needed. Before I could notice, everything went dark and I fell into a deep sleep.

As I slowly blinked my eyes open, the soft amber glow of the lamp enveloped Sofia's living room, casting a warm and comforting light over the space. The events of the evening came rushing back to me in a hazy blur, the memory of my fainting spell still fresh in my mind.

I shifted slightly on the couch, the cushions conforming to the shape of my body as I took in my surroundings. The coffee table before me told the story of our evening together: two mugs, their surfaces stained with the ring marks of numerous refills, stood as silent witnesses to our conversation. A tattered box of tissues sat nearby, its contents depleted from the tears shed in moments of vulnerability. And scattered amidst it all were the remnants of hastily eaten takeout, a testament to our shared comfort in the face of uncertainty.

As I slowly sat up, the room seemed to spin around me, the world tilting slightly on its axis. My head throbbed with the dull ache of exhaustion, my body still weary from the ordeal of the evening. But despite the lingering sense of unease, there was also a quiet sense of relief, a reassurance that I was not alone in facing whatever challenges lay ahead.

With a deep breath, I pushed myself up from the couch, my movements slow and deliberate as I steadied myself against the dizziness that threatened to overwhelm me. Sofia's presence beside me offered a silent source of strength, her unwavering support a reminder that I was not navigating this journey alone.

Sofia's gentle voice floated through the room, breaking the silence like a beacon of reassurance. "You scared me there for a moment," she said softly, her eyes filled with concern as she reached out to offer me a comforting hand.

I managed a weak smile. "Sorry about that," I murmured, my voice barely above a whisper. "I guess I just needed a moment to catch my breath."

Sofia's hand tightened around mine, her touch grounding me in the present moment. "Take all the time you need," she replied, her voice filled with warmth and understanding.

Thirty minutes later, I was finally able to sit up with no struggle.

"Okay, so what do we know for sure?" Sofia asked, her hazel eyes searching mine with a clarity that pierced through the fog of my emotions.

I recounted the news. "Jake is engaged to Eleanor. And... he's not even 'Jake.'" The name felt foreign on my tongue now, tainted by the lie it represented.

"Dylan, then," Sofia corrected gently, her fingers drumming a silent rhythm against the ceramic mug cradled

THE SECRET

in her hands. "What about your feelings for him? Where does that leave you?"

"Confused." The word was a mere whisper, but it carried the torment of the whirlwind in my heart. "Betrayed."

"Understandable." She reached across the space between us, her touch grounding. Sofia smiled warmly and reached out to touch my hand. "Forget about it, Mads. You have Steve now, and that's all that matters. Remember when you started your own event planning business? Look how far you've come since then. It's time to leave this uncertainty behind and focus on your happiness."

Her reminder stirred something within me—a memory of strength I had drawn from a well deep inside myself. It was that same resilience that I needed to tap into now.

"True," I conceded, a tentative smile playing on my lips. "Maybe it's time to reclaim that part of me. The one who takes risks, who stands up for herself."

"Exactly!" Sofia's enthusiasm was contagious. "You're Madelyn Montgomery. You craft beauty out of chaos for a living. If anyone can navigate this mess, it's you."

Our conversation wove through the tapestry of possibilities, mapping out scenarios.

"But why would he lie about his identity? I still don't get it." I shook my head."Now I understand why he made sure to never meet me in person at the office."

"Do you think he left Eleanor at the altar for you?" Sofia asked.

"I don't know. I need answers. But how will I get them?"

Sofia leaned back against the couch cushions, her expression thoughtful. "You could confront him."

I shook my head immediately. "No, that's not an option. I can't just barge into his life and stir things up again."

"Then what about talking to Eleanor?" Sofia suggested, her voice gentle but persistent.

My mind raced with objections. It wasn't fair to involve someone else in this mess, especially not Jake/Dylan's past bride-to-be that was just left at the altar. But then again, didn't she have a right to know the truth?

"I don't know," I admitted helplessly.

Sofia reached out and squeezed my hand reassuringly. "You'll figure it out, Mads. Just remember that whatever happens, you have people who love and support you."

I nodded.

Her words were more than a promise; they were the foundation upon which I could begin to rebuild my sense of self. I rose from the comfort of her couch, feeling the solidity of the floor beneath my feet. The act of standing seemed symbolic, a physical manifestation of the inner shift that had taken place within me.

"Thank you, Sof. For everything." My voice held a new determination, and I saw the spark of pride in her eyes.

"Always," she replied, walking me to the door. "Are you sure you don't want me to drive you home?"

THE SECRET

"I'm sure. I need some fresh air. I'll be fine, I promise."

Stepping out into the cool night air, I paused for a moment. The city lights twinkled in the distance, their steady glow mirroring the flicker of hope that now ignited my spirit. Walking away from Sofia's house, my thoughts crystallized into plans, actions, decisions. The road ahead might be fraught with challenges, but I no longer felt adrift in a sea of unpredictability.

The rhythm of my footsteps on the uneven pavement matched the cadence of my racing heart, a silent percussion to the chaos of thoughts tumbling through my mind. Streetlamps cast elongated shadows that stretched out before me, like dark fingers trying to pull me back into a past now tainted with deception.

I wrapped my arms tighter around myself, as if I could physically hold together the fragments of the life I once knew. The cool breeze whispered through the trees, carrying away the remnants of warmth from Sofia's comforting embrace. Leaves rustled, speaking in hushed tones to the night, and for a moment, I felt as though they shared in my restless contemplation.

With each block passed, the image of Eleanor's mantel flickered behind my eyelids—Jake, or rather Dylan, smiling beside her. That picture, an innocent snapshot to any other eye, had razed the landscape of my reality. My mind struggled to reconcile the tender moments we had.

How could the man who looked at me with such genuine affection be the same person who stood by another woman's side, hidden behind a mask of false identity? The questions spiraled, threading doubt through our encounters.

But beneath the torrent of confusion and hurt, a quiet strength began to take root. It was a resilience forged in the fires of unexpected betrayal, watered by the tears shed onto Sofia's shoulder.

This wasn't just about unmasking the truth of Dylan's duplicity; it was about rediscovering Madelyn Montgomery. The woman who planned grand events with precision, who could find beauty in the details others overlooked. If I could create worlds for others to revel in, surely I could craft a path for myself—one not defined by the whims of a man with two faces.

A car horn blared in the distance, jolting me from my thoughts, and I realized I had reached the familiar stoop of my home. Lifting my gaze, I saw my reflection in the glass door. Past the pain, beyond the uncertainty, there was a determination in those green eyes that had not been there before.

My hand pushed against the cold metal, the click of the latch granting me entry to more than just my home—it was the threshold to a future of my own making. The journey up the stairs was less of an ascent and more of a declaration with every step. By the time I turned the key in my door, Dylan's secret had transformed from a shackle into a stepping stone.

THE SECRET

Inside, the silence welcomed me, a blank canvas waiting for the first stroke of a new beginning. I stood there, in the entryway of my home, knowing that tomorrow would bring its challenges, but for the first time in a long while, I faced them not as Madelyn, the deceived, but as Madelyn, the undeterred.

CHAPTER 16

Doubts

I HAD to get my mind off of what I had just discovered, so I dived into some comforting family time. The soft clink of silverware against china and the rich aroma of garlic and basil filled the warm kitchen as I dished out generous helpings of homemade spaghetti onto each plate. Lauren's chatter about school projects mingled with the sizzle of the garlic bread browning under the broiler, creating a cozy symphony of domestic tranquility. Steve's appreciative smile as he took his first mouthful of pasta warmed me from the inside out.

"Maddie, this is amazing," he complimented, and my heart fluttered like it used to in the early days of our marriage.

"Thanks," I replied, tucking a stray chestnut curl behind my ear and forcing myself to meet his blue gaze. "There's something I need to tell you about the wedding."

Lauren, sensing a shift in the atmosphere, paused with her fork mid-air. Steve's expression sobered, and he nodded for me to continue, his attention now fully on me.

"The groom, Dylan, he didn't show up." I watched his jaw tighten, the muscles working beneath the surface of his smooth skin. "It was... embarrassing, standing there waiting to coordinate a wedding that wasn't going to happen."

"Wow, that's rough," Steve said after a moment, reaching across the table to cover my hand with his own—a gesture so familiar and yet so distant lately. His touch sparked a glimmer of something forgotten but not lost.

"Is there more to it?" His question was gentle, prodding, laced with concern.

I hesitated, torn between revealing the tangled web of emotions and keeping Jake—or Dylan's—secret just a little longer. Deceit pressed on my shoulders, and it was uncomfortable to say the least.

"Nothing I can share right now," I admitted, offering a sheepish half-smile. "Just... wedding chaos, you know?"

"Of course," he said, though I could see the questions dancing behind his eyes.

Lauren resumed eating, the tension broken by her innocent oblivion. Steve's reassurance wrapped around me like a security blanket. It had been too long since we connected like this—openly, honestly. A surge of hope washed over me, cleansing some of the doubt that had been clinging to my spirit.

"Hey, what do you say about us getting away for the weekend? Just the two of us?" Steve suggested, the corners of his lips tilting upwards in an inviting smile.

"Really?" My voice held a mixture of surprise and excitement. The idea of being alone with him, away from the daily grind, reignited a spark of anticipation in my chest. "Like a romantic getaway?"

"Exactly." His thumb caressed the back of my hand, sending shivers down my spine. "Somewhere we can just... be. You and me, Maddy."

The glimmer in his deep-set blue eyes was like a beacon in the night, guiding me back to the safe harbor of our love. Something inside me fluttered—hope, perhaps, or the beginnings of trust being rebuilt, piece by delicate piece.

"Lauren, sweetie, how would you like a weekend at Grandma's Paula?" I asked, turning to our daughter with an encouraging smile. Steve's mother, Paula, became a widow when Steve was just nine years old. Despite life's trials, she radiated warmth and kindness, making her the epitome of a sweet seventy-year-old. From the moment we met, I felt a deep affection for her, as she often expressed how I filled the void of the daughter she never had.

Living a mere ten minutes away from our home, Paula graced our lives with her presence frequently. Her sons had long since moved out, venturing into their own lives and families, leaving her with occasional bouts of loneliness. It was during these times that she found solace in our company, as we were the closest family she had nearby.

Lauren, too, held a special place in her heart for Paula. Their bond was undeniable. I'd always been grateful of the love and affection that Paula effortlessly bestowed upon us all.

"Can I bake cookies with her?" Lauren's face lit up at the prospect, her youthful enthusiasm untouched by what weighed on my heart.

"Of course, honey," Steve chimed in, "You'll have a great time."

As we cleared the table, the normalcy of the moment felt precious, fragile. We moved in tandem, a dance we had perfected over the years but had recently neglected. The clink of dishes and the hum of the dishwasher underscored the rhythm of our synchronized routine.

"Steve," I began, pausing to lean against the counter, "this means a lot to me. More than you might realize."

He wrapped his arms around me from behind, pulling me close against his chest. His touch was warm, solid, reassuring. "I know we've had our rough patches lately. But I'm here, and I'm not going anywhere. We're in this together, remember?"

"Remember," I said, allowing myself to relax into his embrace. The fears and doubts that constantly nipped at my heels seemed to recede into the shadows, if only for a moment.

DOUBTS

"Let's make this weekend special, okay?" His voice was soft, a whisper meant just for me. "We deserve it."

"Okay," I agreed, the word a vow, a promise to focus on us, on what we could be once more.

We parted with a kiss that spoke volumes, a silent conversation of renewed commitment. As he stepped away, a sense of determination settled within me. This weekend would be our chance—a small window of opportunity to rekindle the flame that once burned so brightly between us.

"Let's start packing," I said, already envisioning the secluded cabin and the stretches of time that awaited us, free from the outside world and its relentless demands.

"Sounds perfect," Steve replied, his hand finding mine as we walked together toward the promise of something rediscovered, something cherished—our love, still there, waiting to be awakened.

The soft clink of dishes being stacked, a domestic melody, as I began to clear away the remnants of our dinner. Lauren had already scampered off to her room, lost in the universe of a child's imagination, leaving Steve and me alone in the quiet aftermath.

"Madelyn?" Steve called from the hallway, his voice a gentle interruption. "I'll be right back, just need to use the bathroom."

"Sure," I replied, my attention focused on scraping the last bits of food into the trash. The rhythmic motions were calming, meditative, allowing my mind to drift toward the upcoming weekend, toward hope.

I was rinsing a plate when the sharp buzz of a phone shattered my tranquility. Instinctively, I glanced over at the counter where Steve's phone lay, the screen lighting up with an urgency that seemed out of place in our tranquil kitchen. Francesca, the name glowed, accompanied by the preview of a message: "Can't wait for…"

A frown creased my forehead as the text vanished into the secrecy of the locked device. Francesca? I couldn't recall a mention of her before, a seed of concern taking root amidst my thoughts. My hand hovered over the phone, the urge to delve deeper wrestling with the trust I was trying to rebuild.

The bathroom door clicked, and I withdrew my hand as if burned. Pressing my lips together, I forced my breathing to even out, striving to maintain a façade of normalcy.

"Everything okay?" Steve asked, emerging from the bathroom, oblivious to the nervousness he'd inadvertently caused.

"Fine," I said, offering him a smile that felt brittle. "Just thinking about what to pack for the weekend."

"Ah, right." He picked up his phone, sliding it into his pocket without a second glance. "You know, whatever you bring, you'll look beautiful."

The compliment, sincere and sweet, calmed my nerves. Could this be just an innocent exchange? A work thing, perhaps? Steve was always so guarded, but not unfaithful—of that, my heart was desperate to be certain.

"Thank you," I murmured, leaning against the counter as I watched him move around the kitchen, energy and confidence in every step. This was the man I loved, the one I wanted to believe in, flaws and all.

"Let's make it unforgettable," I added, my words a request to the universe more than to him.

"Absolutely," he agreed, the room filling with his unmistakable presence, a force that both comforted and commanded.

As he wrapped his arms around me once again, I made my choice. I would bury the whisper of doubt that Francesca's name had sparked. This weekend wasn't about suspicions; it was about us, about rekindling the ember of our love until it roared to life once more.

"Unforgettable," I repeated, choosing to immerse myself in the here and now, with him, without shadows between us.

The suitcase clicked shut, a definitive sound that marked the beginning of our escape. I shouldered my bag which started brushing against my arm in a familiar caress as we crossed the threshold of our home. The city's clamor fell away, replaced by the tranquil hum of the countryside. Steve's hand found mine across the center console, his fingers intertwining with mine in silent solidarity.

"Look at that," he said, nodding toward the window where the sun dipped low, casting an amber glow over the fields. "It's like the world's putting on a show just for us."

I squeezed his hand, my heart swelling at the thought. Yes, this weekend was ours—a canvas waiting to be painted with memories untainted by the shadows of doubt. I let my gaze linger on the horizon, the colors bleeding into each other like watercolor, and felt a tightness in my chest ease.

The cabin emerged from the embrace of pine trees, its wooden façade promising warmth and seclusion. Steve's excitement was evident, a childlike glee that was both infectious and endearing. He unloaded our bags, his movements efficient yet gentle, while I stood on the porch, inhaling the crisp air, tinged with the scent of earth and pine.

"Madelyn?" His voice pulled me back, and I turned to find him standing in the open doorway, the interior light framing him like a portrait. "Come see inside."

I followed him, a deliberate effort to leave Francesca's name behind, locked outside where it belonged. The cabin's interior was a haven, a perfect blend of rustic charm and comfort. A fire crackled in the stone fireplace, casting dancing shadows across Steve's face as he watched me, his blue eyes reflecting the flames.

"Perfect," I whispered, not just for the cabin, but for the moment—for us.

He wrapped his arms around me from behind, his chin resting atop my head. My senses filled with him—the solid presence of his body, the faint fragrance of his cologne blending with the smoky air, the reassuring cadence of his heartbeat against my back.

"Let's forget the world for a while," he murmured, his breath warm against my ear.

I leaned back into him, allowing his strength to anchor me. This was what I needed, what we needed—a sanctuary from the tempests of life. The worries about Francesca could wait; they had no power here. Instead, I focused on the feel of Steve's hands as they traced patterns along my arms, the softness of his lips when they brushed against the nape of my neck.

"Nothing else matters," I agreed, turning within his embrace to meet his gaze. "Just us."

"Only us," he replied, sealing the vow with a kiss that tasted of promise and new beginnings.

In the dance of tongues and the melding of breaths, I allowed the rhythm of our love to wash over me, soothing the disquiet in my soul. Here, in the heart of the wilderness, I rediscovered the connection that had first drawn us together, the profound intimacy that had somehow survived the storms.

And for those precious hours, my heart clung to the joy of being with Steve, fiercely pushing aside the gnawing doubts. We were here, together, and that was all that mattered.

The golden hues of dawn peeked through the sheer curtains, casting a warm glow over the rustic interior of the cabin. I started savoring the morning fragrance that hinted at the pine and earth outside. With Steve still sleeping soundly, I slipped out from the cocoon of blankets and padded quietly across the wooden floor.

My mind was a whirlwind of emotions as I stood at the window, watching the sun's gentle ascent. Francesca's name flickered in my consciousness like a stubborn ember, threatening to ignite a blaze of doubt and suspicion. The thought of confronting Steve about her loomed large, a shadow poised to eclipse the tranquility we had found here.

This weekend was about us, about rekindling the love that had been weathered by time and tribulations. Confrontation could wait; I would not let it mar the beauty of these moments.

"Good morning," came Steve's groggy voice from behind me. I turned to see him propped up on an elbow, his tousled hair and sleepy smile melting my heart.

"Morning," I replied, my decision solidifying.

"Let's go for a walk," he suggested, his blue eyes bright with the promises of the day ahead.

Hand in hand, we set out into the embrace of nature, the forest enveloping us in its verdant tranquility. The crunch of leaves underfoot became the soundtrack to our silent communion drawing us closer without words. The worries about Francesca receded, dwarfed by the towering pines and the vast expanse of sky above.

In the afternoon, the aroma of garlic and herbs filled the cabin as we cooked together, a ballet of synchronized movements born from years of shared meals. Steve chopped vegetables while I stirred the simmering sauce.

The glances across the kitchen island were reassurance to the life we had built—a life worth fighting for.

As evening fell, we sat before the crackling fireplace, the flames casting a warm dance of light across our faces. Our conversation ebbed and flowed, touching on dreams, fears, and the quiet revelations that only come with heartfelt openness.

"Remember when we first met?" Steve asked, a wistful note in his voice. "You were so passionate about everything... you still are."

"Passion can be a double-edged sword," I admitted, my thoughts briefly flitting to the unresolved tension within me.

"Maybe," he conceded, reaching for my hand. "But it's also what makes you who you are—the woman I fell in love with."

His words wrapped around me like a comforting shawl, and I allowed myself to lean into the safety of his presence. The question of Francesca and what it could mean for us was a specter lurking just beyond the firelight. But for now, I chose the warmth of Steve's touch over the chill of uncertainty.

The moonlight spilled through the window, its silvery glow dancing upon our tangled bodies. Our breaths intermixing as we explored the depths of desire and vulnerability. Every touch, every caress, was imbued with a tenderness that spoke of years of intimacy.

My fingers traced the contours of Steve's muscular back, memorizing every dip and curve as his lips trailed soft kisses along my collarbone. The world outside ceased to exist; there was only the intoxicating blend of our bodies merging and the palpable connection that defied words.

His lips met mine in another languid kiss, as if savoring each second and etching it into memory. The taste of him, combined with the heady scent of pine that still clung to our skin from our earlier explorations, intoxicated me. Our bodies moved together in a dance as old as time, surrendering to the yearning that had been building between us.

Time became a fleeting concept as we surrendered to the night, every movement an expression of love and longing. I reveled in the way our bodies moved in perfect harmony, a dance of passion and trust that left no room for doubt.

The soft sounds of pleasure echoed through the room, as if whispering secrets shared between two souls bound by an unbreakable bond.

The morning sun spilled through the sheer curtains, bathing the room in a soft, golden hue. I stirred, feeling

DOUBTS

Steve's arm draped over me, his breath steady against the nape of my neck. For a moment, the serenity of the scene enveloped me, and I reveled in the closeness we had rediscovered in this countryside retreat.

"Morning," Steve murmured, his voice rough with sleep. He tightened his embrace, pulling me closer, and I felt the contours of his body align with mine—a puzzle fitting perfectly together.

"Good morning," I replied, turning to face him, our noses almost touching. His eyes, a clear blue like the sky outside, held mine with an intensity that made my heart flutter. It was moments like these that I wanted to freeze in time, to live in forever, untainted by the difficulties of life.

We rose and prepared breakfast together in a comfortable silence, moving around with an easiness that spoke of years spent side by side. As Steve flipped pancakes, I set the table, laying out plates and cutlery with a precision that satisfied my need for order. The odor of coffee mingled with the sweet aroma of maple syrup, creating a cocoon of domestic bliss.

But amidst the sizzling of the pan and the clinking of cups, my mind betrayed me, wandering back to the text message from Francesca. Who was she? Why did her name unsettle me so? A part of me felt guilty for not addressing it immediately, for letting it fester in the back of my mind. But another part—a more dominant part—urged me to let it go, at least for now.

"Something on your mind?" Steve's question sliced through my reverie, his gaze probing.

"Nothing," I said too quickly, offering him a smile that felt more like a petition for my thoughts to remain hidden. "Just... enjoying this."

"Me too," he replied, returning the smile, unaware of the undercurrents swirling within me. He plated the pancakes, and we sat down to eat, light conversation filling the space between us.

After breakfast, we decided to take a walk to get some fresh air. The land around the cabin stretched out, rolling hills dotted with wildflowers, a postcard picture of tranquility. We walked hand in hand, the earthy smell of nature a grounding force, my senses heightened to the rustle of leaves and the occasional chirp of distant birds. Steve recounted old college stories, and I laughed genuinely, the sound marrying the breeze.

And yet, as we crossed a small wooden bridge over a babbling brook, the ghost of Francesca's name whispered through the trees. After the new discovery of Dylan that I was still trying to push very deep down the smallest corner of my mind to not think about, this woman was the last thing I needed to worry about. I hoped with all my heart I was worrying for nothing. My steps faltered briefly, and I squeezed Steve's hand tighter, fighting the urge to let suspicion taint the beauty around us.

"Look at this," Steve said, pausing to gesture at the landscape unfolding before us. His awe was contagious, and for a heartbeat, I forgot about the shadows of doubt. In that pause, I chose to immerse myself in the present, to drown out the whispering ghosts with the tangible joy of being here with him.

"Beautiful," I agreed. I focused on the love reflected in Steve's eyes, the connection that thrummed between us, alive and insistent. This was real, this was us—imperfect and unsure, but still so full of hope.

As we continued our walk, the sunlight breaking through the canopy above seemed to bless our path, and I silently vowed to keep walking beside him, leaving unanswered questions for another day.

The car's engine hummed a low, steady note as we wound our way back from the countryside. Our hands were casually intertwined on the console; I could almost feel the weekend's healing touch in the air. The past days had been smoothing our relationship with laughter and lingering kisses. Yet, beneath the veneer of newfound closeness, the name Francesca hung in my mind like a stubborn fog that refused to lift.

As we pulled into the driveway, Steve released my hand to kill the engine, and the sudden absence of his warmth made me acutely aware of the looming decision I had yet to face. "Home sweet home," he said, a smile in his voice, but it only served as a reminder that our idyllic escape was temporary, a parenthesis in real life.

"Thanks for a great weekend," I murmured, offering him a smile that felt both genuine and strained. I watched as he unloaded our bags, his movements sure and familiar, and I willed myself to see only the man I loved, not the enigma he might be hiding.

Inside, the house greeted us with its stoic silence, a stark contrast to the vibrant life we'd just left behind. I moved through the rooms, trailing my fingers along surfaces, reigniting my connection with the everyday. But as I passed by the hall mirror, I caught a glimpse of my reflection—green eyes clouded with doubts.

I sat at the edge of our bed, the material of our quilt cool beneath my fingertips. The internal tug-of-war was exhausting. Should I confront Steve about the mysterious woman who had infiltrated my thoughts? Or should I continue in this semblance of peace, cherishing the fragile thread pulling us back together?

My mind replayed the tenderness in his eyes, the way he'd laugh—a sound that filled spaces I didn't know were empty. It was juxtaposed against the sharp sting of deceit that the mere possibility of Francesca represented. With Steve, there was always an undercurrent of something unsaid, emotions hidden beneath the surface. His jealousy, a fiery undercurrent, demanded loyalty, but did he offer the same in return?

"Madelyn?" Steve's voice broke through my reverie as he entered the room. "You okay?"

"Fine," I lied, standing up and folding myself into his offered embrace. His odor, woodsy and familiar, enveloped me, and for a moment, I let it sedate my churning thoughts.

"Good," he replied, pressing a kiss to the top of my head. "Because I was thinking—"

"What?" I prompted, pulling back slightly to meet his gaze.

"Maybe we can make weekends like this a regular thing," Steve suggested, hope flickering in his blue eyes.

"Maybe," I said, the word hollow as I grappled with the crossroads before me. To question him could open up a can of worms, disturbing what we's been working on over the weekend. Yet, to remain silent might mean living with the perpetual itch of unreliability.

With a soft sigh, I realized the answer wouldn't come tonight. For now, I chose to bury my doubts deep, to lock away the name Francesca in a corner of my heart that I wasn't ready to explore. The consequences of that choice loomed large, casting a shadow that I knew would have to be faced. But not today. Today, I would hold onto the illusion of us, unblemished and whole, for just a little while longer.

CHAPTER 17

Again

I OPENED my eyes and Steve had already left for work. I got up from bed and the first thing I thought of was my coffee, my favorite espresso I made every morning from my Nespresso machine I missed while away.

In the living room, the laptop sat closed on the coffee table —a silent witness to late-night emails and early-morning news. It beckoned me with the promise of answers, or perhaps the threat of more questions. I sank onto the couch, the cushions enveloping me in familiar comfort as I flipped the laptop open. My fingers hovered over the keyboard before tapping out Steve's password with reluctant familiarity.

His Facebook page loaded, the blue banner at the top like the sky after a storm—clear yet foreboding. I clicked on his friends list, my eyes scanning for any signs hidden among the familiar names and faces. A friend from college, a coworker, his cousin from Ohio... they passed in a blur of benign normalcy, but my gut told me something was amiss.

My eyes caught on unfamiliar names, pausing, analyzing. Who was this person? How did they know Steve? Each click was a step deeper into the rabbit hole of suspicion, my creative mind crafting narratives from profile pictures and recent check-ins.

"Come on," I whispered to myself, trying to quell the rising tide of anxiety. "You're being ridiculous." Yet I couldn't stop, couldn't look away, as though the next name might hold the key to the uncertainty that clouded my heart.

A flicker of recognition sparked as I scrolled past a profile picture that seemed out of place amidst the casual acquaintances and long-lost school friends. Francesca Ryan. Her name was a stranger's among the list, yet it rang with an inexplicable familiarity. My cursor hovered for a breath before I clicked.

The profile loaded, a montage of life that felt intrusive to witness. But it was the gym photos that seized my attention —a punch of reality in a stream of casual social media narcissism. There, in the background, was the unmistakable logo of Steve's gym—the same one he frequented religiously every morning. My heart stalled, then raced, thudding against my ribs like a trapped bird.

"Francesca Ryan..." The name tasted like a puzzle piece that didn't fit, and I couldn't resist the impulse to probe further. My fingers hovered over the keyboard. Then, determination took hold, fuelled by a need to dispel the fog of doubt that clouded my thoughts.

With the keystrokes, my pulse quickened. I crafted the message from Steve's profile with meticulous care, weaving words that were both cordial and probing. "Hi Francesca, my phone is not working properly to send text. I'm using my laptop to reach out. Can we meet for coffee later?"

I hit send, feeling a surge of adrenaline sharpen my senses. Anticipation curled in my stomach, a mix of fear and curiosity that propelled me forward on this precarious path of discovery. What would Francesca say? Would she confirm my fears or offer relief from this relentless unease? Only time would tell, and every second stretched taut with expectation.

The soft glow of the screen was a beacon in the dim room, casting long shadows across the walls as I waited. My phone lay passive beside me, a silent arbiter of my fate. When it lit up with notifications, my heart leapt, only to plummet when none bore Francesca's name. The constant cycle of hope and disappointment scraped at my nerves, leaving them raw and exposed.

I busied myself with trivial tasks, fluffing pillows that didn't need fluffing and rearranging books that had long found their rightful place on the shelf. But these distractions were feeble shields against the onslaught of what-ifs that plagued my mind. What if Francesca knew something? What if she didn't? The questions ricocheted within the confines of my skull, a reminder of the revenue of doubts I had willingly stepped into.

I checked Steve's laptop again, thumb swiping down to refresh the messages. Nothing. And then, as I contemplated another circuitous route around the living room, it buzzed. It was an alert from Facebook Messenger. My stomach twisted into a tight coil as I tapped on the icon, my breath held captive in my lungs.

"Sure, I'd love to meet for coffee," the message from Francesca read, "How does 5 pm at Starbucks sound?"

A sigh, part relief, part trepidation, escaped me. The reality of the situation sank its teeth in, grounding me in the present. 5 pm. The word echoed in my mind, a drumbeat counting down the time until this clandestine rendezvous.

Nervous energy coursed through my veins as I contemplated what to wear, how to style my hair, which questions to ask. The attention to detail, usually reserved for my event planning, now fixated on this personal encounter. I rifled through my wardrobe, selecting an ensemble that projected casual confidence—a pair of dark jeans paired with a soft blue sweater that made my eyes pop. It felt like armor, a way to shore up the defenses around my fragile composure.

Practicing nonchalant expressions in the mirror, I tried to quell the tremor in my hands. They betrayed the calm I sought to embody, fidgeting restlessly as I rehearsed greetings and reactions. Would Francesca be forthcoming or guarded? Sympathetic or indifferent?

My green eyes, usually so expressive, now held a glint of resolute steel. This was about seeking truth, about quieting the cacophony of doubts with answers, no matter how unwelcome they might be.

Clutching my purse, I ensured my phone was charged, my mind already racing ahead to the morrow. Francesca held pieces to the puzzle, and I was determined to reclaim them.

Inside the Starbucks, the odor of roasted coffee beans battled with the undercurrent of anxiety that clung to me like a second skin. My gaze flitted over the patrons, a mix of students buried in their laptops and friends sharing hushed confidences. Then, like the sudden click of puzzle pieces aligning, I saw her.

Francesca was ensconced at a corner table, her posture relaxed, unaware of the storm approaching her harbor. The steady thrum of my heart escalated into a pounding rhythm, reverberating against my ribcage with such force I half-wondered if others could hear it. She was real, not just an image behind a screen or an abstract threat looming over my relationship.

With each step threading through the maze of tables and chairs, the clamor of the café dimmed. It was as though I walked in a tunnel, the focus of my world narrowing until there was only Francesca, her presence pulling me forward with magnetic certainty.

I paused a mere breath away from the table, my fingers gripping the strap of my purse with a quiet desperation. Closing my eyes for a fleeting moment, I willed my lungs to draw in a deep, steadying breath of air laced with caffeine and whispered conversations.

"Madelyn Montgomery," I introduced myself silently, a mantra to cement my identity before opening my eyes again.

There she was, her attention captured by my approach, and our eyes locked. I slid into the chair opposite her, my movements deliberate, the veneer of casual confidence masking the tremors that threatened to betray my cool exterior. Here I was, face to face with the woman who might just unveil my carefully reconstructed reality.

Francesca's hands wrapped around her coffee cup, fingers tapping an erratic rhythm against the ceramic. My own lay flat on the table, a visible tremor coursing through them despite my attempt to appear composed. I could feel every beat of my pulse as if it echoed through the very surface between us.

"Steve mentioned you were having some... difficulties," Francesca's voice was a careful blend of concern and curiosity, her words slicing through the tension. "But I honestly didn't know you two had sorted things out."

My breath was catching in my throat. The confession hit me with the subtlety of a sledgehammer; their communication was not just casual gym chatter. I felt a cold wash of shock drenching me from head to toe, chilling the confusion that swirled within like a stubborn fog.

Francesca's gaze held a flicker of remorse as she continued, her voice tinged with regret. "I didn't realize you were back together. Steve and I started talking during a time when you and he were having those big issues... and... we had sex on a few occasions." She looked away, her fingers tracing the rim of her coffee cup, leaving thin trails of condensation in their wake.

I sat there, frozen in disbelief, my mind racing to process the what she'd just said. Each syllable threatening to shatter the fragile foundation of trust I had been clinging to. The café faded into a blur around us as the gravity of Francesca's confession settled upon my shoulders.

"How could Steve have kept this from me?" The question slipped past my lips before I could stop it, laced with a mixture of pain and anger. "How could he betray our vows like this, again?"

Francesca's expression was one of genuine remorse as she met my gaze once more. "I don't know," she admitted softly. "I never meant for any of this to happen."

My fingers tightened around the edge of the table, knuckles turning white as I struggled to contain the emotions raging within me. "And what about you?" I asked, my voice barely above a whisper. "Did you know he was married?"

She looked away again, her eyes flickering with guilt. "I did," she said reluctantly. "But at first it was just... flirting, harmless fun between two people who were attracted to each other. And he told me you weren't together anymore anyways." She paused, taking a deep breath before continuing. "But then things escalated and before I knew it, we were having an affair."

A wave of nausea washed over me, bile rising in my throat as I tried to make sense of it all. How long had this been going on? How many lies had Steve told me? And how much more did Francesca know that she wasn't telling me?

"I'm sorry," she said again, her voice cracking with emotion. "I didn't know you were now back together or I wouldn't have interfered. He didn't tell me."

I leaned back in my chair and closed my eyes, willing myself not to scream or cry or give in to the overwhelming urge to run far away from this mess. When I opened them again, Francesca was still there, watching me with compassion and regret.

"I don't know what to do," I admitted, my voice barely audible. "Thank you for being honest," I managed to say, even as my mind reeled. Honesty—such a simple thing, yet so pivotal, its absence the root of countless fissures. This new information demanded to be sifted and sorted, but for now, it simply hung there, suspended in the space between confession and consequence. "So what were the last messages you sent him for?"

"I texted him and called him a few times this past weekend. He disappeared and I wanted to know what was going on. His phone seemed off all weekend. When I received the Facebook message I assumed his phone was broken. But it was you."

"We were on a gateway at a cabin together all weekend." I swallowed hard, the coffee shop's cacophony receding as I fought to steady my breathing. Francesca's words repeated in my head. The emotions churned within me–anger, hurt, disbelief–each vying for dominance. My hands, once trembling, now lay still on the cool surface of the table, belying the storm inside.

"Complications," I whispered to myself, the word morphing into a myriad of questions with no easy answers. Was our reconciliation a façade? Did Steve see it as a mere intermission in his indiscretions? My gaze drifted over the half-empty cup before me, the remnants of my latte forming an abstract pattern that mocked my search for clarity.

The fabric of trust we wove together seemed threadbare now, worn thin by silences. I had prided myself on being astute, insightful, yet here I was, blindsided by facts that should have been apparent to anyone who knew where to look. It was a bitter pill, laced with the irony of my own ignorance.

"Excuse me, I need to go." My voice sounded hollow as I stood up, feeling Francesca's eyes following me. I didn't look back. The chime of the door signaled my departure, a tiny sound that felt like the closing of a chapter.

Outside, the world moved with an urgency I couldn't muster. People bustled by, entangled in the minutiae of their lives, oblivious to the internal disarray of a stranger among them.

"Where do you go from here?" I muttered under my breath, the question hanging in the balance. Dylan's discovery—the realization that my life was intricately woven with more deceit than I could have imagined— weighed heavily on my heart. The man I thought I knew, the love I thought I had, all of it now seemed as substantial as mist.

As I passed by the familiar storefronts, reflecting on the choices that lay ahead, indecision was eating me up. To confront or to retreat? To forgive or to forsake? The possibilities stretched out like diverging paths in a dense wood, and I, lacking the compass of certainty, felt lost amidst the undergrowth of what-ifs.

My steps slowed as I reached the corner, the traffic light blinking its impassive red. I lingered there, caught between the impulse to rush forward and the desire to remain rooted in place, suspended in the amber hue of uncertainty. With a sigh, I realized that no matter which direction I chose, the journey ahead would demand more of me than I ever anticipated.

The light turned green, and I stepped off the curb, my stride echoing the rhythm of a heart unsure of its next beat.

CHAPTER 18

Enough

I PACED across the polished hardwood floor of our living room. Steve's gym bag lay discarded by the couch, an innocuous detail.

"Steve," I started, my voice steadier than I felt. "We need to talk."

He looked up from his phone, his deep-set blue eyes meeting mine with an unreadable expression. He always had this way of cloaking his emotions, but not tonight. Tonight, I needed answers.

"Francesca," I said, the name tasting bitter on my tongue. "I found out about her... about you." My fingers curled into fists at my sides, my nails digging crescents into my palms. The wavy tendrils of my chestnut hair felt heavy around my face, as if weighted down by my disappointment.

"Madelyn." His use of my name sounded like a plea. Rising from the armchair, he closed the distance between us, his athletic frame towering over me. "It's not what you think. I was going to end it with her, I swear. After we talked about giving our marriage another chance, I just... I never got the chance to tell her."

My green eyes must have flashed with skepticism because he reached out, as if to bridge the gulf our words had created. His touch had once offered comfort, but now it only reminded me of the crack that had widened between us.

"Please, believe me, Maddie," he continued, the nickname slipping out in his desperation. "I want us to work, I do. But I didn't know how to bring it up after we decided to try again."

"Try?" I asked, the word hollow. How many times had we tried? How many chances had been squandered? His assurances felt like band-aids over bullet wounds—temporary and wholly inadequate.

"Your promises are starting to sound like echoes," I admitted, the hurt evident in my voice. "How can I trust that this time will be any different? You should've told me about her."

His jaw clenched, a ripple of tension passing through him. "Because I love you, damn it. And I know I've screwed up, but I can fix this. We can fix this together."

Could we? His earnestness tugged at something within me, yet the shadow of doubt loomed larger than his shadow in the dim light. Each disclosure, each apology from him, only seemed to deepen the grooves of mistrust that had etched themselves into my heart.

"Ending it with her should have been the first thing you did, not an afterthought," I murmured, my voice laced with years of accumulated frustration. "Your intentions don't change the fact that you haven't changed, Steve. Not really."

His hand fell away, and the space between us became more than physical—it was a chasm filled with unresolved issues. I watched him closely, searching for the man I had married within the stranger before me.

My fingers curled into fists at my sides; the cool metal of my wedding ring biting into my palm, suddenly feeling unbearable, like a shackle I had willingly worn for years, only to realize now it was made of nothing but false hopes and empty promises.

"This is over," I said, my voice unwavering despite the storm of emotions churning inside me. "I can't do this anymore."

He recoiled as if I'd struck him, his charismatic façade cracking under the strain. "Don't say that. We can get past this. I know we can."

"Can we?" My laugh was hollow, a bitter sound that didn't belong in the home we had built together. "Because all I see is a pattern that you refuse to break. And I refuse to be part of it any longer."

"Does this have to do with that Jake again? Is this an excuse because you changed your mind about us?" The suspicion in his deep-set blue eyes stung. Steve's jealousy, a constant undercurrent in our marriage, surfaced with a vehemence that should have surprised me, but it didn't.

I met his gaze, steady and clear. "No, it's not about someone else. And stop making this about me. We agreed we were going to be honest with each other. This is about me finding out who I am without you defining that. It's about me learning to trust myself again."

Exploring myself and my feelings... The thought played in my mind, a mantra to keep me grounded amidst the chaos. There was a life I had yet to live, experiences I had yet to savor. And I would not find them in the shadow of a man who could not—would not—change.

The room felt like it was shrinking, walls closing in like a tightening vice. My heart hammered against my ribs. I turned away from Steve, staring through the window at the silent, indifferent city beyond. It was in moments like these, fraught with pain, that my mind would betray me too, wandering to Jake.

Jake—or Dylan, with his tousled dark hair that fell into his eyes when he laughed, his warm brown gaze that seemed to see right into me. We had nothing more than fleeting conversations amidst the musty smell of old books and one night of passion, yet his image stayed, haunting my consciousness. But what did I really know about him? Nothing substantial, nothing real.

"Madelyn?" Steve's voice, tinged with desperation, pulled me back to the present. "Please, we need to talk about this."

"Talk?" The word came out sharper than I intended. "What is there left to say?"

"You're not being fair!" His voice rose, a rare crack in his ever-controlled demeanor. "How can you just throw us away?"

"Fair?" I spun to face him, anger igniting inside me. "Tell me what's fair about lies, again. I thought we were starting fresh. Tell me what's fair about finding solace in someone else's arms while pretending to work on our marriage!"

"Is that what you're doing with him? With that... Jake?" He spat out the name as if it were a curse, his jealousy a palpable entity between us. "A bookstore worker, sure... Did you think I was that stupid? Good thing I tracked your phone that night, or I would've never known."

"Jake? Jake has nothing to do with this!" My denial was fierce, protective over something that was, at its core, nonexistent. Yet even as I said it, doubt gnawed at me. Could any relationship be free of the shadows that now darkened my marriage?

"Doesn't he?" Steve countered, stepping closer, the space between us charged with years of unsaid things. "Because it seems like you're ready to replace me without a second thought."

"Replace you?" The laugh that escaped me was devoid of humor. "You think so highly of yourself, don't you? This isn't about replacing anyone. This is about respect, trust—something I can't seem to find with you."

"Madelyn..." He reached out, but I stepped back, unwilling to let his touch sway me.

"Please, don't." My voice broke, a sign of weakness I couldn't afford. "Don't make this harder than it needs to be."

"Harder?" He threw his hands up, frustration emanating from him in waves. "This is our life we're talking about! How could this possibly be easy?"

"Easy?" I asked, choking back a sob. "There's nothing easy about realizing the man you married is a stranger. There's nothing easy about feeling alone in a house full of memories."

"Is that what I am to you? A stranger?" His words cut deep, but they also rang with an uncomfortable truth. If Steve was a stranger, then what was Jake? A comforting illusion? A distraction from the emptiness?

I swallowed hard, pushing the thoughts of Jake aside. This was between Steve and me—our fractured history, our broken promises. And as much as I wanted to flee from the confrontation, from the raw exposure of our faults, I knew it was necessary. Only through facing the reality of our disintegrating union could I hope to find the strength to rebuild myself from the ruins.

ENOUGH

Digging my heels into the worn carpet, I could feel the intricate patterns pressing against the soles of my feet, a reminder that I was still standing, still breathing, amidst the chaos.

"Please." Steve's voice had softened, a stark contrast to the sharp edges of his desperation. "We can fix this. I know we've been through hell, but I swear to you, I'll do better."

His eyes searched mine, imploring, begging for a sign of the forgiveness that had once come so easily. But as I looked back at him, the man who had promised to be my partner in all things, I realized that I no longer saw the future I had once envisioned. Instead, I saw only the reflection of my own longing for something more than the hollow shell of our marriage.

"Doing better isn't enough anymore." My voice was steady, stronger than I felt inside. There was no tremble to betray the fear coiling in my stomach, no hitch to suggest the ache of leaving behind what had once been. "I need to do what's best for me, for my own happiness. And that means letting go."

"But..." He stepped towards me, closing the distance I had fought to put between us. His hands reached out to grasp mine, a familiar gesture that once would have melted me.

"Steve,"—I withdrew my hands, folding them over my chest like a shield—"you've made promises before. How many more chances can we give this before we accept that it's just... not working?"

The words hung between us, stark and irrefutable. I could see the moment they hit home, the way his shoulders slumped, the faint crease that appeared between his brows. This man, who exuded confidence on the outside, was now fraying at the edges, his vulnerability laid bare.

"Please," he implored again, his voice barely a whisper. "I can change. I will change. For us."

Us. The word in my mind, a haunting reminder of the unity we once cherished. But that unity had frayed, thread by delicate thread, until we were little more than two separate entities occupying the same space.

"There is no..." I said, my heart aching with the finality of my decision, "there is no 'us' to save anymore."

He looked stricken, the blue of his eyes darker with emotion. "Don't say that," he pleaded. "Don't give up on everything we've built together."

"Sometimes," I whispered, the truth settling into my bones, "the bravest thing we can do is start over. On our own."

With those words, the last vestiges of doubt crumbled away. I was resolute, determined to carve a new path forward—one where my happiness wasn't tethered to the whims of another. It was time to trust in myself, and in the possibilities that lay beyond the confines of a loveless marriage.

The silence was thick, almost tangible, as I stood my ground. Steve's eyes searched mine desperately, but I could

ENOUGH

feel them digging deeper into the soil of self-worth. His promises were flimsy and insubstantial like dandelion seeds poised for flight at the slightest breath.

"Madelyn, please," he said again, his voice a mix of command and supplication that once might have swayed me.

I shook my head, not unkindly, but with an unshakeable certainty. "Promises are just words. They're air. And we can't build anything on air." My own voice sounded alien to me, stronger and clearer than it ever had within these walls.

He stepped closer, closing the gap I had so carefully measured between us. His presence was overwhelming, as it always had been—his scent, his heat, his very being. But it was no longer what I craved; it was what I was leaving behind.

"Look at me," he urged, tilting my chin up with his fingers. The familiar touch would have left me melting into him in another life, another time. Not now.

"I've seen beyond the horizon of 'us,'" I began, my gaze steady as I met his pleading blue eyes. "There's a whole expanse out there—a life where I'm more than just part of a couple that isn't working."

His hand fell away from my face as if I'd burned him. In the space between heartbeats, I saw the man I had married— the love that once felt eternal—but even those memories were tinged with the gray of old photographs, fading with every passing second.

"Don't do this. We can fix this," he said, his voice raw with emotion.

"Or will we just keep patching the cracks until we're standing in ruins?"

He was silent then, and in that silence, I knew. I knew that we had built our marriage like a sandcastle at water's edge, beautiful and grand, but destined to be washed away by the tide of reality.

"I'm sure of this," I spoke with a calm I hardly felt, "we're done. You need to accept that." My heart thrummed against my ribs, pounding out the rhythm of an ending, of closure.

"But I love you!" His voice broke, shattering the last defense he had.

"And I care for you," I replied, the truth of it bittersweet on my tongue. "But love shouldn't leave us less than we are. It should make us more. And we... we've become less."

The finality was undeniable. It was over—not with a bang, but with the soft click of a door closing gently on a chapter of my life. As I turned away, leaving Steve standing amidst the shards of our fractured union, I carried with me not just the sorrow of what was lost, but also the flickering flame of hope for what was yet to come.

With every step away from the house, my mind began to spiral, tumbling into the cavern of risks that now lay ahead. The cold wrapped around me like a shawl, the gentle whisper of leaves rustling above in somber chorus with my thoughts. I was free, yet tethered to a past I could not unlive, a love I could no longer lean on.

I settled onto an old wooden bench at the edge of the park, beneath the canopy of a grand oak tree. Its branches, though twisted and reaching, seemed surer of their direction than I felt about my own path. The betrayal, not just Steve's but my own—for had I not lied myself by staying so long?—echoed with every beat of my heart. Could I trust again, not just another man, but my own judgment? The very essence of trust now seemed as elusive as the shifting shapes of clouds under the moonlight.

A single tear traced its way down my cheek, fear gripping my chest. It wasn't just the end of us, it was the beginning of me—the real Madelyn, who loved with ferocity, planned with precision, and dreamt of a life where her creative spirit wasn't stifled by doubt or dimmed by disappointment.

"Who am I beyond 'Madelyn Montgomery, the wife'?" The question was a whisper lost to the night. Those empathetic eyes of mine, once so quick to look for the best in others, now turned inward, searching for the strength to rebuild, to be compassionate toward the woman reflected in the mirror.

I would find happiness, even if it meant stumbling through a thicket of trial and error. The green of my eyes, likened to fresh spring leaves by Steve on better days, would bear witness to growth, to change. And though self-doubt might be a familiar companion, I vowed it would not dictate my journey.

The park was silent now, save for the occasional hoot of an owl, wise and unseen. It felt fitting, this solitary moment amidst the slumbering world, a cocoon from which I would emerge, transformed.

As I stood up, my shadow stretched long on the gravel path, a visual echo of the day fading into history. Tomorrow, with its untouched canvas, beckoned with a bittersweet allure. There would be pain, yes, but woven through it, strands of hope, and the unquenchable desire to craft a life rich with fulfillment.

"Goodbye, Steve," I murmured to the empty space beside me, my voice steady, my spirit already reaching for the dawn of a new day. I stepped forward, leaving behind the echoes of what was and walking toward the promise of what could be.

CHAPTER 19

Moving On

I PERCHED on the edge of our plush, cream-colored sofa, fingers tracing the cool, brushed metal of my wedding band. It spun loosely around my finger—a perfect metaphor for how disconnected I felt from Steve, and from the life we'd built together.

"Hey," I began, my voice barely a whisper as he entered the room, the smell of his aftershave preceding him. "Can we talk?"

He sank into the armchair opposite me, his athletic frame causing the leather to creak in protest. There was an expectant tilt to his head, those deep-set blue eyes searching mine, looking for the Madelyn that once found solace in their oceanic depths.

"Of course," he replied with a smile that didn't quite reach those eyes. The pet name, once a term of endearment, now sounded like a stranger's greeting.

I took a breath, drawing in the courage that flitted around the room like dust motes in the sunlight. My heart pounded against my ribcage, demanding release from the pretense. My phone buzzed discreetly from the coffee table, a message from Sofia offering silent support. *It's over with Steve,* I had texted her moments before. *Will tell you everything soon.*

"This... isn't easy for me to say." My gaze dipped to the woven rug between us, its intricate pattern suddenly fascinating. "But I need you to move out."

A flicker of confusion crossed his handsome face, and he leaned forward, elbows on knees. "Move out? Where am I supposed to go?"

"I don't know. It's not my problem anymore." The words trembled on my lips. "Our marriage—it's over."

"I..." His voice caught, and for a moment, that strong exterior cracked, revealing the vulnerability he so often hid. But I couldn't afford to lose myself in his emotions—not when mine were already spilling over.

"We need to move on," I continued, the conviction in my voice growing stronger. "Move on and figure things out, to understand who we really are and what we really need."

My eyes finally met his, holding onto the unseen request that he would see the necessity of this, that he would understand my need for freedom from the suffocating marriage full of trust issues.

"Move on?" His brow furrowed, and I braced for the storm I knew was coming. But for now, for this one fleeting moment, there was still peace. And within that peace, I found a sliver of hope—that maybe, just maybe, we could both find happiness again, even if it meant finding it apart.

Steve's voice rose, a tempest brewing in the deep-set blue of his eyes. "Are you sure you want me to move out?"

I nodded, my hands clasped tightly in my lap to still their trembling.

"We can work this out," he insisted, reaching across the divide, his hand hovering over mine before I subtly pulled away. "You don't mean this."

"Trust me, I've thought it through. I do mean it. We're not the same people who took those vows."

"Damn it, Madelyn!" He slammed his fist down on the armrest, making me flinch. "You're just going to throw everything away? Just like that?"

His anger stoked a fire within me, one that had been smoldering beneath years of doubt and compromise. This wasn't just about throwing something away; it was about reclaiming what we'd lost—or maybe never had.

"Throw away?" I asked back, my voice firmer. "I'm trying to salvage what's left of me, of us. Maybe there's a chance we can find ourselves again, but not like this. Not together."

"There is someone else, isn't there?" His accusation hit like a slap, his jealousy casting shadows across his face. "I know it."

"No," I said, though my heart ached. "It's not about someone else. It's about us not being right for each other anymore."

"Please—" By the low tone of his voice, I could tell his imploration was a mixture of desperation and command, but I shook my head, cutting him off.

"I need happiness. We both do. And it's clear we can't give that to each other any longer."

"Happy?" He scoffed, standing abruptly. "You think you'll be happy without me?"

"Maybe," I confessed, standing as well to meet his towering figure. "Maybe not. But I know I'm not happy now, and staying in this—staying with you—isn't going to change that."

He looked at me then, really looked, as if seeing me for the first time in years. In his gaze, I saw the flicker of understanding, quickly doused by pride.

"Fine," he ground out between clenched teeth. "If that's what you want."

"It is," I said, my heart pounding with a mix of fear and strength. "It's what we need."

Steve stormed past me, every line of his body rigid with resentment. I watched him get his things, feeling the strings that tied us together stretching, fraying, until at last, they snapped, setting us both adrift.

MOVING ON

The bedroom door slammed open with such force it reverberated against the wall, and I flinched despite myself. Steve's hands were fumbling with the top drawer of our dresser, his movements jerky as he yanked out handfuls of clothes without care or precision.

"Is this what you want, Madelyn?" His voice was a ragged blade. "Me packing up my life? Because you've suddenly decided you're not happy?"

"Steve," I began, but my voice faltered, falling on deaf ears.

"Was this your plan all along?" he spat, a sneer distorting his handsome features. "To throw me out like yesterday's trash? Did you get bored? Is that it? I don't think I've done anything *that* wrong."

I watched him, the man I had shared countless days and nights with, now a stranger fueled by rage. His accusations bore into me, but I refused to let them take root.

"Stop thinking your behavior is okay," I said quietly, my own hands clasped in front of me to stop them from trembling. "We've been unhappy for a long time, and once we were finally doing better, you messed up again. We're not good together anymore."

"Unhappy?" He threw a pair of jeans across the room, the denim slapping against the wall. "You're telling me this now? After years together?"

"It's never easy to admit when something's over," I replied, my throat tight. "But denying it won't make it any less true."

He paused, his back to me, shoulders rising and falling with every labored breath. For a moment, I thought I saw the tension ease, a sign of the understanding man I once knew. But then he whirled around, eyes blazing.

"Then go ahead! Find your damn happiness!" he shouted. "See if anyone else can put up with your indecisiveness and your cold feet!"

Despite his cruel words, I remained still, a quiet observer to his unraveling. I understood his pain, the rawness of being left, but I couldn't allow his hurt to undo the clarity I had fought so hard to find.

"This isn't about blame." My voice was steady, even as compassion warred with my need to protect my new decision. "I don't even care about that. It's time we accept that and give ourselves the chance to heal. Separately."

For a second, his expression faltered, and I glimpsed the vulnerability behind the façade of anger. Then it was gone, masked once again by fury as he zipped the duffel bag with a decisive motion.

"Fine," he said, his tone laced with bitterness. "Have your space. Have your freedom. I hope it's everything you wished for."

He hauled the bag over his shoulder, every muscle in his body coiled with tension, and stormed out, leaving me in the quiet aftermath.

The reverberating slam of the front door marked the finality of Steve's departure. I stood motionless in the hallway, the silence that followed felt both oppressive and liberating. My eyes on the empty space he had vacated, a space that once contained our dreams, our conflicts and our happiness. The sadness crept up, unannounced, pooling in my chest and pressing against my ribs with a dull ache. Yet, as tears threatened to spill over, there was also an unmistakable whisper of relief that fluttered through me like a tentative breeze through an open window.

"It's time to let go," I murmured to no one, a soft exhale carrying away some of the heaviness inside. He hadn't looked back, not even for a moment, and that too was a sign. A sign that we were both ready to let go, even if it tore at our insides to do so.

I padded into the kitchen, the click of my heels on the tile punctuating the quiet. I poured myself a glass of water, watching the bubbles rise and burst with a strange fascination. It was a reminder that life continued its relentless march forward, even when personal worlds seemed to crumble.

I was at the office when intrigue arrived by way of a cream-colored envelope, nestled among the usual assortment of bills and advertisements at my office. The handwriting was unfamiliar, looping and graceful, addressing it to Madelyn Montgomery with a flourish. But it was the name "Jake" printed at the bottom left corner that halted my breath for a fraction too long.

"Jake?" I whispered, flipping the envelope over in my hands. The name almost didn't match with my knowledge anymore; I'd been referring to him as Dylan, but I forgot he didn't know about my discovery. With a flicker of curiosity warming my chest, I slipped a finger under the sealed flap and tore it open with a careful motion.

Inside, a single sheet of paper folded neatly, beckoning with possibilities. I drew in a slow breath, steadying myself for the unknown words of Jake.

The crisp paper crackled softly as it unfolded, a whisper against the silence of my office. With hesitant eyes, I scanned the first line, and the world seemed to tilt, the name "Dylan" anchoring me back to reality.

"Madelyn," it began, a simple greeting that thrummed with depth. Every word thereafter was like a brushstroke on canvas, painting emotions hidden beneath layers of cordial encounters and lingering glances. Jake's, or better, Dylan's confession flowed from the pen with an elegance that made my heart skip erratically.

"I've watched you, in quiet admiration, wrestling with choices that no one should make alone." Vulnerability crept through the cracks of my composed façade, as his words reflected the silent struggle I had endeavored to keep from the world, including him—especially him.

"Your happiness has always been of paramount importance to me, and while I wished to be its keeper, I respect your decision to mend what's broken." A breath I hadn't known I was holding escaped in a rush. To know that

MOVING ON

Dylan, this enigma swathed in sophistication, had seen me —not just the façade of the event planner, but Madelyn, the dreamer, the doubter—sent a tremor through my being.

As my gaze traveled down the page, a knot formed in my stomach. "Thus, I find myself at the cusp of a new chapter, as do you with your family. The city beckons with open arms, and I must answer its call." New York City. The words were a cold splash of reality against the warmth of his previous sentiments. I blinked rapidly, willing the sting at the corners of my eyes to recede.

New York City. He was leaving.

A multitude of emotions collided within me, each vying for dominance. There was the sharp pang of loss, so acute it bordered on physical pain, gnawing at the idea of a future without the man who'd inadvertently woven himself into the tapestry of my desires. And yet, beneath the sorrow lay a ribbon of anger—a frustration at the universe for its cruel timing, presenting me with the potential for something beautiful only to tear it away.

But more than anything, there was fear. Fear that in seeking to mend one relationship, I had severed another, perhaps more vital connection. That Dylan, who had silently understood and supported me from afar, would now become just a wisp of memory in the vastness of a city that never sleeps.

"Be well," the letter concluded, those three words a gentle release, setting me adrift in a sea of doubts. Dylan's signature, "Jake," stood boldly beneath, a revelation that left me reeling with the knowledge of his true identity.

I sat motionless, the letter resting in my lap, a tangible proof of love and timing's twists. In the quiet aftermath of the letter, I allowed myself a moment to mourn the possibilities that drifted away towards distant city lights.

Dylan's words blurring as tears threatened to betray the composure I fought so hard to maintain. I stood up, pacing the room—a caged animal torn between the instinct to give chase and the wisdom to let go. Every single step was a silent conversation with myself, deliberating over what I knew of love and what it asked of me.

"He escaped his marriage and he is now moving to New York City. Why? Did he do it because of his feelings for me? Is there some other reason? Figure out what you want," I whispered into the stillness. My reflection caught in the windowpane, green eyes searching for answers in the twilight's gentle embrace. Steve's laughter echoed through my memory, a reminder of joy once present. But Dylan's silent understanding had been a cure to my wounds I hadn't known were there until they began to heal.

Should I call Eleanor and ask her if she talked to Dylan after the wedding fiasco? Should I just drive to her house? Should I go find Dylan directly? Is it too late? I need answers. Now.

"Enough," I chided myself, straightening my spine. I couldn't allow the what-ifs of Dylan's departure to cloud the reality of my present.

I folded Dylan's letter carefully, a ritual of closure, and tucked it away in the drawer of my writing desk. A deep breath filled my lungs, and as I exhaled, a sense of purpose steadied my trembling hands. It was time to confront the end of one chapter before I could consider the beginning of another.

"Clarity, Maddy," I encouraged myself, using the nickname Sofia often called me in moments of endearment. The task at hand was simple, yet colossal—reclaiming my space, my life, after Steve's exit. There would be logistics to manage, silences to endure, but I was ready.

In the quiet of the house, I began to imagine it as a canvas for my solitude. Tomorrow, I would start fresh, sorting through belongings, reorganizing spaces infused with memories of Steve and I. It was an act of reclaiming, of setting boundaries within the walls that had witnessed the rise and fall of our union.

"Step by step," I told myself. "You can do this." Determination was a flame within me, fragile but persistent. I would nurture it, protect it from the gusts of doubt and regret. For now, Dylan—and the heartache of his impending absence—would have to wait. I had a more immediate healing to attend to, one that started with goodbye.

I stood in the center of the living room, the silence echoing around me like a blank slate. The walls, stripped of Steve's photographs and memorabilia, now expanded with possibility. My gaze drifted to the empty shelves, the cleared tabletops, and I felt a surge of empowerment rush through me. This was no longer the home we had built together; it was my sanctuary, my domain to redesign.

"Alright, Madelyn," I whispered to myself, "it's time to sketch your future, one line at a time."

With purpose, I strode to the kitchen, its countertops gleaming under the warm light. Out came the notepad, its pages crisp and inviting. I penned down thoughts that had been simmering in the back of my mind—ideas for a new layout, a fresh coat of paint, maybe even that herb garden I'd always envisioned by the window.

Each word I wrote was a declaration, a commitment to transformation. I could host dinner parties, start a book club, or simply relish the quietude with a glass of wine and a good novel. I allowed myself to daydream, to weave fantasies that were mine alone to fulfill.

Steve was gone. Sad yet oddly liberating. A part of me longed for the comfort of what was familiar, but the burgeoning sense of freedom whispered of new horizons. I closed my eyes, letting the silence envelop me, a blank canvas awaiting the first stroke of color.

My mind drifted to Dylan—no, Jake. His letter had shaken the foundations of my world, his words etched into my heart with an artist's precision. How strange it was that someone could see you so clearly, could understand the layers of your soul with such clarity. I hugged myself, feeling the warmth of his confession in the letter still heating my skin, despite the paper's absence.

"Jake," I murmured, testing the name, letting it roll off my tongue. It felt right, somehow, as though this piece of the puzzle had been missing all along. Confusion mingled with the budding shoots of hope in my chest. Could there be something real there, something worth exploring?

A sigh escaped me, laden with the difficulties of the day. I had set one life adrift to possibly chart a course for another. But was I ready? Was I brave enough to step forward into this new chapter without looking back? These questions danced at the edge of my consciousness, daring me to leap into the unknown.

I pushed away from the wall, my legs carrying me to the window where the evening sky painted streaks of purple and orange across the horizon. It was as if the universe itself was affirming the beauty of beginnings and endings, the natural rhythm of life's ebb and flow.

"Here's to new beginnings," I whispered, a pledge to the reflection staring back at me with those expressive green eyes. They held stories untold, adventures uncharted, and love yet to be discovered. I smiled, a soft, tentative thing, as hope took root once more. "And to me!"

In that quiet moment, I allowed myself to grieve the end of what had been and embrace the potential of what might be. Every day was a new day, and with it, the first step of a journey that was truly mine to shape.

CHAPTER 20
Letting Go

I passed Dylan's letter into Sofia's waiting hands.

"He's moving to New York City," she murmured, eyebrows knitting in concern. "That's quite the distance. Are you alright with this? With no closure before his departure?"

Restlessness seized me, propelling me to my feet. I began to pace the expanse of the living room, a storm of emotions brewing within. "I'm at a loss, Sof," I confessed. "Ever since Steve..." My words trailed off as I caught Sofia's gaze, realizing with a start she was at a loss too. Her silence spoke volumes; she had no words to offer, no comfort to give. "I have to face him," I declared, more to myself than to her.

"Dylan?" she questioned, seeking clarification.

"Yes, Dylan. I need answers," I stated.

Sofia nodded, her support unwavering. "Then what are you waiting for? Confront him. Call him."

A flicker of determination ignited within me. "I know what I need to do. I'll be back," I promised, stepping towards a decision that could change everything.

Quill Haven's door bell announced my arrival like a herald of my intentions. I stepped inside, the familiar odor of aged paper and coffee-infused air wrapping around me like an old, comforting blanket. My heart hammered against my ribs.

I knew Jake—or Dylan, the name that still tasted of betrayal on my tongue—found refuge among these towering shelves. This was where we first collided in serendipitous chaos, my stack of novels scattering across the floor, his warm brown eyes meeting mine in amused apology. It was here, amidst the whispering pages and quiet conversations, he'd become more than a stranger, weaving himself into the narrative of my life.

Now, with every step echoing softly on the worn wooden floorboards, I searched for him. My gaze flitted from face to face, bypassing the patrons lost in literary worlds. The store was a labyrinth of knowledge and imagination, every aisle a tunnel veiling potential disappointment. But he was not nestled in the nooks lined with leather-bound classics, nor was he perusing the latest bestsellers that adorned the front displays.

"Jake?" The name slipped from my lips, a hopeful incantation dissolving into the sound of rustling pages and

LETTING GO

murmured words. No answering call came, no familiar chuckle or soft-footed approach. Just the steady rhythm of other lives continuing undisturbed.

I wandered deeper, past the corner where children sat cross-legged, their wide-eyed wonder at storybook tales so distant from my own reality. The cozy armchairs by the fireplace stood empty, their cushions devoid of his presence.

A knot tightened in my chest, a blend of longing and apprehension. It tugged at the corners of my mind, fraying the edges of my composure. Would I find him here, in this haven that had once felt like a secret? Or would the empty spaces between the books only echo back my own undecidedness?

Quill Haven held whispers of countless stories, but today, it seemed, it would not grant me mine.

Tucked a strand of chestnut hair behind my ear, I stepped out into the crisp air, the chime of Quill Haven's door marking my departure. My fingertips danced across the screen of my phone. The message, stark against the bright backdrop, was simple: "Can we meet at Java Jolts? Need to talk before you go to New York."

The 'send' button felt like a cliff's edge; with a tap, I leaped.

Leaning against the cool brick of the bookstore, I watched a parade of people pass by absorbed in their own narrative. The small device in my hand became the focus of my world. I imagined him, Jake—or Dylan—his warm brown eyes scanning the words that could bridge the distance between us or widen it infinitely.

What would I say when faced with him? The words that had seemed so clear became a jumble, like the mixed-up letters that fall from a Scrabble bag. I wanted to speak of hurt and hope, of confusion and a desperate need for truth. But beneath it all lay the raw need for closure, a way to stitch up the wound left open and bleeding.

"Please," I whispered to the phone, to him, to the universe. "Just... please."

The coffee shop's sign flickered in the corner of my vision, a beacon of normalcy that seemed an ocean away. I pictured us there, two figures at a table cluttered with mugs and past remnants of our intertwined story. Would he offer explanations wrapped in soft apologies, or would his silence be the final chapter of us?

"Madelyn," I coached myself, channeling the event planner who knows how to navigate crises. "You'll handle this, one way or another."

But as the minutes trickled by, hope waned, leaving me to cling to the last threads of what might never be resolved.

My fingers trembled slightly, betraying the anxiety that was mounting with every single passing second. The cool screen of my phone felt detached against my warmth as I navigated through my contacts, seeking the one person who could tether me back to sanity, Sofia. I pressed 'call' and brought the phone to my ear, listening to the ring that cut through the silence of Quill Haven like a lifeline.

"Hey babe, what's up?" Sofia's voice was soothing, vibrant and filled with an undercurrent of strength that I so desperately needed right now.

"Hi, Sof... I'm at Quill Haven," I started, my voice sounding more brittle than I intended. "I messaged Jake—or Dylan, God, it's still so weird—and asked him to meet me. But there's no sign of him, and he hasn't replied yet."

"Okay, take a deep breath for me, Maddie," she instructed gently. "Talk to me. What are you feeling?"

"Scattered," I confessed, my gaze slipping over the spines of books that stood regimented on the shelves around me. "I'm scared he'll leave for New York without us even speaking, and I'll be left with all these unanswered questions."

"Remember why you're doing this," Sofia reminded me, her voice a soft command. "You want closure, right? You deserve that much. So, let's think this through. If he doesn't show up, what's your plan B?"

I chewed on my bottom lip, considering her question. "I don't know," I admitted. "I hadn't thought that far ahead. I was so focused on confronting him face-to-face."

"Then it's time to start thinking about it," she advised, practical as ever. "You're strong. Don't let this unreliability undo you. You've handled tougher situations, and you've always come out on top."

Her words were like anchors, grounding me amidst the storm of emotions. "You're right. I just... I can't shake off the fear of not knowing how it's going to turn out. It's that moment before the event starts, where everything is uncertain."

"Except this isn't an event, Maddie. This is your life," Sofia said firmly. "And whatever happens, you'll handle it with the same grace and composure. Trust in yourself."

"Thank you, Sof," I whispered, gratitude mixing with the remnants of fear. "I needed to hear that."

"Anytime," she reassured me. "Keep me posted, okay? And remember, no matter what, you've got this."

With those parting words, Sofia's presence receded, leaving me alone with my thoughts once again. Her unwavering confidence in me acted as a beacon, guiding me through the fog of my own doubts. If Jake—or Dylan—failed to appear, I would find another way to seek the answers that haunted me. Because Sofia was right: I was strong, I was capable, and I would face whatever came with the same determination that had carried me this far.

I clasped my phone—a lifeline to the man who held the missing pieces of my puzzle. My thumb hovered over his name, Jake/Dylan, a duality that mirrored my own confusion. The push of a button, and his voicemail greeted me, indifferent to the tempest within.

"Hey, it's Madelyn," I started, my voice a mix of strength and vulnerability. "I'm standing here in Quill Haven, surrounded by stories, but none as incomplete as ours. I need to see you, to talk to you. There's so much left unsaid, Jake... Please, call me back."

LETTING GO

The message sent, an echo in the digital void, I released a breath I hadn't realized I'd been holding.

But one voicemail morphed into a series, steps deeper into my exposed heart. In the privacy of my apartment, with sunset casting long shadows across the floor, I poured out my feelings like spilled ink on parchment.

"Jake, I keep replaying our moments together, trying to understand where the lines blurred between truth and pretense. Your warmth, your smiles—they felt real. Were they? I just... I need closure before you leave for New York. Please, reach out. We can meet at that coffee shop around the corner, the one with the little wind chimes by the door. Just... please."

Each plea was a petal plucked from the flower of hope, and with each unanswered call, the bloom withered.

Hours stretched into aching silence, punctuated only by the habitual glance at my phone. Sunrises and sunsets passed, whispering the possibility of a missed call, a notification, any sign that he heard me. But my screen remained as barren as my hopes, its glow a false promise in the quiet of my room.

I clung to routine like a raft in these uncharted waters—work during the day, restless evenings filled with distractions. Yet, nothing quelled the persistent urge to check my phone, the muscle memory of disappointment growing stronger with each futile attempt.

"Maybe tomorrow," I murmured to myself, thumb brushing over the cold glass once more. But like a mantra losing its meaning, the words fell flat, the silence from Jake/Dylan becoming a presence in its own right.

The leaves outside my window transitioned from vibrant green to the fiery hues of autumn, a season changing before my eyes while I remained tethered to a single, unchanging wish—that he would hear me, that he would respond. But as the hours piled up, they built a wall between the past and the present, a barrier that seemed increasingly insurmountable.

My heart, once buoyant with anticipation, began to sink under the weight of reality. Yet even as hope dimmed, I couldn't extinguish the small flame completely—not until I'd heard his voice, not until I'd seen his face. Not until I'd said goodbye.

I tossed my phone onto the bed, its bounce mirroring the leap of my stomach—a cruel mimicry of the hope that once danced there. My fingers traced the edge of the nightstand, lingering on the cool wood as if I could draw strength from its solidity. Every message I left for Jake—for Dylan—was a plea cast into the void.

"Was it all for nothing?" The whisper barely escaped my lips, the question clawing its way through my chest, leaving behind a hollow echo. The rawness of not knowing gnawed at me, the possibility that closure might just be a myth, a story we tell ourselves to justify the ache of unanswered questions.

My mind replayed our last moments, searching for signs, for words unsaid. But the more I dwelled, the more elusive peace became, slipping through my fingers like the autumn leaves that fluttered past my window.

"Enough," I commanded myself, the word a sharp cut through the fog of longing. It was time to shed this skin of sorrow, to step beyond the confines of waiting and wanting. I sat up, rolling my shoulders back as if I could physically cast off the burden of heartache.

I rose, feet planting firmly on the ground. My reflection in the mirror caught my eye—green eyes that once shone with secrets now reflected a newfound determination. I saw the contours of a woman reshaped by trials, edges worn but not broken.

"Move forward." The name grounded me, a reminder of who I was beyond this pain. There was an event tomorrow that required my attention, details that only I could finesse into perfection. Life beckoned with a thousand little threads, a promise that the tapestry was not yet complete.

So I chose to weave new patterns, to create moments rich with potential. Maybe some threads would remain loose, some patterns unfinished. Acceptance didn't come easy—it was a bitter pill, coated with the reality that not every story had a clear ending.

But as I turned away from the mirror, determination settled over me. It was time to embrace the unknown chapters, to find fulfillment in the narrative I crafted for myself, with or without him. Closure, I realized, wasn't always an answer received; sometimes, it was simply the decision to stop asking the questions.

And so, I decided to let go—not just of him, but of the very notion of expectations, those silent demands we place on life's unpredictable script. Embracing unknown felt like stepping out onto a stage without a script, the audience waiting, breath bated. Yet, I stood tall, ready to deliver lines crafted from authenticity, from the raw and unscripted heartbeats of existence.

As night claimed the day, my footsteps carried me back towards the world beyond—one filled with possibilities yet to be explored, events yet to be planned, and a self yet to be fully discovered. The road ahead was shrouded in mystery, the endings unwritten, and that, I realized, was where true freedom lay.

CHAPTER 21

Real Life

I WAS READING one of my favorite books, 'Ready or Not' by Lara Martin on my bed when I heard my phone ring. I approached the counter top in the kitchen where the phone was charging and I couldn't believe the name that appeared on the screen. It was Jake.

My hands trembled as I fumbled with the phone, its shrill ring slicing through the quietude of my meticulously planned afternoon. "Madelyn," came his voice, strained and distant, "there's been an accident."

"Jake?" I whispered, the name catching in my throat, a knot of fear coiling tight in my stomach. My hands were slick with sweat. My heart raced with anxiety. My mind immediately went to worst-case scenarios. "What happened?" I asked urgently.

"I'm at the hospital," he replied, his voice distant and shaky. The line went dead and my world felt like it was crumbling around me. What had happened? Who was

LORAIN RIZK

hurt? And why was he at the hospital? The questions raced through my mind as I frantically tried to gather my thoughts and make sense of the situation.

"Please come," was all he managed before the line went dead.

Heart hammering against my ribs, I dropped everything—a cascade of papers fluttering to the floor like wounded doves —and grabbed my keys. My mind raced, images of Jake— no, Dylan—flashing before me: our accidental meeting among the musty stacks of books, the way his laughter resonated just for me, the warm brown of his eyes cradling secrets I yearned to understand. Now those same eyes might be closed in pain, that laughter silenced by twisted metal. *Am I dreaming?*

I barely remembered locking the door behind me, my feet carrying me faster than thought, propelled by a single, all-consuming need to reach him. The world blurred into streaks of color as I wove through the streets, the city's cacophony dull against the pounding in my ears.

The hospital loomed ahead, a monolith of white and steel, but it was the chaos encircling it that drew a gasp from my lips. Flashbulbs popped like strobe lights in a nightmare, casting stark shadows across my path. A sea of bodies pressed forward, a barrage of voices clamoring for attention.

"Madelyn Montgomery! What can you tell us about Dylan Dalton's condition?"

"Is it true he was set to marry someone else?"

REAL LIFE

"Madelyn! Over here!"

Their questions pelted me like hailstones igniting fresh sparks of panic. My green eyes, usually so observant, now darted frantically, searching for escape. I pushed through, the crowd's energy jarring against my own tumultuous thoughts. My chestnut hair clung to my forehead, damp with perspiration and the mist of anxiety that hovered around me.

Dylan's plea was a siren call that drowned out the media frenzy. It didn't matter that just hours ago I had been steeped in self-doubt, wondering if I was making the right choices, the right sacrifices. In this moment, nothing mattered but the beating of my heart and the breath in my lungs, both syncing to the urgency of reaching him.

"Let her through!" someone shouted, but the words were distant, muffled by the blood rushing in my ears. I stumbled, regaining my balance by sheer will. And then I was through, past the gauntlet of lenses and microphones, into the sterile stillness of the hospital corridor.

Jake. Dylan. The names merged inside me, a reality still too tender to touch. I ran on, every step bringing me closer to uncovering the mystery that had twined itself around my life, binding me to a man whose true identity was the final piece of the puzzle.

The hospital corridor, a stark contrast to the clamor outside, hummed with its own form of chaos. Nurses darted past, their faces set in grim lines, while somewhere nearby the relentless beep of a heart monitor played an eerie counterpoint to my racing pulse. I slalomed between gurneys and medical carts, every room number I passed ratcheting up the tension knotted within me.

"Excuse me!" My voice sounded foreign amidst the clinical buzz. "I need to find Dylan Dalton's room."

A nurse, her scrubs a blur of pastel colors, glanced up from her clipboard, eyes narrowing as if to shield herself from yet another emotional onslaught. "Family only," she said, words clipped, but her gaze softened, just for a moment, as it met my anxious stare.

"I am family," I lied, or maybe it wasn't a lie at all. What is family, if not the name we give to those who hold pieces of our hearts?

"Fourth floor," she relented, gesturing towards the elevators, where a security guard was holding back a journalist, his camera like a weapon of intrusion.

Gratitude flashed through me as I turned, feet finding new purpose. The elevator doors parted with a sigh, welcoming me into their brief sanctuary.

The doors opened, and I stepped out into another hallway, this one lined with doorways that promised relief or heartbreak behind them. Room 402... 403... 404. Each heartbeat, a drumroll to the moment of truth.

And then there it was: Room 407. Dylan's room.

A deep breath did little to steady my trembling hands as I pushed open the door, the quiet click of the latch unbearably loud in the hush that enveloped me. There, surrounded by a tangle of wires and the soft hum of machinery, lay Dylan—no, Jake. Pale, bruised, but unmistakably alive.

"Madelyn," he murmured, his voice a fractured whisper that managed to slice through the fog of my worry.

In two strides, I was at his side, my fingers seeking the warmth of his hand. The cool touch of his skin against mine anchored me to the here and now, away from the what-ifs that threatened to consume me.

"Jake," I breathed. His eyelids fluttered showing his struggle, and in the dim light of the room, I could see the strain etched into his features."What happened? Are you okay?"

"Sorry," he said, a word so infused with meaning that it seemed to carry the weight of both our worlds. "I'm alright. I had a car accident this morning."

"Shh, save your strength," I whispered, brushing a lock of hair from his forehead. The gesture felt intimate, natural— as if I'd been doing it for years instead of standing on the precipice of a truth only half-revealed.

Relief, sharp and sweet, flooded through me as I watched him settle back against the pillows, his breathing steady under the watchful eyes of the monitors. He was alive, and for now, that was all that mattered.

The steady beep of the heart monitor was like a metronome to the chaos of my thoughts, grounding me in the reality of Dylan's hospital room. He looked frail beneath the stark white sheets, a shadow of the enigmatic man I thought I knew.

"Madelyn," he murmured, his voice rough with pain or emotion—I couldn't tell which. "There's something I have to tell you."

I held my breath, waiting for him to continue. In the fluorescent light, his eyes looked like galaxies of unspoken words.

"My name... I'm not Jake. I'm Dy— Dylan Dalton." He interrupted, his gaze piercing me with a force that left me breathless.

"I know. I've known since the day of your wedding when I accompanied Eleanor to her house. I saw a picture of you two."

"I'm sorry," he whispered, his grip on me loosening. "I never meant to hurt you."

"But why? Why did you lie about your real identity?" I asked, waiting for the answer I had been waiting for weeks.

"The engagement... it was never real. Not for me at least." His confession spilled out in a rush with the words punctuated by the hitch in his breathing. "A charade set up by my family. They wanted... control. Influence."

My heart skipped a beat, refusing to understand. "But the wedding–"

"Was never going to happen," he cut in, his gaze locking onto mine with an intensity that felt like a physical touch.

REAL LIFE

"I didn't show up because I couldn't stand there and lie. Not to them, not to myself, and especially not to you. Not anymore. I lied about my identity because I wanted you to see me for the real me and not 'Dylan Dalton,' the man and family everyone gossips about. I was your client and I was supposed to get married. How could I've told you about who I really was? I would've lost you, although I ended up losing you anyways."

"Me?" The question was a fragile thing, barely audible over the crescendo of my pulse in my ears.

"Madelyn," he continued. "I've been in love with you since the first day I saw you. Before we even talked for the first time at Quill Haven, I had been admiring you from afar. I knew you were the woman planning my wedding; I had seen pictures of you. I couldn't tell you I was Dylan. You are the first woman who has seen me for the real me, and not for my name."

The room spun slightly as his words washed over me, and I grasped the edge of the bed to steady myself. My mind raced to piece together our encounters—the lingering looks, the charged silences, the warmth of his smile, the passionate love making at the beach. Had it all been real?

"I didn't show up at the wedding because I couldn't do it. I couldn't let my family decide on my future; not anymore. My heart belongs to you. And I understand you decided to go a different route prior to my decision to not marry Eleanor, but that's where my heart was. And it still is."

"Dylan, I—" The name tasted foreign on my tongue, a reminder of the secrets between us. My emotions were a whirlwind, picking up fragments of confusion, disbelief, and the faintest flicker of hope. Could it be possible? Dare I let myself believe in the depth of his feelings?

"Please say something," he implored, his hand finding mine.

I searched his face, looking for the answers in the lines of pain and sincerity etched around his eyes. The green of my irises reflected back at me, filled with questions and the beginnings of understanding.

"Dylan, I don't know what to say," I admitted, the truth of his words still settling. "This is all too much." I took a sip of water. "And... Steve and I are done. We had been done for a while, but I was finally brave enough to let go. But I need time to digest what's happening."

Dylan smiled. "Take your time," he said gently, the corners of his mouth lifting in the ghost of a smile. "We have all the time in the world."

For a moment, I allowed myself to lean into the possibility of this new reality. A world where the man lying before me wasn't just an illusion wrapped in deceit, but someone who had seen me, truly seen me, and loved me from afar.

"Okay," I whispered, squeezing his hand. "Okay, Dylan."

The sterile smell of the hospital room brought me even more uneasiness, a stark contrast to the chaos that churned just beyond the walls. I stood by his bedside, my hand

REAL LIFE

enveloped in his, as if our fingers intertwined could shield us from the world outside. Dylan's gaze held mine, unwavering, the beats of silence punctuated by the soft beep of the heart monitor. This was the first time I met Dylan and it was the strangest feeling ever.

"Madelyn," he murmured, the sound of my name on his lips anchoring me back to the moment. His eyes, pools of earnest blue, were windows to a soul laid bare—a soul that had defied the constructs of wealth and expectation for something deeper, something real. "If you never want to see me, I get it. I was ready to move miles away to New York City because I wanted you to be happy with your family. I couldn't deal with the fact that I'd never be with you. And I decided to move to get away from my family and start a new life. Staying here without you was too much for me. Everything reminds me of you in Keystone."

I exhaled slowly, the breath I'd been holding releasing doubts and fears that had shackled my heart. In this quiet space between heartbeats, I found clarity. He had risked it all for me. Family, legacy, security—all forsaken in the name of what? Love?

"Dylan," I began, my voice barely a whisper, "I see you. And I believe you." The words felt like a vow, an acceptance of his sacrifice—and with it, a forgiveness for the tangled web of deceit that had brought us here.

A smile flickered across his bruised face. Yet, through the pain, there was hope—a hope that mirrored the hesitant flame within me.

"Madelyn?" Dylan's voice was weak but threaded with earnestness.

I moved closer. His hand found mine, a fragile yet determined grip. His injuries were stark against the stark white of the hospital linens, a visual reminder of the chaos that had brought us to this precipice.

"Thank you," he whispered, his thumb brushing across my knuckles in a gesture so tender it threatened to undo me. "For understanding... for being here."

I wanted to tell him that no thanks were needed, that the depth of what I felt for him transcended gratitude, but the words lodged in my throat, too big and too raw to escape.

"I'll be here," I managed to say, the promise feeling like a vow.

Dylan's gaze held mine, a myriad of emotions flickering there—relief, pain, hope. In that look, I saw the reflection of my own heart, the echo of a love that had weathered storms in silence but now spoke its name aloud.

He nodded slightly, the motion careful but deliberate. "With you here... it feels like everything might just be okay." The hope in his voice was fragile but unyielding. I could now feel the strength of what had blossomed unexpectedly between us.

"Okay is a good start." My response was soft, my fingers tracing the lines of his palm—a map of the journey he had been on long before our paths converged. A journey that now, against all odds, included me.

"More than okay," Dylan corrected, his grip tightening just enough to send a surge of courage through my veins. "We have a future. One that starts with honesty and a love that doesn't have to hide anymore."

I felt the truth of his words resonate deep within me, a promise of something real and unfettered by the expectations we had both been shackled to. It was a future ripe with possibilities, daunting in its newness but exhilarating in its potential.

"Let them talk," I found myself saying, a newfound determination steeling my spine as I thought of the clamor beyond these walls. "Let the world watch and wonder. We know our truth, Dylan. That's all that matters."

"Exactly." He smiled, and even through the pain, it was the most beautiful thing I'd seen. "You and me, Maddie. We write our own story from here."

As we sat there, hands clasped, hearts tentatively entwined, the cacophony of the outside world—the insistent flashes of cameras, the shouted questions, the relentless pursuit of a narrative that no longer held sway over us—faded to mere background noise. They were on the outside looking in, but we had traversed to a place where only we existed, a realm crafted from mutual understanding and the tender threads of a love born in the shadows but ready to step into the light.

I leaned back against the cool sterility of the hospital wall, Dylan's warm hand still enclosed in mine. My mind raced with the velocity of a tempest, thoughts colliding and reforming into new shapes, forging a reality I could never have anticipated when I woke up this morning.

Lauren. Her name surfaced amidst the tumult, her bright smile a beacon that both warmed and pained me. How was I to explain any of this to her? She was the heartbeat of my world, and yet here I was, on the precipice of upheaval that would shake her foundations as surely as it had rattled mine.

"Hey," Dylan's voice was tender, his thumb brushing over my knuckles, "whatever happens, we'll face it together."

I closed my eyes, breathing in the truth that while the landscape of my life had irrevocably changed, I wasn't alone. Dylan understood the complexity of love and duty that bound a mother to her child.

"Lauren," I said softly, my voice a fragile thread in the vastness of the room, "if we really do this, she's going to need time. To understand. Steve just moved out."

"Of course." He nodded, and there was no mistaking the resolve in his eyes. "We'll give her all the time she needs. And," he added, a touch of fervor lining his words, "we'll be honest with her, with everyone. From now on."

Honesty. The word reverberating against the walls I'd built around my heart. I'd played a role for so long, the dutiful wife, the perfect event planner, always anticipating others' needs while neglecting the quiet pleadings of my own soul.

But this... This was my awakening.

"Let's start again. Let's move anywhere you like, or let's stay here. As long as I'm with you, nothing else matters." Dylan held my hand tighter.

I refused to repeat my mother's mistakes with Sebastian, wasting a life not shared with whom truly holds your heart. Life's tumultuous journey would not catch me off guard. I was ready to face it head on and take responsibility for the choices that brought me to this moment—in this room, with the man whose heartbeat echoed mine.

"I'm ready for this," I whispered, my voice carrying a newfound strength that surprised even me. "Together."

Dylan held my hand and pulled me closer. His lips met mine in a deep, passionate kiss that left no doubts or questions. And as we pulled away, he whispered those three words that I had been longing to hear, "I love you."

"I love you too, Dylan."

Ready or not, our story begins.

LORAIN RIZK

CONTINUE THE ADVENTURE IN BOOK TWO:

SATIN SHADOWS

Madelyn and Dylan's story unfolds further in the next installment of the Keystone Series.

Afterword

As I close this chapter on Velvet Shadows, I find myself reflecting on the journey that led me here. Writing this book has been a voyage of discovery, not just into the lives of Madelyn and Dylan, but into the heart of what it means to find real love.

This endeavor would not have been possible without the unwavering support of my husband, who believed in this story even when it was just a flicker of an idea.

I owe a huge thank you to The Paper House, my publishing house who made my dream come true.

My hope is that Velvet Shadows resonates with you, that it sparks curiosity, conversation, passion, and perhaps even change. Change to always seek what your heart whispers and never settle. The worlds we've explored together within these pages are a testament to the power of storytelling, to its ability to bridge gaps and to illuminate the shared threads of our humanity.

AFTERWORD

I invite you to share your thoughts, to connect with me through social media, email, or my website.

www.instagram.com/lorainrizkauthor

lorainrizk@gmail.com

www.lorainrizk.com

Thank you for allowing me to share Velvet Shadows with you. It has been an honor and a privilege.

About the Author

Lorain Rizk, a captivating romance author, was born in Italy and embraced the magic of storytelling after moving to the United States at 17. A graduate of William Paterson University, she traded a career in her field for the world of romance writing.

As a dedicated wife and mother of two, Lorain infuses her stories with the warmth of family and the passion inspired by her love for salsa dancing. A globetrotter at heart, she adores exploring new cultures, adding a touch of wanderlust to her vibrant life.

Beyond her literary pursuits, Lorain serves as the CEO of her own company, infusing an entrepreneurial spirit into her creative journey. Lorain Rizk's novels are a fusion of Italian charm and American romance, inviting readers into worlds where love takes center stage. Join her on a journey where every heart finds its own melody, and love knows no boundaries.

Connect with Lorain Rizk and let her transport you into the enchanting landscapes of her heartfelt stories.

www.lorainrizk.com

lorainrizk@gmail.com

Printed in the USA
CPSIA information can be obtained
at www.ICGtesting.com
LVHW091435160524
780333LV00013B/39